Before It Happens

By Boyd Hastings

Published by
Spiritbuilding Publishers
9700 Ferry Road, Waynesville, OH 45068

BEFORE IT HAPPENS
By Boyd Hastings

ISBN: 978–1–964–80554–2

Cover Design by Adam Hastings

Spiritbuilding
PUBLISHERS

spiritbuilding.com

Dedication

Young people will cross paths with many adults before their high-school graduation. Perhaps none of those will have more influence on their later lives than their teachers. Within the agriculture education programs, offered in over eleven thousand schools across America, a key component is the FFA organization. It is within the FFA that teachers work with students to learn skills in leadership, personal growth and development, competition, and career skills. Today the National FFA can boast as the largest youth organization in America with a membership of over 1,000,000 students.

Thanks

Many thanks to my wife Jeri, for her encouraging words to write this book, instead of the "how-to" book on food security I had already started writing. *"Put a little romance in it,"* she said. *"It'll sell better and more people will read it."*

It was about that time we were leaving the farm and moving to a little house in the city. She knew the move would be difficult for a guy who thrives in open spaces, and flourishes on the sights and sounds of nature. She also knew that writing a lengthy Christian novel, instead of a short how-to book, could serve as a much longer and needed distraction within the process of surviving the move.

So to Jeri, my wife of fifty-seven years, I thank you. Not just for your help with the manuscript, but for being the love of my life, the mother of our children, and my fellow sojourner on our pathway headed home.

—Boyd

Prologue

The child's body bolted straight up in his bed—screaming and crying and gasping for air. His mother ran as fast as she could from down the hall. It was the same nightmare he had been having since the night of the crash that killed his father. The family was on its way home from visiting friends when it started raining. There was no moon, and there were no stars—just the blackness of a warm, rainy night in May. As the car rounded the corner on the hillside road, a tanker truck was in their lane. The blinding lights and the truck's deafening horn left his father no time to think. Instinctively, he swerved to avoid a head-on collision. The car went through the guardrail and careened down the hillside into the ravine below. In the darkness of night, the vehicle rolled over and over and over until it came to rest at the bottom. The boy and his mother had somehow survived; the father had not.

It was that nightmare that still haunted the boy six months after the accident. Every time he screamed, his mother would rush to his side and pull him close. Then, with arms securely around him, she would rock back and forth and say, "It's okay, baby. I've got you. It's okay. I've got you."

As the gasping for air subsided, she would whisper in his ear, "I want to tell you a story about a little boy named Tommy, but I need your help, okay?" She would then take her index finger and place it gently in the center of the boy's back. "Tommy and his dog Rufus lived right here in a little brick house on Market Street. One day, Tommy and Rufus went on an adventure." The adventure would begin from there. As Tommy and his dog left their house, the index finger on the boy's back would start to move. With each imaginary street they took, with each imaginary place they went, the finger made an ever-increasing, larger circle on the boy's back.

Sometimes, a second finger would join in if Tommy and Rufus were climbing or running. Sometimes, Mother would *accidentally* forget an obvious, important detail and ask her son for help, thus engaging his mind in the story and disengaging him from the thoughts of the nightmare. Before long, the tension in his body would relax, and his breathing would return to normal. Soon there would be a yawn. His mother would suggest they finish the story with him lying back down in bed. As she continued the story, her voice would become softer and softer. The finger would move slower and slower, and the boy would soon slip back into quiet and peaceful sleep.

Chapter 1

Rise and Shine

Chicago, Illinois

Tap-tap-tap. Tap-tap-tap. "There's my morning wake-up service—again," groaned Lucy. *I am quite sure this free service was not mentioned when I signed the apartment rental agreement,* she said to herself. She had recently asked another renter how she might discontinue the *service.* He just laughed and said, 'Lots of luck!' Lucy rolled out of bed and walked to the kitchen. Looking in the refrigerator to explore her breakfast options, she heard it again. *Tap-tap-tap.* She turned and stepped over to the kitchen window, and in an agitated voice yelled, "WHAT DO YOU WANT? I HEARD YOU THE FIRST TIME!" Her *favorite* pair of fourth-floor, ledge-walking pigeons were determined that Lucy would not be going back to sleep today.

After a slice of toast and a bowl of Cheerios, Lucy went to the bathroom to get ready for work. She was looking in the mirror and putting on some light makeup when she saw them. They had traveled from my bedroom window to the kitchen window, and now they were peeking through the bathroom window. She kept getting ready, and they kept watching. At least they had stopped the *tap-tap-tapping.* Maybe she should start feeding them and get to know them better. If she brushed up on her conversational pigeon, she could do an interview and write a column on the plights of pigeons now living in the big city. After all, everyone needed someone to help tell their story—someone to help them survive going through their story—someone to make a difference in their life. For Lucy, that someone had been Granny.

Lucy was only three when both of her parents were killed by gang members who broke into their house one night. Her parents had resisted and were killed, so Granny took her in and raised her. Times were tough both emotionally and financially. All of their clothing came from the thrift store or from folks at church. The neighborhood grocery owner would save food about to expire and give it to Granny. They never went hungry, but Granny gave a whole new meaning to *leftovers*. Looking back, Lucy could have written a best-selling cookbook, *10 New Ways to Serve Leftover Meatloaf*. Granny was something else—special in so many ways.

Granny was the one who had helped Lucy survive the tragic story of her parents' death. After all, it was her story too. Lucy's mother had been her only child. Granny always said that as long as they had each other, they were more blessed than those who had no one. She said that together they should keep our eyes open for those other folks who were alone, and then ask if they could help. 'It's the neighborly thing to do. Sometimes all you need to do is ask,' she would often remark.

By the age of four, Lucy started asking everyone who crossed her path if she might be able to help. She interviewed stray cats and dogs that wandered through her backyard. One day, she even interviewed a squirrel in the park who kept crossing back and forth in the grass beneath a big oak tree. He would stop, dig a little, then move to another spot and repeat the same action over and over. Lucy felt sure he had buried a nut, but could not remember where he had buried it. Granny said that when folks get old, they start to lose their memory, so perhaps he was a very old squirrel and needed help, too.

By the time Lucy was in middle school, she volunteered to be the reporter for the school paper. Once again, she became the interviewer. Whether the person was the janitor, the librarian, the principal, or another student, she would always ask one common question: "Who has helped you get through a difficult time in your life?" It was a personal question, but it also encouraged them to find an opportunity to do the same for someone else. By the time she was a senior in high school, Lucy had permitted herself to say the words, "I want to be a writer." The journey had been a most interesting one.

Today, however, helping the pigeons would have to wait. Today, she had a manuscript ready for her editor and sometime friend, Lenny Dekoskie. He would take the manuscript, do the editing, and then he would find the best place to have it published. The story was about a rash of fires at smaller meat-packing companies. Since none of the big corporate companies have been bothered by the fires, people were starting to point accusing fingers toward the big boys.

****

While Lucy continued getting ready for what she hoped would be a positive meeting, her editor, Lenny, was having a very anxious, worrisome morning. He was pacing back and forth in his tenth-floor office on Twenty-Third Street. Even though it was in an aged commercial building in an older section of the city, his office was clean and very nice. What it lacked in location, Lenny was determined to make up for with a stately office interior. However, at the moment, Lenny was not being consoled by his grand surroundings.

Last night had been another short night, as tensions were high at home. There had been another explosive argument with his wife for the same reason as always—money. Lenny was so very tired. He sat down in his big leather chair at his mahogany desk. He was one of those guys who believed that sometimes *you have to fake it till you make it*. The problem for Lenny was that his *faking it* was costing him more than the *making it* was making.

Lenny had a few freelance writers who brought him decent material from time to time, but those barely paid the bills. Lenny was hoping for a really big story … a huge, unbelievable, Pulitzer Prize-winning story that would last for weeks—maybe even months. It would be a story that might become a book on the best-seller list and would fly off the shelves of every bookstore across America! That was what Lenny Dekoskie dreamed about when he went to bed at night.

He also knew that his best hope of that dream ever happening was in the hands of one of his stringers—his friend Lucy Moore. She could easily interview a story right out of a speechless mime, and she was an exceptional writer! Her work on America's food insecurity had been published in several national magazines, and her research had been cited in a half-dozen professional journals. She had even been asked to testify before Congress regarding her research, and you could always find her work near the top of any internet search results. He knew she could easily get her work published without him, but he would never be

5

the one to tell her that. Down below at street level, Lucy Moore had just stepped into the elevator and punched the button for floor number ten.

A minute later, there was a knock at Lenny's office door. Lucy let herself in. Lenny didn't have a receptionist; they cost money that he didn't have. He stood up from behind his big, beautiful, expensive desk and gave a great big Lenny smile. "Hey Lucy, great to see you! What's up?"

"I'm dropping off a few pages for your review. So far, I think what I've found is just the tip of the iceberg. I've titled it: "Who Smokes Your Meat." It's about a rash of fires hitting meat processing plants, but only the smaller, independent plants are having the fires. As you might expect, some are thinking it might be foul play."

"Be careful, Lucy," he said with genuine concern in his voice. "I worry about you getting in the middle of the story to write the story. You could get hurt." Lenny paused for a second and took a deep breath. He knew what he was about to say could escalate into a familiar battle that, someday, might jeopardize their business relationship.

In an effort to sound like he was innocently changing the subject, Lenny continued, "Hey Lucy, did you hear that they finally got the rebels in Kenya to surrender, and the war there has been officially declared over? The Pentagon says we can see our troops start to come home within a few weeks. Not only that, I heard that a new Taiwanese-American partnership is in the works. The two countries will share in the technology and production of the most advanced, affordable cars that have come off assembly lines in decades. Then the White House …"

"Stop it, Lenny!" Lucy interrupted him in a tone of frustration. In a softer but exasperated voice, she continued, "Lenny, please. We've been through this before. For good or bad, I'm a one-story girl. You just don't understand. I have been in parts of the world where I've seen children, old people, and average hard-working people go to bed hungry every night of the week. I know how fragile our own plentiful food supply is, and I don't want anything to ever happen that might jeopardize it."

"I get it," said Lenny. "I really do. But I also know that right now this country is basking in good times. America is tired of reading about pandemics, inflation, and the corruption in government and in corporations. No one is interested in reading stories of doom and gloom."

"*Hmmm* … you could be right, Lenny. Maybe I need something fresh and positive to write about … but what?"

Lenny did not respond.

"Well, I'll take a few days and see what might click," Lucy stated. "In the meantime, look over what I've left you, and let me know what you think. I'm really sorry, Lenny, but I need to head out. Talk with you later." And with that, she left his office and headed back down the elevator.

Chapter 2

Right on Time

Welcome, Indiana

I t was still dark outside. *Buzz-buzz-buzz-buzz. That's not the phone,* Caleb thought groggily. Reaching for the communicator on his nightstand, he quickly sat up in bed. The screen showed two things: 4:30 a.m. and the message, SECURED COMMUNICATION— CONFIRM. Confirming the message, it then opened: Hey C.B., Hope you can join us for lunch today at the CUPBOARD. Planning on eating at 12:30 p.m. Cousins Via and Ria also coming. Louie will get you here if you can be at his place in Atled by 9:45 a.m. Reservations made. See you at lunch.—Mother.

Intel had thought it prudent to always practice message encoding, yet Caleb Burns was confident he understood the message. It was from Mother Hubbard. The CUPBOARD meant that the meeting would be held somewhere within the D.C. area. The time would be 12:30 p.m. Via was simply "via", by way of, and RIA meant Reagan International Airport. He would get to RIA by way of Louisville airport, and airline tickets would be with Atled, which spelled backwards was Delta Air Lines.

It would be tight but doable. Leave Welcome by 5:30 a.m. Fly out of Louisville by 7:45 a.m. Arrive at Reagan International by 10:00 a.m., and be at the meeting by 12:15 p.m. *Sure, piece of cake,* he thought to himself as he quickly dressed and grabbed an old backpack. Ready to leave the house moments later, he paused and scribbled a note on the kitchen table. Eating breakfast on the run. Lunch with Janice. Be home by late evening. Tell Sadi not to wait up for me.

Twenty minutes later, Caleb arrived at the National Guard Base just outside of Welcome, Indiana. In another eight minutes, the chopper lifted off and set course for Louisville. As the pilot banked the aircraft to the right, Caleb looked through the window at the still sleepy town below. Welcome was just beginning to wake up. At that moment, a feeling of uneasiness swept over him, like a parent looking down on sleeping children who were about to experience an unexpected change in their lives.

Two hours and ten minutes later, now listed as passenger 32B, Major Caleb Burns was safely buckled in his seat and ready for takeoff. The massive jet engines of the Delta 757 were still in their earthbound voices as they began to taxi the plane down the runway. Then the familiar *thump-thump-thump-thump* as the wheels moved over the runway pavement faster and faster. The huge turbos started screaming as the plane continued to pick up speed. *Ca-plump.* The wing flaps went down, and the nose of the plane began to lift higher and higher.

A few seconds later, the friendly little *ding* sounded. That sound assured all on board, who had not already done so, that it was okay to release the seat belt. When Caleb first boarded the plane, he had noticed the seat behind him was empty. *Lucky him!* He reclined his seat and began to get comfortable. Yesterday had been a full and very physical day. Last night's sleep had been brief and interrupted. He was ready for a nap.

Two minutes later, passenger 32B, retired Major Burns, was sound asleep. He would need to be fresh and alert when he arrived at his meeting. It would be a meeting often referred to as a *quiet* meeting. Simply put, it meant this meeting would never be found on anyone's calendar. There would be no government vehicles chauffeuring attendees and no Secret Service protection. Everyone there, including the lady in charge, would be armed. By tomorrow morning, this quickly called meeting will never have happened.

****

The group of eight that had been summoned by Mother Hubbard referred to themselves simply as The Board of Directors of the Hubbard Foundation. The genesis of the group came from Janice Hubbard Higgins, the current acting Secretary of the DOP, Department of Provisions. This was a new cabinet-level department formed after the last presidential election. It was for this new department that retired

Rear Admiral Janice Hubbard Higgins had been brought on board as Secretary. It was she who had called the meeting.

The Department of Provision's main focus was serving all other departments with respect to their potential emergency needs. It was all about the *what-if questions*. What if multiple hurricanes hit multiple cities at the same time, and our nation's response efforts were overwhelmed? What if a hostile government used imported seeds or pharmaceuticals to deliver biological agents and infected our nation's food crops or livestock? There were a lot of *what-if* scenarios to consider. Very little press had been given to the activities of this new department, since to do so would only fuel the imaginations of those who would fixate on conspiracy theories and who could profit by taking advantage of a potential crisis.

Higgins' previous job before heading the Department of Provisions had been that of Undersecretary of the Navy. It was while serving there that she became aware of how easy it was to divert budget dollars into little special-interest projects without a trace of their origin or accountability. A million dollars from here, a million or two from there, and pretty soon this little ambiguous project that no one knew anything about became very well funded. On the books, Higgins' project was the Urban Food Statistical Analysis Group and required the Secretary's personal clearance to access it.

****

One-and-a-half hours later, the plane landed right on schedule and without incident. The engines quieted down, and the passengers soon began to exit. The last passenger to disembark was passenger 32B. He wore a plaid flannel shirt, khaki work pants, and he carried a bright-orange hard hat. His only carry-on baggage was a well-worn backpack. Passenger 32B looked like any other young construction worker on his way to the next job site.

Once through the exit doors of concourse C, he spotted his ride. It was a white work van parked in the nearby passenger pickup lane. On the side of the truck was written Miller Bros. Construction Co. He slid open the side passenger door, threw in the backpack, and took a second-row seat in the van.

"Good morning, Gentlemen," he said as he closed the door.

"Good morning, Major," the driver responded.

Burns leaned forward, "Good to see you again, Richard. Who is riding shotgun with us today?"

"My name is Jack, sir. Pleased to meet you," said the young man in the passenger seat.

"Where are we working today?' Burns asked as they left the terminal and headed out toward Maryland Highway 28W.

Richard replied, "There's an old campsite about two hours from here. Miller Brothers is making some preliminary plans for upgrades on a few of the outbuildings."

"Does the campsite have a name?" Burns asked.

"The place is called Camp David, sir", replied Jack as the young man opened a large center console compartment, reached in, and passed a handgun back to Burns.

Burns thought quietly to himself, *Camp David? Janice must have gone to the top to reserve a play date at Camp David. Whatever it is, there is an obvious sense of urgency.* Burns then re-engaged in conversation, "From the looks of our new vans, I would say Miller Brothers' Construction is doing quite well these days."

"Yes, sir," said Jack from the front passenger seat. "You might also appreciate one of the added features in the console compartment beside you, sir."

Burns shoved his backpack over to the outside seat and lifted the lid to the console. He found a mini cooler on the left side and a mini microwave on the right. Within the two units, Burns saw a large coffee, a small orange juice, two breakfast sweet rolls, and a sausage-egg English muffin.

Richard glanced back and saw a big smile on Burn's face. "It was Jack's idea," he said. "You know, new on the job—trying to make a good impression."

Smiling, Burns added, "Well, Jack, thank you very much for your exceptional service".

"My pleasure," replied Jack.

"Jack, where was your first job out of school?" Burns inquired.

"Uh, Chick-fil-A, sir".

"I thought so," smiled Burns as he began to eat his much-appreciated breakfast.

As the van rolled along the winding roads of Virginia's hill country, Burns tried to avoid the obvious—his apprehension of a meeting called so quickly and the absence of any agenda. Even without the agenda, he knew the meeting would have national— if not international ramifications.

Suddenly, Richard announced, "Major Burns, we have a problem. There's a roadblock ahead—three cars in front of us. It looks like there's a tree across the road, maybe from the morning storm. It's not a very big tree, but it is a traffic-stopper just the same."

Jack said, "I'll check it out; be right back."

As he jumped out of the van, Burns asked Richard, "Does the van come with any tools?"

"There should be a chest of tools included for props in the back, but I have no idea what we've got, Major," Richard replied.

Burns climbed over the center console and into the back of the van. He started looking through a chest of tools and found a small battery-powered chainsaw. "It's not much, but it's all we've got."

Jack climbed back into the van. "In the car nearest the tree are two old people in their late seventies or eighties. The middle car has three college girls. The car in front of us has a mom with three little kids."

Burns instructed, "Richard, pull around the three cars and stop near the tree."

Seconds later, the three men were out of the van and surveying the situation. "Okay, guys, it's showtime. Richard, you start breaking off the branches as big as you can and pulling them to the center of the road. Jack, you get the three girls from the center car and have them help pull the freed branches off the road and into the side ditch. I'll take this little chainsaw and work on the main limb crossing the road. If we can get rid of the branches and the battery gives out, we can all still push on the main limb and either break it or move it enough to get the van through."

Jack stood there frozen for a second. Richard looked over at him and said, "You heard what the man said. We're running out of time. Go get us some help!"

Jack ran over to the car with the three girls. The driver rolled down her window. "Hi, handsome!" she cooed. "How long do you think it will take you boys to get us out of here and on our way?"

"That depends," said Jack. "Maybe you didn't get the text? You three are helping us pull the branches into the side ditch."

"WHAT?" they all yelled in unison.

Jack smiled, looked at each one, and said, "It's like this, Ladies. I am going to start counting down from ten, and if you sweet things aren't over there pulling branches before I get to three, I will begin letting the air out of your tires." He began: "Ten, nine, eight ..." The doors flew open, and in seconds, they were all pulling branches to the side of the road.

A few minutes later, the three men and three girls were pushing on the remaining limb, which had almost been sawn through. Richard ordered, "Okay, one more try. Give it all you've got!" Above the sounds of great groaning, a sharp *SNAP* was heard. The large limb broke, and the road was now open on one side. There was no time for celebrating, though. The three men jumped back in the van and maneuvered it over and through the remaining branches on the road.

Richard looked over at Jack. "What did that blond stick in your shirt pocket when she bumped into you?" With a puzzled look on his face, he reached in and pulled out a paper receipt from a fast-food restaurant. On the back was written *Joanie 945-687-9923* along with a happy face. They all laughed out loud as the van sped on toward Camp David.

Richard was now trying to make up for lost time. "Don't worry, Major. We'll get you there on time."

"I do not doubt that, Richard. The boss lady sends only the best. It's all yours." With that, Caleb Burns looked out the window and tried not to think of anything but the beautiful spring landscape that flew past. The images of trees and fields had soon blurred his mind into a trance. As the van rolled on, he started to think of his family he had left behind just a few hours earlier: Uncle Joe, Aunt Millie, and Sadie. Earlier that morning, he had left the house without saying a word to anyone. Joe and Millie would understand from the note he left on the kitchen table. On the other hand, Sadie would make it a point not to understand and would demand his total attention when he got back home.

He had also left behind his very special team—a team that he had personally chosen. No one could ask for a more devoted and committed team in any walk of life. He led them, but not as in the army, where the expectation had been one of command and control. His team and their mission were now advanced by an atmosphere of trust and encouragement. He knew they would do anything for him, and they knew he would, likewise, do anything for them.

Burns' five-member team back in Welcome had been very successful in blending in, becoming regular folks in Indiana's southern rural landscape. Their project was all about people still having access to food when all the conventional ways were eliminated. The driving force of the project was out in the open, in plain view to all. Yet, at the same time, it was quite invisible to anyone who might be looking for it. Regardless, if questions arose, their activities would only serve as a great distraction from what was happening two stories beneath Uncle Joe's old barn.

His team was made up of five members: Marcus the chemist, Pete the photographer, Maria the house cleaner, Zachary the bike shop owner, and Jenny the nurse. It was only with Jenny that Caleb had had a previous relationship.

Jenny and Caleb had served together in the same unit in the war in Africa. As with many who serve together in combat, there was a special connection unknown and unfelt by others. It was a union of shared thoughts and fears, of joy and tears, and of victory and loss. It was a relationship void of romantic memories or physical attraction. It was a relationship that would last until something yet unknown would dissolve the need for such a relationship.

Burns had been in his private little trance longer than he realized. Suddenly, the truck slowed down and made a sharp turn. "We're almost there, Major," Richard said. "Right on time, if I might add."

"You did a great job driving, Richard," Burns said with true appreciation. Then he spoke to Jack, "And Jack, I just want to say, again, what a wonderful breakfast you surprised me with."

Jack smiled and said, "My pleasure, sir." Richard and Burns started laughing again. With a quizzical frown, Jack said, "Whaaat?

What's so funny?"

Richard pulled the van up to the compound's security checkpoint, put down his window, and handed the guard their authorization papers. A minute later, he waved them through, and they proceeded to cabin number four. The van stopped in front of the main door, and Burns got out. The van went on, and Burns walked up the wide steps and onto the big front porch. Before turning the knob, he whispered to himself, "What's up, Mother Hubbard? What … is … up?" He turned the knob and walked in.

Chapter 3

Camp David, Maryland

Burns scanned the spacious meeting room from left to right. On the left side were eight conference tables forming a tight circle. One chair at each table facing inward suggested the meeting would be open for discussions. On the right side of the room, the other attendees were standing around a long banquet table. On that table were several boxed lunches, drinks, and a great assortment of snacks.

With a slightly elevated voice, the lady in charge said, "May I have your attention? Please pick up a lunch, a drink, and whatever snacks you like, then have a seat at any one of the tables." After she did the same, she stepped to the only remaining table and chair. She was wearing jeans, a sweatshirt, and a pair of slip-on shoes. Standing at only five-foot-five, she was in better shape than most women half her age.

As Secretary of the Department of Provisions, she had always advocated that the first and most important way for citizens to be prepared for the unknown was to be prepared physically. If a person is obese or lacking physical strength, their ability to adapt and execute any plan of survival will be greatly jeopardized. She had lived as she had preached. As a cadet at the Naval Academy, she had often been among the strongest competitors in both women's swimming and cross-country events.

"Good afternoon," she began. "First, I want to thank all of you for doing whatever had to be done to get here on such short notice. It is truly indicative of your dedication and devotion to your country and to this special group. You may have noticed by now that there are no handouts, notepads, pencils, or pens at your tables. I am confident you will remember what I have to say in our short time together today."

She paused and then continued. "It was at the beginning of

the Atomic Age and the development and use of the atomic bomb that Albert Einstein was quoted as saying: 'I know not what will be the weapons of WWIII, but I am quite sure that the weapons of WWIV will be sticks and stones.' It is regarding his prediction that we gather here today."

"As members of the Hubbard Team, your missions have always been about helping people prepare for an unknown aftermath. All of the *what-ifs* that your teams are working on are within either a *possible* or *probable* status."

"I know that all of you recognize EMP as the acronym for Electromagnetic Pulse, and that EMPs are most often associated with nuclear bomb explosions. You also know that depending on the size and strength of the pulse, these EMPs have the potential to wipe out all the electronic or digital networks that connect and ultimately sustain us. A high-altitude nuclear weapon detonated twenty-five miles above North America could destroy most, if not all, unshielded electronics, high-voltage transformers, vehicles, and all other machinery and equipment with electronic components."

"The federal government has nearly thirty separate initiatives researching ways to deal with such a crisis. If the power grid goes down, everything that is electronic without protective shields will, within a very short time, be wiped out. It will happen quickly and without warning. Unfortunately, the AI models being developed to deal with such a scenario are currently being slow-walked. The funding for those programs is now being redirected to yet another, even more probable, crisis on the horizon."

"The immediate focus has turned toward the constant, unrelenting cybersecurity attacks on our digital grid. Our enemies are obviously more interested in controlling us than in destroying us. Why destroy the physical infrastructure if you can control the digital grid, which ultimately gives one control over all those who use it?"

"All the players in this game of chess have so far avoided Einstein's prediction of self-annihilation. Words like treaties, accords, alliances, negotiation, and even retaliation have kept mankind from self-destruction. There is one superpower, however, that will never be receptive to a treaty, nor interested in negotiations, nor intimidated by threats of retaliation. It is regarding that power that we now turn our attention."

While everyone looked at each other with a puzzled look on their faces, wondering who might have this superpower, the Secretary paused. She reached into her lunchbox and took out a twin-pack of cookies. "Please," she said, "If I can eat and talk at the same time, then feel free to eat and listen at the same time. Go ahead and resupply your snacks." A couple of the attendees stepped to the snack table and retrieved plenty for everyone.

The Secretary continued. "The superpower in question is not of any familiar family of nations. Its destructive power comes from ninety-three million miles away and will inflict damage so fast there will be no time to respond." Heads started slowly nodding up and down, acknowledging they now knew who she was talking about.

"Each of your individual programs is linked to one or more of our forty-two national security satellites. Most recently, you were also connected to one of NASA's older solar-observation satellites, Stereo A. Beyond Stereo A, there is yet another solar-observation satellite unknown to the rest of the world. She goes by the name of Starbright and orbits at an altitude much farther out in the upper atmosphere. She is monitored by a combined team of members from NASA, SpaceX, and the U.S. Space Force."

"Three days ago, Starbright began sending back a flurry of scrambled data. Yesterday, the initial data was finally decoded. We already knew that the sun has been going through another one of its mid-life crises with increasing hot flashes. These solar flares, with very small and limited energy, have been entertaining millions of people over the past several months. As minor invasions, we call them The Northern Lights. But when those same solar ejections become much more powerful, we potentially have a very real and dangerous problem."

With all the recent activity of The Northern Lights and now the data coming back from Starbright, I am raising the status of a solar EMP to either *probable* or *likely*. Even with our current technology, we still cannot predict a status of either *very likely* or *imminent*. However, in either of those two cases, humanity will have no time to prepare. If we can help people to survive a world without digital technology, then that preparation must be now — *before it happens*. I'll take any questions you might have at this time."

For the next two hours, Secretary Higgins took questions and continued to update everyone with what information she had. Finally, she stood and looked over her team leaders. "If there are no other questions, I wish you all God's speed in your efforts to prepare for the unknown. May you all have safe travels home." With that, the chairs were pushed back from the tables. Eight contractors stood up and began to exit the cabin. Caleb Burns was the last to approach the door when Higgins quietly said, "Caleb, can I have a word with you?" The two stepped away from the door as the others walked on toward their vehicles.

Higgins walked back to one of the tables and sat down. Caleb followed, grabbed another chair, and sat down across from her. The Secretary smiled as she reached into her vest pocket and pulled out an envelope. She handed it to Caleb, who proceeded to take out a single sheet of folded paper from inside. On the paper was a photo of an attractive woman with honey-blonde hair and green eyes. She could easily pass as a model for hair and eye products. Perhaps she was in her early thirties—just a few years younger than Caleb. Below the photo was her name, Lucy Moore, along with a few lines of personal and professional data.

"Do I know her?" asked Caleb.

"Not likely," responded Higgins. "But you will. She is your new incoming recruit."

"Okay...." said Caleb, "Anything else I should know about her?" he asked with a hint of foreboding caution in his voice.

"Well, there is one other little thing," Higgins said. "She doesn't know she's being recruited yet."

Higgins continued, "Caleb, right now, your efforts in Welcome, Indiana, offer the best possible hope of significant survival. If we have a big SEMP, people will still instinctively realize they can walk to get from A to B. They will instinctively find or create shelter, but they will not instinctively know how to grow, preserve, or prepare their food. Your project in Welcome does all of that in a very basic and sustainable way. We desperately need something like that to give the masses at least a chance—a reason to have hope."

Caleb stroked his chin and then said, "I want to make sure I've got this right.

You want us to train a few million people in an unknown but probably very short period of time to grow their own food, and the person who is to connect our work with those millions of people doesn't even know she's going to do it yet. Do I have it about right?"

Higgins smiled. "I have always admired your ability to grasp the obvious so quickly, Caleb." Then her smile faded and was replaced by a very concerned and serious look on her face. "You have every right to feel unfairly overwhelmed, Caleb. I don't know how much time we have. If we are lucky, the SEMP will miss Earth completely, like it did back in 2012. Of all the projects we currently have in place, your Welcome project offers the best chance of helping people prepare."

Higgins continued, "I have followed Lucy Moore and her publications from well before there was a Domestic Preparedness cabinet position. As a research writer, she has written about the insecurity of our food system for a long period of time. She's not shy about going to the top to ask the hard questions, and she's not afraid to write the answers once she knows them. She has the drive and the intellect to design a way to tell the story of how to survive. If she needs something to do that, don't worry. Your petty cash box from Uncle Sam will take on a significant weight increase, so you can help her with whatever resources she needs to get the job done. I cannot overstate the sense of urgency, Caleb. We must get the information and experience into the hands of the masses as soon as possible."

With a hint of exasperation in his voice, Caleb said, "It will take us at least one growing season, Janice. We're not talking about training people to make shoeboxes. Besides, how do you plan on getting her on board without telling her all the details to begin with? The security of Mother Hubbard is too important to add an unknown risk when we don't even know for sure that the SEMP will hit us."

"She has a publishing agent in Chicago who has neither the resources nor the drive to get something this big delivered in adequate time. We feel quite certain that if he hears there's a secret government project regarding the nation's food supply taking place in Welcome, he will encourage Ms. Moore to go there and check it out. Your people in Welcome can then help her *accidentally* find you, and you and your team can take it from there."

Higgins closed her eyes and let out a long, slow breath. "Even if time is short, we have to do everything possible to give people hope." Another long pause. "Ms. Moore is good, Caleb. You and your team down in Welcome are the best. I ask only that you promise to give Lucy Moore a chance—a chance to help you and your team give America the gift of hope." She rose from her chair and motioned for Burns to follow.

She stepped over to the table of food and picked up three of the remaining boxed lunches. Then she filled three bags with snacks. "These are for you and your drivers to get you back to Reagan. I hate government waste." They both started walking toward the door. Once there, she turned and faced him, "Your mission is clear, Major. Make it happen." With that, they both walked out through the door and left cabin four.

Chapter 4

Chicago, Illinois

Lenny was happy that the clash with Lucy last Thursday had ended in a truce. That was four days ago. On this particular morning, his increasingly familiar problem was shouting for full attention. The night before, his wife had once again threatened divorce. She had reminded him that his credit cards were maxed out, the family hadn't had a vacation in three years, she couldn't afford to do any clothes shopping, and she had no intention of getting a second job to support his floundering business.

Lenny wasn't lazy. He had no vices like gambling or drinking, or drugs. He just liked to live about twenty percent above his income. What Lenny was quickly starting to grasp was that his lifestyle of twenty percent beyond his income was starting to show up as a forty percent greater debt year after year, which was making it eighty percent harder to get out of debt. If things didn't change in a big way in a big hurry, Lenny was going to be one hundred percent broke by the end of the year.

That was the problem that Lenny Dekoskie was thinking about when his phone chirped. He struggled to clear his mind and then reached into his pocket for the phone.

A less-than-refined male voice on the other end spoke first, "Is this Lenny Dekoskie?"

"Yes, this is Leonard Dekoskie. Who is calling?"

"Let's just say I'm an old acquaintance that owes you a big favor, Lenny, and I'm callin' to clear the debt. You're still in the writin' business, aren't you?"

"I'm a publishing agent," said Lenny.

"Close enough," said the caller. "So here's your tip. It seems as though our dear old Uncle Sam has a little secret project down in southern Indiana being conducted as we speak. It has somethin' to do with people havin' food to eat when there ain't any food to eat – some kind of doomsday project. The thing is this—the people I represent would like to know what is happenin' before everyone else finds out. And Lenny ol' boy, let's just say that the people I represent have *very* deep pockets. So, if you get the scoop for them first, you will never have to work the rest of your life. You will be a very, very rich man."

The caller continued, "Look, here's what I got for ya, Lenny. The town is called Welcome over next door in Indiana. There's no big commercial airport nearby, so if you got a writer to check it out, tell him he'd better plan on driving. My source says there are not many motels either, but there is a little old-fashioned B&B on the west side of town on the main road going in. He says it's clean and cheap. It's called the Chicken's Nest, or Birds Nest, or something like that." With that, the man on the other end of the conversation simply said, "Well, good luck, Lenny ol' boy. We are now officially even. You have a great day," and the call ended.

Lenny sat for a moment, trying to process what had just happened—but only for a moment. Then he took the phone and immediately called Lucy Moore. "Lucy, this is Lenny. You will not believe what just happened." He filled her in on most of the call but left out the part about how he could become rich if she got the scoop.

"I know it's not much to go on, and it sounds like a long shot," Lenny cautioned." He knew Lucy loved the challenge of a long-shot story. "Maybe there's nothing to it," he continued, but I thought I should let you know."

"Lenny, why the sudden change of heart about my compulsion to write about food security?"

"Lucy, I just felt really bad about the friction in the office the other morning, and I wanted to pass along a peace offering to say I'm sorry. So if you want the story, it's yours."

"Are you kidding? I'll be packed and headed south in less than two hours. I'll check in with you in a few days to see if there's anything there for a story or not. Thanks, Lenny. Wish me luck. Bye."

Chapter 5

The Road Trip

Chicago, Illinois

Lucy quickly began her plans for the unknown. She would take all her writing materials, her older laptop, and her new, latest, and greatest tablet. She packed clothes enough for a week without going to a laundromat: one change of nice dress clothes, two or three casual outfits for day-to-day work (even though she didn't know what that would be), rain gear, boots, and a sunhat. She always over-prepared for the unknown. But that was okay. After all, there was no one in her life to pass judgment on what she did or did not do.

She decided to leave instructions for Carl, who was one of the few people she *did* interact with. Carl was the apartment garage attendant and general go-to guy for any issues within the apartment complex. Carl had a heart of gold, and everyone loved him. He was in his early seventies but with no hope of any retirement. She considered him a neighbor-friend and a friend of mutual respect. He was the great-grandson of a Georgian slave. He was someone who would always share with you what he considered the blessings in his life, but he would never spoil your day by dwelling on his own problems and difficulties.

Lucy would ask Carl to set out the trash and to do two or three other housekeeping chores for her while she was gone. She had decided to leave a letter of instructions in his mailbox explaining the things she wanted him to do, especially if she was away for any length of time. Along with the letter, there would be two hundred dollars in twenties—sufficient for a tip in advance. When Lucy first met Carl, he was someone for her to interview to get to know. Now Lucy considered Carl a close friend. She knew if Granny were alive and living with her, Granny and Carl would be great friends. Sometimes Lucy would double the tip and tell Carl the extra was from a secret admirer. He would ask, "Who?"

Lucy would shrug her shoulders and say, "I think she just calls herself Granny."

It took Lucy a very short time to pack her clothes and personal things, locate Welcome, Indiana with her navigation app, and pack a lunch: a sandwich, a bag of Cheetos, and a Diet Coke. She grabbed her writing materials, locked the door behind her, and headed down to the parking garage.

Max was there waiting for her, as she knew he would be. He was always there in space number nine. Max was a vintage 2020 Mazda Miata MX-5. The little sports car was the only luxury she had ever allowed herself to enjoy. She liked Max a lot, but had never dared to tell him she was writing him off as a tax deduction.

Twenty minutes later, she took the Wilson Parkway exit onto I-90 and headed south toward Gary, Indiana. According to Max's GPS, to get to Welcome would be a little over five hours of driving time, but she was in no hurry—so long as she got there before dark.

Lucy enjoyed the long drives that her work sometimes required, as it gave her time to think, time to reflect, and, of course, time to talk. It was on those long drives that Lucy had her longest talks with God. Her whole life was about writing words— not saying words. She had no family to talk to and no close friends or neighbors to really talk with, so Lucy Moore enjoyed talking to God. She didn't just think the words in her head. She didn't say the words softly or reverently. She just talked out loud to God as though He was sitting right there in the seat beside her.

"So God, are You going to let me in on what's happening here? Is this little road trip from You, or is someone just messing with our old buddy Lenny? Or, am I out for a long ride to some third-world American city just to put a *little excitement* into my life? Lord knows I could... oh, I'm sorry God, what I meant was, You know better than anyone, that this girl could use a little excitement." On and on it would go, Lucy talking with her dear friend God about all sorts of things, including her work.

Lucy loved her career. It gave her life some meaning and a sense of purpose, but more and more lately, she felt like something was missing. She knew what that something was. Everyone she had ever loved or cared for was gone. Now she was scared to ever love anyone, or to care for any one person again. She was scared of being hurt again.

To make sure that would never happen, Lucy had decided it was okay to care about and write about the masses—the non-personal, non-individual masses. After all, she couldn't get hurt by the masses, right? Disappointed, sure, but not hurt. So it only seemed natural for her writing and her stories to be about the masses. If they listened, then great. And if not … no harm, no foul, and no hurt.

Lately, though, it seemed some of the masses were starting to have names and faces. They had personal hopes and dreams, personal worries and fears, and she was starting to care about the individuals within the masses. She was starting to wonder what it might be like to care for someone again. More than that, she was starting to wonder how it would feel to have someone care for her. So when Lucy talked about a *little excitement* in her life, she knew God understood what she was talking about. She was resigned to be patient and let Him help her know when the time was right.

It seemed like no time at all had passed when the bypass around Gary, Indiana, was in her rear-view mirror. The road sign ahead said West Lafayette, eighty miles. It had been more than two years since she had been there, though it seemed like only yesterday. It was the home of Purdue University, but Lucy's time there had not been to watch the Boilermakers win or lose a football game. Instead, it had been to interview the people in white lab coats in the College of Agriculture.

Like all other agriculture colleges, Purdue's College of Agriculture was focused on food, fuel, and fiber. Lucy's focus had been on the food sector of their research. Like all other such colleges, with their reputations as premier research centers, came millions and millions of research dollars from the big agricultural corporations.

The seed companies needed validation that their new genetically modified seeds, or GMOs as they were called, were safe for both humans and the environment. The petrochemical companies needed similar confirmation about their herbicides and pesticides. The food processing companies needed research data to show that their new extended shelf-life additives were not only safe but also made the food tastier than ever before.

On and on it went. To no one's surprise, if the results came back in favor of the corporations' new products, then the universities could count on a steady flow of research dollars in the form of grants, facilities, and supplies. And, of course, the corporations could count on someone independent of themselves to validate their products. It truly was a marriage of mutual dependency.

Lucy had interviewed the corporate executives from all the big players in the American food industry. They were referred to as The Big Six, or sometimes as The Big Four. Honestly, it made no difference, four or six, because regardless of the names or numbers, they were all the same.

They each had several smaller, familiar corporations under the parent corporate umbrella. Every three or four years, there would be a redistribution of the smaller corporations. Selloffs, buyouts, name changes, and stock trades were just a few of the ways that the deck would get reshuffled. When it was all over, each would have its own share of profits and losses to keep the corporate accountants happy. Each would also have its fair share of seed companies, herbicide and pesticide companies, fertilizer companies, pharmaceutical companies, and food processing companies. Each would have a big enough slice of the pie to stay in the game and to keep any new players from getting in.

Their congressional lobby efforts were in the billions of dollars, and they made sure that the laws were written to their benefit. There was so much power in the hands of so few. They had convinced themselves that they were invincible. The technologies that each had either developed or bought would feed the world. Their technologies would save the world. They worshiped their technologies. Sometimes, they worshiped themselves.

As she passed the university exit, her thoughts returned to last week's argument with Lenny. It had been the same challenge every time. "Who cares?" Lenny would always say. "So long as the grocery shelves are full of food, and the choices are plentiful, who really cares?"

To that, Lucy would always respond with her but *what-if* questions: "What if someday their technologies failed? What if there were unintended consequences of those technologies within the food stream, and something goes terribly wrong? What if a hostile country hacked our power grid or launched a nuclear EMP event large enough to take everything down?"

She was pretty sure those were good questions, but she also knew that she did not have the answers. Maybe Lenny was right. Maybe she was starting to sound like Chicken Little—sounding the alarm but having no good solutions. And yes, maybe her writings of late were starting to have a flavor of fear with a pinch of paranoia.

She hated to admit it, but she was starting to feel a little burned out with the one single subject that had always fueled her passion and energized her as a writer. The deeper she went in her research, the more depressed she became. So much power was in the hands of so few. She had started to consider that the answers to all of her *what-if* questions might not be found within the power of the few, but rather in the hands of the many—the masses, and even more specifically, in the efforts of the individual.

Max was cruising around the Indianapolis bypass when Lucy finished the Cheetos, emptied the can of Diet Coke, and was ready to take a break. She would get a bite to eat, something more nutritious than her snacks, and change the channel inside her thinking cap.

Looking down at the gas gauge, she saw that Max was getting thirsty too, so at the next exit, she pulled into a service center with a little store. Fifteen gallons later, she walked inside and got a hot sandwich, fries, and a drink. She took the food back outside and sat down at an outdoor eating area.

She sat there eating her food and watching the people come and go. After all, she was a people watcher. It was one of those things that gave her extra insight for her writing, so it was okay to just sit and watch people. There were young parents with children, people in business dress, construction workers, and truck drivers.

She watched an old couple in their eighties holding hands like newlyweds as they helped each other into the store. She couldn't help but smile. Then she saw an elderly woman, worn by too many days and by herself, slowly make her way toward the store. Lucy's smile faded as she watched the woman struggle to get the door open and go inside—alone.

Would that be her someday down the road … all alone and without anyone to open the door for her? Then, without warning, a loud, stern voice inside her head said, *Lucy Moore, stop that right now. You know better than to think thoughts like that.*

It was Granny's voice, right on time. When Lucy was little and would get sad about losing her parents, her Granny would hold her close and say, "Lucy, child, so long as we have memories, we still have our yesterdays. As long as we have hopes for the future, then tomorrow is out there just waiting for us. But most important, as long as we have love, then today is always going to be beautiful."

Granny would hold Lucy real close and whisper in her ear, 'Lucy, I love you.' And with that, the little fragile girl would give her Granny a big hug back and say, "I love you too, Granny."

Lucy wiped her tears away, gathered up her paper trash, and headed back to the car.

Chapter 6

Welcome to Welcome

Welcome, Indiana

Lucy continued south through changing farmland and rolling hills. It was mid-spring in southern Indiana. The farmers were getting back in the fields to begin the annual cycle of tillage, sowing, and harvest. High in the sky were the sights and sounds of thousands of migratory birds making their way north one more time. Lucy smiled as she considered what the view might look like if the Federal Aviation Authority were responsible for booking all those flights. She had finally cleared her mind of work and began to simply enjoy the drive.

An hour and a half later, Lucy exited the interstate and continued onto a state highway. She turned east, and with the evening sun to her back, she settled in for the last leg of the trip.

WELCOME TO WELCOME, INDIANA, said the sign, but where was Welcome? Slowly, a few houses and small businesses started to appear. Then ahead on the left, she saw the sign, THE ROBINS' NEST- BED & BREAKFAST. She pulled into the off-street parking area and went inside. "Good evening, young lady," said a cheerful, corpulent woman in her sixties. "Can I help you?"

"I need a room," replied Lucy, "If you've got one, that is. I looked online to make a reservation, but I couldn't find a motel in Welcome."

"Not to worry, young lady, I have a couple of rooms. My nicest room is upstairs, first door on the right. How many nights will you be staying? It's cheaper by the week, you know".

"I'm not sure yet," said Lucy, "Just one night for now."

The lady smiled and said, "If you want to charge for the room, I need some identification." Lucy handed her some ID and a credit card. The lady looked at it and said, "Well, Lucy Moore from Chicago, welcome to Welcome. My name is Ms. Robins. I'm the owner, housekeeper, and cook at The Robins' Nest B & B. Most folks around here just call it The Nest. I'll go open up your room while you get your things from your car."

When Lucy came back in, Ms. Robins was getting fresh linens and keys to the room. "House rules are posted on the back of your door, and breakfast is promptly at 7:00 a.m."

"Oh, I'm not much of a breakfast person," answered Lucy.

"Suit yourself," said Ms. Robins. "It makes no difference in the price though." She continued, "I'll be up till ten o'clock, so if you need something, just come down and ask. Have a good night's sleep, and welcome to Welcome!"

Then Angela Robins stepped into her office and woke up her computer. Seconds later, through a secured line, she sent the message: SHE'S HERE.

****

The next morning, when Lucy came downstairs, she was greeted by Ms. Robins. "Here's your copy of the Welcome morning paper," she said. "You know, the only reason we still have a printed newspaper is that old man Jasper left an endowment of a few million dollars to keep it going. He said that to be a good citizen, you needed to be an informed citizen. Of course, that was a century before digital technology. Anyway, today the Historical Society manages the endowment and runs the newspaper. If you ask me, if they don't get some decent writers soon, they might as well close up shop. But then, I suppose it's like everything else, hard to find good writers."

"Well, that's what I do, I'm a writer, said Lucy, "That's why I'm here."

"No kidding?" said Ms. Robins. "You're going to work for the Welcome paper?"

"Oh no," said Lucy, "Actually, I'm here because…" she paused and then continued, "because of a tip about a possible government project dealing with food security. But truthfully, I have very little information to go on. I don't suppose you've had a recent group of government guests here at the B&B, have you?"

"No, can't say that I have. Let's see, there is a guy I know who could maybe help you. His name is Caleb Burns. He brings me some mighty fine homegrown food for the B&B every once in a while. Seems like he and his friends always have food to share with those who need it or who appreciate real, good-tasting food."

"Where can I find him?" asked Lucy.

"Most mornings, he eats over at K's restaurant. It's a little diner on Market Street— just a couple of blocks from here. It might be a place to get a start," said Ms. Robins.

Lucy grabbed her notepad, picked up a Robins' Nest business card for contact reference, and began to walk the two blocks to K's. Glancing at the card, she read The Robins' Nest B&B, Angela Robins, proprietor.

K's was one of those little hometown restaurants that appeared to be stuck in a 1950s time warp. To stop in at K's was like going through an interactive museum, but it was all very real. There was a little bell that *dinged* when anyone walked through the front door. There were ceiling fans instead of air conditioning. There was a jukebox that still played old songs for a quarter. Red vinyl-covered stools still swiveled at the counter. K's was different, and the people of Welcome liked it that way.

For Caleb Burns, it would be a morning unlike any other of his mornings at K's. A great deal of thought and planning had been put into play for this morning. Angela had been in place to direct Lucy to the diner. The waitress was prepped, and the team was on standby. Caleb was on his second cup of coffee, sitting in his favorite booth, enjoying breakfast, and waiting. The little bell over the door did its thing, and Caleb looked up to see who had come in.

Kay, the owner, had gone back into the kitchen, and Alison, the waitress, was clearing tables. There was no greeter at the door to ask: *Table, booth, or counter?* Lucy stood there and began scanning the seating area. The breakfast folks were mostly cleared out by now, except for one man who she saw sitting alone in a booth. She began walking toward him and stopped at booth number seven.

"Excuse me," she said, "Are you Caleb Burns?"

"Who's asking?" he said.

"Oh, sorry. My name is Lucy Moore. Ms. Robins over at the

B&B, where I'm staying, said I might find him here."

"And why would Lucy Moore want to find Caleb Burns?" he asked.

Looking a little frustrated, but pretty sure she had found Caleb Burns, she said, "Mr. Burns, may I sit down?"

"Don't see why not", he said.

She slid into the vinyl-covered seat across from him and placed both hands on the table. "That's good," he said.

"What's good?" she asked.

"Both hands on the table means you're probably not going to try to rob me."

"No, Mr. Burns, I don't want to rob you. I just want to ask you a few questions."

"About what?" he said.

"About Welcome's food supply," Lucy responded.

"Is there a problem with our food supply?" he asked.

"I don't think so … I mean, no, of course not," she said, sounding even more frustrated. Lucy was accustomed to being in total control of her interviews, but this guy was getting the best of her. It was time to get the conversation back online and get to the point.

"Mr. Burns, I am a writer, and I am researching material for a story on the safety and security of America's food supply."

"Okay," he said, "But my question still stands—why does Lucy Moore want to talk with Caleb Burns?"

"Well," she began, "my publisher in Chicago got a tip that something most unusual was going on in Welcome regarding some local food production project, so I drove down to check it out. When I checked in at the B&B, I told Ms. Robins why I was here, and she suggested I talk with you. She said you seem to always have extra fresh, local food. I guess she figures you must have one really big garden and know what you're doing."

"Actually, Miss Moore," Caleb said, "I don't even have a garden. I just know a few people who are very good at growing what they grow. They often have a surplus and don't mind sharing with others, that's all." He continued, "So, Ms. Moore, you say you are a writer. Let me ask you one simple question. Why this subject? Why is this story so important to you? Last time I was in a grocery store, it looked like we had plenty of food on hand."

"Of course, they're full of food today," Lucy responded, "but what if something interrupted the daily delivery of that food. How long would the store shelves be full? With our just-in-time delivery systems, our grocery stores depend completely on a daily delivery of fresh produce. There are few, if any, cities that have over a day or two of fresh produce in stock. If their daily deliveries were interrupted, or worse yet, stopped altogether, can you imagine the chaos that would ensue? And what if the interruption wasn't just local, but all across America … and it lasted not for days but for weeks. Do you know what our country would look like after two or three weeks, Mr. Burns?"

Caleb rubbed his chin a little and said, "You know, Ms. Moore, it sounds to me like you should write a book on why everyone should become a Mormon and learn how to stock up a couple of years' worth of food. That would solve the problem, wouldn't it?"

Lucy rolled her eyes in total exasperation, thinking to herself, "This is not going well".

Caleb, sensing her level of frustration, said, "I tell you what, I need to be out of town for the rest of the week. Before I leave, let me connect you with those friends of mine who grow all that food. I'm sure you can interview them, get their perspective, and see if there is anything for your story here in Welcome. How does that sound?"

"That sounds wonderful!" said Lucy, surprised at the change in the direction of their conversation.

"My flight leaves early in the morning, so I'll contact one of my friends by the name of Jenny. She can meet you at The Robins' Nest tomorrow morning, and from there you two can put together a schedule for the rest of the week."

"Thank you so much, Mr. Burns!"

"Not a problem," he said. "I'd love to stay and talk about the perils of Welcome's food supply, but I've got some things I need to do today before I leave. I've been promising my girls I'd spend some time with them, but I've been so busy lately, I've neglected them, and that's not a good thing to do."

"Oh, please, Mr. Burns, by all means, I don't want to keep you from your girls. Besides, it was a long drive down from Chicago yesterday, and I need to get a few things done to settle in if I'm to start on interviews tomorrow. So, I'll see you a week from today?" she asked.

"Don't see why not. Same place, same time—if that works for you?"

"Yes, and thanks again, Mr. Burns."

At that, Caleb Burns slid out from behind the booth's table and walked to the cash register near the front of the diner. As he did so, he looked in the curved mirror behind the counter and saw Lucy Moore watching him intently. What Lucy did not know was at that very moment, the tall curly-haired blonde waitress behind her was giving an understanding nod to Caleb. As Burns stepped out the door and into the warm morning air, he smiled and said softly, "Ah, yes, Sherlock, the game is afoot".

Chapter 7

BISCUITS, BUTTER, AND HONEY

The next morning, Lucy came down the stairs and was greeted by Ms. Robins. "Morning. You have a visitor." She motioned for Lucy to follow.

Seconds later, Lucy stood in what a century ago would have been called the parlor. Standing there dressed in jeans, a T-shirt, and a lightweight jacket was a very attractive black woman. She smiled. "Hi, I'm Jenny Reece, a friend of Caleb Burns."

Lucy reached out to shake hands with Jenny. The woman might have been forty, maybe even forty-five, but the strength in her hands and her striking appearance was that of a woman clearly ten years her junior. After exchanging the common pleasantries between two strangers meeting for the first time, they turned to walk out the door. Suddenly, a voice from behind called out, "Where do you two think you're going in such a hurry? You can't leave until you have had some hot biscuits and fresh clover honey from Mr. Caleb's girls. He brought it by yesterday late afternoon."

Jenny smiled and looked at Lucy, "There's no arguing with Ms. Robins. We might as well not even try." They sat down at the kitchen table, and Ms. Robins pulled from the oven the fluffiest biscuits Lucy had ever seen. A bowl of fresh butter and a jar of light-amber honey were placed on the table.

Jenny proceeded to explain the Welcome way to eat biscuits, butter, and honey. "This is the way Caleb insists on eating his honey for maximum effect: First, take your knife and put a nice big pat of butter on the plate. Now, pour a generous amount of honey over the butter—about half and half. Then, take your knife and begin to blend the two in this swirling, circular motion. After that, when the two are a creamy blend, then, and only then, do you dare put it on a hot biscuit."

"A little much, don't you think?" said Lucy, in a condescending tone.

"You be the judge," said Jenny as she spread some on a biscuit.

Lucy did the same. She put a bite in her mouth. "Wow! That has got to be the best tasting breakfast treat I have ever eaten!"

The two women sat there for several more minutes— two strangers enjoying the moment together. It would be the beginning of a very strong bond between the two—a bond of sharing more than biscuits, butter, and honey. As they wiped their mouths and stood up, Lucy started to speak, then stopped.

Jenny looked at her and said, "Yes?" as though permitting her to continue.

Lucy said, "Well, I'm not even sure why, but I do have a question. It's a personal question about Mr. Burns."

"I hope not too personal," said Jenny.

"I was just wondering how many girls does Mr. Burns have?"

Trying to keep a straight face, Jenny said, "You know, I don't think he even knows for sure."

"What?" Lucy's face filled with a look of disgust and shock.

"Well, let me think," Jenny continued as she rolled her eyes up in her head as though calculating great numbers. "He has eight hives, and this time of the year each hive might have between forty to fifty thousand bees, so let's see....I guess Caleb would have somewhere between three hundred to four hundred thousand girls."

"What?" Lucy's shock turned to confusion. "You mean Mr. Burns' girls are his honey bees?"

"Well, of course, Lucy," Jenny started to laugh a little. "Caleb is not married, and he has no children. The bees are his girls. Then Jenny continued, "There's one other piece of personal information about Caleb Burns I should share with you. He doesn't like being called Mr. Burns— just Caleb. But he's too traditional to ever ask you to call him that. So maybe the next time you two are together, you might think of a way to ask him to call you Lucy, and then he can ... well, you know."

"Sure, Jenny, thanks for the tip."

They left the house and walked to the curb where Jenny's old pickup truck was parked. "Hop in," said Jenny. "He may not look pretty, but he's the most dependable truck I've ever owned. His name is Rufus."

As the truck pulled away from the curb, Jenny began to update

Lucy on her phone call from Caleb the night before. "We decided it might be more efficient if all of us met with you first thing this morning. We can do introductions, and then you can tell us about the work you've been doing and what you hope to accomplish while you're here in Welcome.

****

The neighborhood was obviously in an old section of town. The houses were well-kept, and most were set on large lots. The streets were lined with old trees that had seen better days but still gave shade to the new, young trees planted as future replacements. Jenny turned the truck into the driveway of a stately, old two-story brick house that had to be at least one hundred and fifty years old.

Parked at the curb at the front of the house were one late-model pickup truck, an older minivan, a motorcycle, and a bicycle. Jenny led the way as they passed through a squeaky, old yard gate and into the backyard. Sitting at a table under a massive, old sugar maple were four people. They all stood as Jenny and Lucy walked toward them.

"Hey, good morning everyone," Jenny said as they approached the group. "I want you to meet Lucy Moore, a freelance writer from Chicago." They all responded with smiles and good mornings, then sat back down at the table.

Jenny spoke up, "Why don't each of you quickly go around the table and say your name?"

In that ten-second moment, Lucy's mind took a snapshot of the four people she was meeting for the first time. To her left was a tall, thin, dark-haired man with bushy eyebrows. "Hi Lucy, my name is Marcus ." He was wearing khaki pants and a college sweatshirt.

Beside him was a petite Latina girl. "Good morning, my name is Maria Sanchez". She was dressed in jeans, a flannel shirt, and a tractor-advertising ball cap.

To her left was a fair-complexioned young man with rusty-orange hair. He was stout but not overweight, strong-looking, but not like a bodybuilder. "Morning, Lucy, I'm Zachary Blair. Zack for short."

To Lucy's right was the last of the group. He was trim, with short, sandy-brown hair, and a charming, pleasant smile. "Welcome to

38

Welcome. My name is Pete Mullens." All of this visual data was now imprinted on Lucy's mental hard drive. She was, after all, a people watcher.

Jenny continued, "As I shared with each of you, Lucy ran into our buddy Caleb at K's diner yesterday. Lucy here must have had a very compelling conversation with him because, even though he was leaving town for a few days, he wanted to continue the conversation."

Lucy tried to hide the curious smile on her face as she thought to herself, "Is she talking about the same conversation I remember having with Caleb Burns?"

Jenny continued, "Caleb asked if we would make her feel welcome and help her in any way we could until he gets back. I've asked Lucy to share with us what brings her to Welcome and what she hopes to find here for a future story. It's all yours, Lucy.

"First, I want to thank all of you for taking time out of your day to hear the rants of a total stranger. As Jenny told you, I am a freelance writer from Chicago. For whatever reason, it seems like almost all my work has been in some way about the American food story. I've researched and written about our nation's food production, processing, and safety, as well as its access and affordability to the consumer. I've written about corporate farming and the family farm, about chemical farming and organic farming, and about the growing interest in urban and suburban food production. Lately, however, my research has taken a turn toward the very real possibility of disruptions in any or all of those systems that I just mentioned."

"As of today, we are the most successful nation in the world when it comes to having enough food for its people, and we even have enough to share with other countries all around the world. However, our amazing success is very dependent on two things: First, on high energy inputs, and second, on a very complex and integrated network of digital technologies. If those two twins of energy and technology were ever disrupted or separated for even a few days, our entire food system could quickly collapse."

At that point, Pete interrupted, "So, Lucy, I have to ask, are you aware of some soon-to-be apocalyptic event that none of us have heard about?"

"Oh no, Pete," said Lucy, "No, not at all. But I am concerned about the increasing number of cyber hacking events in many of our supply chain components. I know that our systems are so large and cumbersome that when something does happen, everything could collapse into chaos very quickly. When that happens, it will be too late to start the conversation. Sadly, I do not think that we can leave it to the government or the corporate giants to solve the problem. I'm thinking maybe smaller community-based initiatives, maybe even small groups within a community."

Lucy paused and took a deep breath. "All I know is that I'm trying to take a break from writing about potential doom and gloom. I'm looking now to write about something that can actually give people ownership in their daily food supply. Please, don't laugh, but as I told Mr. Burns, my publisher in Chicago got a tip. The tip was something about the government conducting a secret project here in Welcome. The project had something to do with people still having food to eat when, otherwise, there would be no food. So yes, I am also very curious about what this ambiguous government project might be about as well."

"What if you don't find this secret government project? What about those other small groups you mentioned earlier—the homesteader, the urban farmer, or even trying to get people to have a few weeks' supply of prepared food on hand for what you seemingly see as the inevitable?"

Lucy began, "So let's take a look at those you just mentioned. Let's see if the solution to my problem is found in any of them."

"First, you've got the Preppers, also known as Survivalists. They turn their home sites into fortified compounds with weapons and surveillance equipment to stop anyone at any cost from getting to their stockpile of emergency food. Most of them have some paranoia as to what the crisis would be to trigger the need for their prepping. Some think it would be a currency collapse. Others think it would be a natural disaster, another pandemic, or even a biological warfare agent. Some think it would be a collapse in the electrical grid or a long-term interruption of essential goods and services. Whatever their reason, they all have a hefty dose of paranoia and a self-centered reasoning in their approach to their methods of preparedness."

"Then there are the homesteaders, or smallholders as they are called in other parts of the world. These folks are characterized by their determination to be self-sufficient. They get a nice little patch of ground, maybe a large suburban lot, or maybe two to five acres. The amount of ground isn't as important as their determination to produce most, if not all, of the food that they need to survive. They usually, but not always, ascribe to a mindset that everything should be grown organically. I might add that the life expectancy of a homesteader staying a homesteader is only three to five years."

"Their biggest problem starts when they come down with what I call the *Noah's Ark Fever*. The symptoms are expressed by having to have some of everything: two or more goats, chickens, rabbits, pigs, fruit trees, a big garden, solar panels, a windmill, and a score of other amenities they find advertised in their hobby farm or back-to-the-land books and magazines.

These well-intentioned people have, for the most part, lived their entire lives in an urban setting. Their sweat has come from riding a stationary bike, not physical labor in the sun. A cold winter day may have been enjoyed on the ski slopes, but not from carrying buckets of water to the animals in the barn because the pipes froze when temperatures dropped to ten below zero. They have no experience or exposure to what it really takes to raise and care for animals intended for consumption. Add to that the emotional hurdles of harvesting and then eating the rabbit known by the family as *Flopsy*. They have never grown vegetables or had to wait for years to enjoy the benefits of their efforts, as is the case with fruit trees or nut trees. But no problem—all the answers and all the experience needed are close by. All they have to do is ask their all-knowing virtual farmhand, Mr. Google."

"After a few years of more failures than successes, of more confinement than freedom, and more cost in producing food than buying it in the store, the disillusionment stage of *Noah's Ark Fever* sets in. The fever begins to ease as all the animals and related supplies are sold off at a fraction of their cost. Hopefully, the sales will bring enough to buy that new zero-turn, farm-size lawn mower required to mow the now three acres of lawn."

"The third example is the urban farmer. Those who are

interested usually have very limited opportunities or resources, so they do it as a pastime or for some social cause, but with very little real impact on their own food supply. Eighty-five to ninety percent of their meals are still eaten outside of the home. Even if they could produce a significant amount of food, no one cooks anymore; no one even knows how to cook."

"I think I've about run out of models to even consider as a viable solution to what I consider to be a very precarious national food system." At that, Lucy looked at everyone, shrugged her shoulders, and said, "So … what do you think?"

Chapter 8

Everybody's Part

Before Pete began to speak, he poured a big glass of sweet tea from a pitcher and offered the same to the others. He looked over to Lucy and said, "Before I tell you how we function and succeed as a group, I think I need to tell you how we completely fail as individuals."

"As individuals, we do not know how to do everything, but we all know how to do something and do it well. As individuals, none of us has enough land or other resources to be self-sufficient, but we each have some unique soils and other resources to grow things or raise animals that the others cannot. We each contribute what we can, and by all of us doing that, then as a group we reach our goal of *group sufficiency* or *group reliance*."

Pete continued, "As we begin to tell you what we do individually, you will start to see why we have plenty of food for ourselves and to share with others. My contribution to this group comes mostly from my fruit trees. I have three dwarf apple trees, one peach tree, and one pear tree. I am also the bramble guy. I have both black and red raspberries, as well as everyone's favorite, my strawberry patch. I am also the seed saver. I cross-pollinate some varieties and isolate others. I collect the seeds at harvest and prepare them for the next year's crop. Since everyone here has to have some sort of real job, I happen to be a freelance photographer. So, if you ever need photos for your publications or seeds for your garden, I'm your guy."

The second to speak up was Zack. "Good morning, Lucy. As I said earlier, my name is Zack, and my background is in mechanical engineering. My contribution to our little group has two parts. First, I design, construct, and maintain some of the equipment we use in our efforts to produce our food. Most of that equipment is pedal-powered or handheld. My food contribution to the group is raising rabbits. I hope you are not vegan," He said with a grin.

Maria, who appeared to be the youngest in the group, was next. She again introduced herself and began telling Lucy about her two goats, Angelina and Bonita. "They give us milk, and from that we can also make cheese and butter, and Zack's favorite, homemade ice cream. My other contribution to the group's collective pantry is the tilapia fish. I'm sure you will find my backyard fish production system unlike any you have ever seen. I also have a small home cleaning business that provides me with sufficient income."

The tall, slender, dark-haired man stood and introduced himself once again as Marcus. "I am Marcus, an adjunct chemistry professor at the nearby community college. For this strange little group, I make explosives." Lucy's face filled with a look of disbelief.

"I'm sorry," said Marcus. "What I should have said is that I grow potatoes and raise a few chickens. From the potatoes I make alcohol, and from the chicken manure I make methane gas." Lucy still looked confused. Marcus shrugged his shoulder and said, "What did you expect—French fries and chicken nuggets? I told you, I'm a chemist." With a mischievous look in his eyes, he said, "Can't wait to show you what I do with the alcohol and methane gas."

Jenny interrupted, "Okay, Marcus, that's enough. Don't scare off our guest before she even decides whether to visit or not." Jenny continued, "I guess it's my turn now." She pointed Lucy's attention to a small but professional-looking sign attached to the porch railing of the house. "Like the sign says, I'm a nurse practitioner."

"My training is in human health care, but, with all the animals in this little group, I have been designated as the group's vet tech as well. In addition, I am the greens grower. We're talking about all kinds of greens, from lettuce to kale, from spinach to turnips, and a whole host of others that most people have never even heard of. My goal is to produce them year-round with no supplemental heat source. That's a real challenge when you consider that Welcome can get down to single-digit temperatures in the winter, but it is doable."

"There are six of us altogether, counting Caleb. Other than the bees, Caleb doesn't grow any food, but he helps us in lots of other ways. What we are trying to do is develop a workable model of fresh food production. We want to do it without all those problems inherent with the homesteaders, urban farmers, or the stock-and-store preppers that you spoke of earlier."

"We are striving to grow delicious, healthy, affordable, fresh food year-round for ourselves and others. Perhaps most of all, we want access to that food without worry of disruption or dependency on others."

Jenny then said, "Why don't we break for the day. I know the rest of you have places to go and things to do. Lucy and I can spend a little more time here at my place. Then, if she likes, we can make a schedule for her to visit each of you throughout the rest of the week." With that, the others all stood, said their goodbyes, and left through the backyard gate.

Jenny stood and said, "Let's stretch our legs while I show you around my little place." As they walked toward what looked like an old carriage barn in the back of the property, Jenny continued, "Medicine is my background. That big brick house I call home is also where I have a small clinic. I serve as a very part-time nurse practitioner. I have very few patients, and that's the way I like it. That is because I also have some not-so-human patients that keep me busy enough. They are over here in the old carriage barn."

The two walked toward a beautiful, old stone building likely built more than a hundred and fifty years ago. The large two-story barn looked as though it sat on a lush green carpet. The green extended out three feet from the base of the building on all four sides. Jenny opened a heavy wooden door, hinged with the most ornate hinges one would ever expect to see on a barn. Lucy stepped in and was greeted by a dozen newly hatched chicks, one small goat, and a pair of rabbits.

Jenny said, "Since I am the healthcare person in our little group, my philosophy is that our own safe and nutritious meat must come from healthy animals. Healthy animals come from clean and healthy spaces. You mentioned you had visited the big farm feedlots, so you know what I am talking about. Overpopulation breeds disease and requires a great deal of medication to prevent or control those diseases. That is neither healthy nor sustainable."

The two stayed in the carriage house for several more minutes. Lucy watched as Jenny fed and charted each of the animals, much like in a hospital ward. When the chores were finished, Jenny motioned with her hand and said, "Let's go back up to the house and get a bite of lunch. After lunch, we can finish the tour and make plans, if you like, to meet with the others throughout the rest of the week at their own homes."

Lunch consisted of a large Caesar salad made with the most crisp and delicious mix of lettuce (beet greens and Asian greens) and homemade sourdough breadsticks. Dessert was a slice of strawberry-rhubarb pie. After all, it was springtime in Welcome.

After lunch, Jenny showed Lucy the lush, green carpet at the base of the carriage house. There were several varieties of lettuce, kale, collards, Asian greens, cabbage, and Brussels sprouts. There were only a few of each variety, but successive plantings of each insured a continuous harvest throughout the months ahead. Jenny then gave a quick in-service on how her greens were watered with drip hoses connected to rainwater barrels attached to the barn's gutters. That was followed by another mini-class on how the cold frames and other structures protected the greens from freezing in the coldest months.

It had been a long day, and Lucy had worked up a real appetite. As they were headed back to The Robins' Nest, Lucy asked Jenny to drop her off at K's diner.

Moments later, Jenny pulled to the curb, and Lucy got out. "Thanks for such an amazing day, Jenny. It was wonderful! If the rest are willing, I would indeed like to visit with each of them during the rest of the week."

"That's great, Lucy! I will put together a schedule with them this evening and text it to you late tonight or first thing in the morning. See ya." Lucy waved bye and just stood there a minute, trying to comprehend the day she had just had.

When she walked inside the diner, she noticed that booth number seven, the booth where she first met and talked with Caleb Burns, was empty. Not sure why she seemed to be drawn to that booth, she slid into the same place she had sat before. The location of booth number seven might give her a chance for a little more people-watching and a wee bit of eavesdropping. You never know what leads you might pick up when people have their guard down. *You never know*, she thought to herself. *K's just might be the place to hear about a secret government project happening somewhere in Welcome.*

A waitress came over, handed Lucy a menu, and suggested the

Wednesday evening special. "And what might that be?" asked Lucy.

"Meatloaf and mashed potatoes", the waitress replied.

Lucy said, "Fine, and add a large Diet Coke, please." As she sat there waiting for her food, she began to scan the diner as though it would be a base of operations for her undercover work. By the time her food came, she had decided that booth number seven should do just fine.

A few minutes later, after she had finished her meal, she got a Diet Coke to go and grabbed a bag of Cheetos from the rack at the cash register. Passing through the door, the little bell above it did its *ding-ding* again. Lucy decided she liked it. It said *thanks for coming* when she walked in and *come back soon* when she left. K's was different. Like her Granny used to say, 'If you can make people smile coming and going, you must be doing something good.'

Turning right, she started walking back toward The Nest. She knew she had to write in her journal tonight, but she was in no hurry. The air was warm and filled with new sights and sounds. Birds were chirping in the trees, dogs were barking, and children were playing outside by themselves. People were sitting on their front porches. Some people waved when cars passed by while horns were honked. For sure, this was not Chicago. Whether she ever found the secret government project or not, Lucy was starting to think Welcome might be just what she needed right now, and that was alright with her.

When she got back to her room, she took a quick shower and prepared her things for the next day. She then did her journal entries, and, after that, it was time to read her Bible. Although not always possible, Lucy tried to read from her Bible every night before bed. She feared that if she read in bed, she might fall asleep while reading.

Lucy believed that reading from her Bible was as though God was talking to her personally. With that in mind, she thought He might consider it very rude of her if she fell asleep while He was talking to her, so she read sitting up in a chair. Thirty minutes later, she had finished her reading and set her phone alarm. It had been a long day, and she was quite sure tomorrow would be just as full.

Chapter 9

Greeting, Feeding, and Weeping

The sun was peeking over the horizon, and Lucy's phone began chirping. Thirty minutes later, she was sitting in booth number seven doing a little people-watching. Her phone chirped again. It was a message from Jenny with the schedule for visiting the others. She would visit Maria, the girl with the goats, this morning, and Marcus, the chemistry teacher, in the afternoon. Jenny's message also included each of their addresses and contact numbers.

The same tall, curly-haired blonde who had been there when she first met Caleb came over and handed Lucy the morning menu. She then stepped back a bit as Lucy began to scan the menu. With a southern drawl that came from a lot farther south than Welcome, she said, "So you're keepin' Mr. Caleb's booth occupied till he gets back from bein' out of town, huh?"

A little taken aback by the waitress's seemingly personal comments, Lucy said, "Well, should I move? I mean, there was no one sitting here when I came in."

"Oh no," said the waitress with a big smile. "Goodness gracious, no, I was just making small talk. You just stay right there … and, I am so sorry," she continued. "Where's my manners? My name is Alison, the mornin' waitress," she said as she put her hand out to Lucy. Lucy started to return the gesture just as Alison quickly pulled her hand back. Alison again began to apologize. "I'm so sorry again, but I forgot. I'm not supposed to shake hands with the customers—just greet you with a smile."

"It's okay, Alison, I'm Lucy Moore… from Chicago."

"Pleased to meet ya," said Alison. Lucy gave Alison her order and settled in to wait for her food: coffee, two eggs, sausage, biscuits, and honey. She had been in Welcome only three days and already had developed a growing interest in breakfast, a favorite place to eat it, and even a favorite breakfast treat—biscuits and honey.

Her food came, and while eating, she got a text from Maria asking her to meet her in the little barn when she arrived. Lucy finished her breakfast and, seeing no one at the cash register, left her money and tip on the table. As she was about to walk out, she heard a voice from behind. "Hey girl, see ya in the morning," It was Alison with a great big smile on her face. Lucy gave her a big thumbs up and walked through the door. *Ding-ding.* Lucy smiled. Moments later, she was in the car and on her way to Maria's.

Maria lived on the south side of Welcome in an older but well-kept neighborhood. Her home was a single-level ranch with a good-sized concrete block building and a very spacious backyard. The very visible sidewall of the block building faced the street, where bright, lively colors depicted a village setting in Latin America. Scenes of children leading goats, feeding chickens, and running and playing covered the building's entire wall. *Had Maria left all this behind in search of a better life?* Lucy thought as she approached the building.

Shouting louder than she had intended to, Lucy yelled out, "Maria … It's Lucy!"

"In here," came a voice from inside the building. "Come through the yard gate to the right, and around to the back of the barn." Lucy walked around to the back of the barn. From there, she walked through another yard gate, allowing access to a small corral attached to the barn. When Maria heard the gate swing closed, she called for Lucy to come through the only open doorway.

Lucy stepped inside just as Maria was leading a goat up a ramp and onto a milking stand. "Good morning," she said as she handed Lucy a small scoop of feed. "Please dump this in the feed pan just below the neck yoke so Angelina can have her breakfast."

Lucy did as asked and handed the scoop back to Maria. "Now we get another scoop of feed for Bonita, who is still in her pen. Bonita is not producing milk these days, so that makes her a *dry* goat. She will stay *dry* until she has her babies in a few months, then she will give milk again. By then, Angelina will be going *dry*, and we will re-breed her to start the process all over again."

As they walked from Bonita back to Angelina, Maria continued, "Each goat will produce just over a gallon of milk a day. Their babies need only half that amount for just a few weeks, then they are weaned and sent to a farm in the country. I trade a farmer my little goats for his bales of hay to feed my mama goats in the winter. It's a win-win for both of us. Right now, Angelina is giving me over a gallon of milk per day. That's seven gallons of milk each week—almost twice as much as the six of us will consume."

Lucy stepped back over by Angelina to watch her eat. The goat was using her upper lip and tongue to retrieve the grain. "Fascinating …" said Lucy as she watched in amazement as the goat ate her feed.

Maria spoke up, "Hey Lucy, have you ever milked a cow or a goat before?"

"Can't say that I have," said Lucy.

"Well, then, Lucy Moore from Chicago, this is your lucky day."

Maria explained and then demonstrated the process. Without hesitation, Lucy gave it a try and found it was not as simple as it looked. A few squeezes later, she heard the first *squirt* sound in the milk pan. After a few more minutes, she was milking two-handed and making great progress in filling up the milk pail. Soon, the chores were finished. They took the milk into the house where Maria strained it, ice-chilled it, and put it in the refrigerator.

"You know, many people say goat's milk has a funny taste. Well, it does taste different than cow's milk. However, skimmed cow's milk, two percent, and whole milk all taste a little funny too if you are used to only one and not the others. We use the goat's milk not so much for drinking as we do for making butter and cheese and, of course, ice cream." After her crash course in the attributes of goat's milk, Maria suggested they go check out the fish farm.

Leaving the house, Maria explained that, currently, the most popular and affordable fish eaten in America is the Tilapia. "I buy the fish that I will raise as babies, called fingerlings. Even though they are only two inches long, they can grow very quickly. The warmer the water, the faster they grow. In this part of Indiana,
we raise Tilapia only in the warmer months—outside in those big watering tanks." She pointed over to four big tanks under three huge sugar maple trees. "First, we need to swing by the goat barn to pick up the fish food, and then you can watch them eat." Lucy figured the fish

food would be in containers that looked like goldfish food dispensers, but much larger. They stepped inside the barn, and Maria grabbed two burlap bags that each appeared to be only half full. Each bag had a Styrofoam flotation piece attached snugly to one side of the bag. She handed one of the bags to Lucy, and they started walking toward the tanks. Not wanting to seem impatient, Lucy waited to ask Maria what was in the bags.

When they arrived at the tanks, Maria set the two bags on the ground. She proceeded to pull two similar wet bags from the two corners nearest them. They were replaced with the ones they had just brought from the goat barn. The bags began to soak up the water in the pool, but remained floating half in and half out of the water. Maria started toward the other end of the tank, where there was an obvious turbulence in each corner. Lucy couldn't wait any longer. "What was in those two bags we just put in the pool?"

Maria smiled and said, "Goat manure."

"What?" questioned Lucy. Maria smiled again and motioned for Lucy to follow.

When they arrived at the end of the pool where the water had been churning, it was easy to see what was happening. Dozens of much larger fish in each corner were at the edges of the bags that were floating in the water.

Maria explained that these bags had been floating for three weeks. Once the bags had soaked up enough water to make all the manure very moist, the flies showed up. "It's a simple and free source of high-protein feed for the fish. The flies deposit their eggs through the burlap into the moist manure held inside. Eight days later, the eggs hatch into fly larvae, which grow very fast. They work their way through the burlap for the next stage of their development. But before they have a chance to turn into the pupa, dozens of fish are waiting at the *maggot bar*—waiting to eat those plump little organic, tasty treats. We monitor the water to make sure no pathogens are present, and we end up with pounds and pounds of healthy, protein-rich, organically raised Tilapia fish. The spent manure inside the bags is then added to the compost pile, and the process starts all over again."

Maria looked at her watch and said to Lucy, "I would love to keep you here all day and show you so much more, but I have a client's house to clean in forty-five minutes. Lucy quickly added she still needed to get some lunch and then make it to Marcus' place by one o'clock. They went back to the house, washed up from the chores, and said their goodbyes. Lucy got into Max and headed down the street, and on her way to K's diner.

****

Five minutes later, she pulled in behind a yellow van parked on Market Street. As Lucy walked beside the van, she noticed the words, WATERSON SCHOOL DISTRICT. She headed for K's front door, worried there might be an extra number of guests for lunch today. As she opened the door and went inside, it was as she had expected. K's was packed. Lucy looked around for a seat and found a little two-chair table still open at the far end of the diner. She made a rushed effort to get to the table and quickly sat down.

The restaurant was full of high school students all dressed in blue FFA jackets. On the back of their jackets was embroidered the name of their home school, either Waterson or Welcome. This was Lucy's first encounter with FFA kids up close. She had to admit they left a good impression. They were well-behaved and very respectful to an obviously overworked waitress. As Lucy watched them closely, her first urge was to interview a couple of them, but she decided not to do that today. Today, she was intent on making a few notes from her morning visit with Maria. There was so much to capture while it was still fresh in her mind. Besides, she knew it would be a long time before the lunch waitress would even make it to her table. As Lucy began on her notes, she heard the little bell over the door. *Ding-ding.* Lucy looked up.

In the open space between the check-out register and the entry door stood a little old man, all alone. Weathered by time and crowned with white hair and beard, he set his canvas travel bag on the floor. Lucy felt quite sure he was not a part of the school group.

As he began to survey the busy diner looking for a place to sit down, his body began to slump. *Why not?* Lucy thought to herself and motioned for the old man to come and sit with her.

He put his hands to his chest and raised his eyebrows in the universal, unspoken question, *Who, me?* She once again waved him toward her table. He picked up his bag and slowly made his way down the crowded aisle. He sat down, placed his bag on the floor, and turned to Lucy. "Thank you," he said, "That was very neighborly on your part."

Lucy smiled back, "Well, that's what neighbors do for each other, right?"

Again, he smiled at her and said, "Someone taught you very well as to what it means to be a neighbor."

"Oh, that would be my Granny," said Lucy.

"Ah, yes, your Granny, indeed." He said. Lucy was touched by the way he said Granny's name, as if he had known her personally, in another time.

"So, what brings you to Welcome, if you don't mind me asking?"

The old man let out a very long and tired breath as he began his story. "I'm looking for my boss's boy," he said. "He left home some years back. Something very tragic happened in his life, and he blamed it all on his father. The boy thought his father could have or should have prevented it."

"If I find the boy, I am supposed to tell him that sometimes life can be very hard for both father and son. Even though it happened a long time ago, his father has never stopped loving him and trying to reconnect. He wants the boy to know that he still loves him as much as the day he was born. He wants the boy so much to be his son again."

In the blink of an eye, Lucy reverted to Lucy Moore, the little girl, always looking for someone to help. Her heart began to ache as she heard the old man continue his story. "My sources say he was last seen around these parts, and I just thought, well, you know, maybe I could—"

Lucy interjected, "If there is anything I can do for you, I promise I will, but I don't even live here, and if I did run into him, how would I recognize him?"

The old man put a finger to his lips as though he was thinking, and then said, "I know… if you come across the kindest man you have ever met and get close enough to him, you will see that he has a big hole in his heart."

A confused Lucy said, "What?"

He replied, "Oh, don't worry over the details. If you find him, leave a note over there on the business card board that says, FOUND HIM! I will know it's you, and then I will get in touch with you."

"But how will you know where to find me?" Lucy asked.

"Like I said earlier, I have my sources," replied the old man with a smile.

With that, he stood, picked up his bag, and said, "I think I need to step out for some fresh air. I'm starting to feel a little claustrophobic in here." Lucy watched him walk down between the tables and toward the door. He stopped at the cash register and picked up a bag of Cheetos. As he paid for the snacks, he turned back to face Lucy, lifted the Cheetos, smiled, winked at her, and left the diner.

"What in the world just happened?" thought Lucy. She was trying to comprehend the conversation of the past few moments and the old man's departure. Abruptly, her consciousness was interrupted by a repeating voice, "Order please … your order please."

Her meal finally came just as the last of the students were leaving to get back in their vans and on their way. She struggled to clear her mind, eat her meal, and refocus on her schedule for the afternoon. *Okay, Lucy Moore*, she said to herself. *Just put it on the shelf for now, and figure it out later. In five minutes, you have an interview with a guy named Marcus.*

****

Lucy left the diner and headed east on Mulberry Street. With each passing cross street, she found herself driving further back in time. She passed the closed shopping center, the abandoned commercial buildings, and now a closed manufacturing building. It was as though this part of Welcome was an area that the city council was content to forget. She next saw the guardrail barricade across the road ahead, with a sign that read DEAD END. *Now what,* she thought as she started to slow the car and turn Max around. Max's navigation system chirped in with "*Turn right, now.*" Only then did Lucy see the street sign she had been looking for. Bent over and almost touching the ground was an old, rusted sign that read BICKETT ROAD.

She slowly turned the car onto what once had been a drivable road but now was a patchwork of potholes and broken pavement. As soon as she was on the roadway, the navigation system once again chirped, *"In five hundred feet, your destination is on the right."* She continued down the road toward the only house in sight. She was nearing an old brick farmhouse when Max once again chirped in, *"You have arrived."*

She stopped the car, got out, and looked around. Had there been some kind of mistake with the navigation system? There were just three other buildings visible on Bickett Road before it also came to another dead-end barricade. Across the road from where she stood were two block buildings with rusty tin roofs. Attached to one of the buildings was a tall silo, indicating that at some time in the distant past, both structures had been barns. She turned around to view the old brick house that she now stood in front of.

Chapter 10

The Unpredictables

She saw an old, two-story brick house with a wraparound front porch. It was tall and imposing with a slightly higher elevation than the road. The main thing that gave Lucy concern was the fact that all its windows were covered with sheets of plywood. On the far side of the house was a driveway occupied by a very old blue pickup truck.

Lucy had just started walking toward the truck when she saw Marcus step out from one of the buildings across the road. He waved and, with a big smile, said, "Congratulations, Lucy, you found me. As you may have guessed by now, I don't get a lot of visitors out this way. Let's go to the house, and I can give you the quick version of my part in our little group. Then if you like, we can go back across the road to the lab."

Lucy was not sure she even wanted to go inside the house. How could a college professor live in a place like this, unless he had some sort of mental issue? Visions of rodents running across the floor, sinks backed up, and piles of trash from wall to wall flashed across her mind's eye.

"Coming?" asked Marcus as he turned to make sure she was still following.

"Right behind you," she responded. She took in a long, deep breath, exhaled, and said silently to herself, *Here goes.* As she continued up the porch steps, she quickly and silently prayed, *Dear Lord, please protect me from whatever I am about to endure, and return me into Your service safely.*

As Marcus opened the porch door to the living room, he motioned for Lucy to go in. Lucy stepped inside … and could not believe what she saw. As she tried to regain her composure, she heard a very warm and friendly feminine AI voice, *"Good afternoon, Lucy. We are so happy you could come. Marcus has been looking forward to your visit ever since he met you at Jenny's on Tuesday. If there is anything I can do to*

56

make your visit more enjoyable, just tell Marcus." With that, the welcome greeting ended.

The floors were not as she had suspected, either. They were, instead, polished hickory floorboards on which the finest occasional rugs and runners were strategically placed. The walls were wainscoted with stone paneling on the bottom and beautiful wallpaper up to the high ceiling. The window wells were not darkened by the plywood attached to the outside of the house. Instead, each window space had a full-length, vertical plasma screen monitor!

Each window was framed with traditional wood window sill framing. Marcus saw the confusion on her face and began to explain. "The view from the window in each room of the house is determined by a simple voice command. Today's view has the house set near a cliff, overlooking a valley below. The hillsides are covered in the foliage of spring trees and blooming rhododendrons, appropriate for this time of the year. Step closer to the window so you can appreciate the detail."

As Lucy approached the window, she gasped for fear of losing her balance. It was all so very real … and yet, not real at all.

She was startled when her trance was interrupted by Marcus. "So, what do you think, Lucy? Maybe not quite what you expected?"

She turned to him, "I-I don't understand. How…. Why?"

Marcus smiled and said, "The how is just technology; there's nothing special about that. The why is a little more complicated. I guess it's just to make a point."

Lucy tilted her head and slowly said, "And the point is…"

"Isn't it obvious?" asked Marcus. "The point is that things are not always what they appear to be."

Lucy couldn't resist. "Are we talking about the house or the chemistry professor?"

Without answering her question, Marcus said, "Why don't we go out on the porch and continue our conversation there?" He poured a couple of glasses of iced tea, and they went outside. They each sat down in high-back rockers, the kind that used to be at Cracker Barrel restaurants. Marcus rocked and sipped his tea, saying nothing.

Lucy restarted the conversation. "I think we left off with things not being as they seem, and then I asked—"

"Oh, that's right," said Marcus. "I was about to explain that. That's why I love chemistry. Chemistry is always so predictable."

Now Lucy was really getting confused. Marcus went on. "You see, chemistry is very predictable; people are not. The conclusions of chemical observations, of chemical reactions, are very predictable. People are so very unpredictable. For example, you observed the outside of my house and concluded that I was a hermit with no concern or appreciation for the nicer things in life. But when you went inside, had your earlier observations been accurate?"

"Well, I don't know," said Lucy, "I observed two very different things regarding the same person, so to this point in time, I cannot make an accurate conclusion."

"Exactly," said Marcus. "But with chemistry, you can get exactly what you predict every time." He went on, "The behaviors of people are so unpredictable. Many motives can alter their behaviors. For example, if I were to— ." He stopped in mid-sentence and scanned his eyes beyond Lucy, first left, then right. "Lucy, if you will please excuse me for just a second, but be very still. There is something I need to do."

Marcus slowly reached for a BB gun that was leaning up against the porch wall near his chair. He slowly turned back around and pointed the gun toward a brush pile about sixty feet away out in a field. "Do you see that robin perched on the branch sticking out of the left side of the brush pile?" he asked.

"Yes," said Lucy, "But why—"

BANG! The gun fired, and the robin flew away.

"Why did you shoot at the robin? She wasn't hurting anything," said Lucy, becoming irritated.

Marcus turned to Lucy. "That robin has started building her nest in that brush pile three different times in the past two weeks. I have gone out and torn the nest out each time, and she's back again."

Lucy was obviously getting upset with Marcus by this time. "Do you really hate robins that much?" she asked with a tinge of anger in her voice.

"No, Lucy, I don't hate robins at all. I actually like robins very much. The problem is this: I have a county burn permit to burn that brush pile next week. If I let her build her nest, then she will lay her eggs in the nest, and they will all be destroyed in the fire. So I've been trying to encourage her to build her nest somewhere else, that's all."

"Oh," said Lucy apologetically. "I didn't know."

"That is why I say people's behaviors are so unpredictable, because of all the unknown motives behind those behaviors."

To that, Lucy responded, "Yes, Marcus, I grant you that people are often unpredictable. And yet, that is one reason I find people so wonderful and enchanting. They are, indeed, full of surprises."

Marcus countered, "You know, I never get upset or angry with chemicals. Their behaviors or reactions are always so precisely predictable."

As Marcus continued, Lucy felt like she was sitting in a psychology class debate instead of in an interview with a chemistry teacher. A moment later, Lucy asked, "And what was it, that third reason you liked chemistry so much—something about people's motives in relationships?"

To that, Marcus abruptly suggested they should go over to the lab and see how he turned animal waste into methane gas and food waste into alcohol. They stepped down from the porch, crossed the road, and approached the first of the two barns. Both barns were quite large and clothed in weathered wood siding. Once again, Lucy was not sure if she even wanted to go in, but she did. And once again, she could hardly believe her eyes. Just as the outward appearance of his house had been deceptive, so now also the outside appearance of the barn had been deceptive.

She was standing in a spacious, open area that looked more like a huge surgical operating room in a hospital instead of a barn. What she saw in the center of the space, she felt sure was the equipment in which he made his methane gas.

Marcus beamed from ear to ear when he saw the expression on Lucy's face.

"Welcome to Miracle Marc's methane gas refinery; one of the most efficient, personal-sized methane gas production units in the world. My name is Marcus, and I will be your tour guide today." He was quite animated as he pretended to be giving a personal tour to a potential investor. "Before we go any further, I must remind you, from this point on, no photos, no videos, and no voice recording." Lucy raised her hand.

Marcus acknowledged and said, "Yes, Miss … Miss … *ahh,* it looks as though you have lost your name tag."

You've got to be kidding, Lucy thought as she rolled her eyes with an obvious sense of annoyance.

The former excited expression on Marcus' face drained out completely. He stood there like a little boy whose game of imagination had been called to an abrupt halt. Marcus swallowed hard and said, "I'm sorry, Lucy. I just got caught up in the excitement of showing an outsider what I've got here."

"It's okay, Marcus," Lucy said quickly, trying to minimize the collateral damage inflicted by the way she rolled her eyes. "I'm not a chemist, so why don't you give me the quick *hundred-word or less* explanation of how the methane gas is made from the manures and how the alcohol can be harvested from the potatoes and unusable fruit. After that, I can do some research if I need any more information."
She continued, "But I would like to come back sometime, if that's okay, and get the advanced class on burning and blowing up things."

Marcus smiled and said, "Sure, that is one of my favorite classes to teach."

A short time later, they left the two barns and started back toward the house. Halfway across the road, Lucy stopped and pointed further down to the DEAD END sign. She asked, "What's beyond that sign, and the other one that says DO NOT ENTER?"

Chapter 11

Negotiations and Relationships

They both stood looking down the road at the guardrail across the road and the two signs, DEAD END and DO NOT ENTER. Lucy put her hand up above her eyes so she could see better. "It looks to me like at one time this road actually kept going on past the roadblock."

Marcus replied, "It did."

Lucy responded, "It did, but not now?"

"Well, it is a rather long story," he said.

Her curiosity had been sparked. "I like stories," she said.

"Well, maybe I can give you the short version. When I moved to Welcome, I was looking for a place to live that was private and secluded. I came across this parcel, which was made up of six different lots. This end of town had become dead in a lot of ways for many reasons. No developer wanted to take a risk, and no individual or group of individuals was interested, so it was placed on the city's surplus lands list. Those properties are sold at auction just to get rid of them. The auction came and went, but no one even offered a bid. The city was still stuck with it—a blighted area with no city services of water, sewer, natural gas, or fiber-optic lines."

"I went to the city soon after the auction and made my offer. It was a ridiculously low price and was to include all six parcels and, most importantly, the Bickett Road right-of-way. They jumped at the offer in order to get rid of the site."

Lucy interrupted, "But the road looks like it continues past the roadblock. Why would the city give you control of the road if the road actually continues past this property?"

"Ah, yes, Ms. Moore, you are indeed the writer with questions. The answer to your question will reinforce my earlier comments about unpredictable people. Do you remember the part about their behaviors being often entwined with unknown motives? Well, Lucy, I had ulterior motives for locking in control of Bickett Road."

He continued, "Even before I made an offer to the city for this property, I checked to see who owned the properties beyond the roadblock. As it turned out, none of that land is within the city limits of Welcome. Instead, it was in the neighboring jurisdiction of Madison Township. My inquiry also turned up that there was only one parcel through which Bickett Road enters before it makes a big turnaround circle, sending you right back out this way again."

Lucy was really confused now. "So, who owns that land?" she asked, trying to make sense of it all.

"We're almost there," said Marcus. "What I found out was that the eight-acre parcel had, many years ago, been the home of Camp Clifton, a regional 4-H camp. As a summer camp, it had eight sizable cabins, four outhouses, one dining hall, and an implement shed for the grounds equipment. It had its own well for water, and propane gas was used for stoves in the dining hall. Electrical service had gone to the camp but had been disconnected years ago."

"As the years went by, the organization that owned the camp acquired enough funding to relocate and build a new camp with much newer facilities and amenities. That organization, in turn, donated Camp Clifton to Madison Township's Park District. Years passed, and interest in using the camp faded. The township lost interest in providing upkeep on a facility that was not being used. As a result, Camp Clifton had been put on the township's surplus lands list as well. After acquiring this six-acre parcel that I call home, I then went to the township to make an offer on the campground acreage."

"I offered three thousand dollars for the land and all the structures. 'You have to be kidding!' They protested. 'It's worth a lot more than that'. I responded, "Not if people can't access it through Bickett Road, and I own Bickett Road."

Again, they protested. 'The city cannot sell you its land and give up the right of way through that land. We will sue the city.'

"Go ahead," I said. "You will have more money tied up in legal fees than your land is worth. That should make all the taxpayers of Madison township eager to re-elect you when your terms expire."

They went into a huddle, came out smiling, and said, 'You got yourself a campground.'

Lucy just shook her head and said, "That's amazing! So what do you plan to do with the campground?"

Marcus replied, "I didn't buy it to do anything with it. I bought it so no one else will ever do anything with it. That way, I can pretty much stay out of sight and out of mind—away from all those unpredictable people."

By then, it was starting to get late in the afternoon. Marcus apologized for needing to prep for a class he was teaching the next morning, so they said their goodbyes. Lucy got in Max and turned the little car around in the middle of the driveway, known as Bickett Road, and headed back toward Mulberry Street.

A great puzzled expression came over her face. Had she spent the afternoon with a teacher of chemistry, or a psychologist of people's behavior, or maybe a commercial real estate broker who liked the game of political chess? Marcus was, indeed, very different. Maybe that was why he kept avoiding the topic of relationships as part of their afternoon discussion.

****

Lucy turned back onto Mulberry Street and headed back to The Nest. She found it very difficult to focus on any one part of the visit. The afternoon had been both exhausting and exhilarating, both enlightening and ambiguous. If only Marcus had been willing to share his frustration about relationships. Maybe she could have helped in some way. She had driven a couple of blocks, still thinking how she might approach the topic with him, when she glanced over toward her friend in the seemingly empty passenger seat.

"Okay, okay, I know what You're saying, Who am I to talk about relationships?I don't even have a goldfish, let alone a cat or dog. But don't you see, God, I can't have those kinds of relationship responsibilities with the kind of job I have. I am on the road so much of the time. What do you mean, The job is just another excuse?"

The tension in her voice was beginning to grow stronger. She began to blink back tears. "Do you really think it is all about being afraid of losing someone I might care for?" More tension, "someone I might love and then lose?" Her breathing was rapid. "Really? I mean, REALLY, God?" Then the conversation with God abruptly stopped. She wiped the tears away from her eyes, pulled the car over to the curb of the street, and parked. With both hands at the top of the steering wheel and her forehead resting on her hands, she began to cry … and cry … and cry.

Several minutes later, she started the car again and headed toward K's restaurant. Realizing then how red her eyes must be and perhaps how distraught she might appear, she turned and headed back home to The Nest. Once inside the B&B, she heard Ms. Robins in the parlor. As she walked past the door, Ms. Robins yelled out to her, "Hey Lucy, if you're hungry, there is a batch of freshly baked cookies cooling in the dining room. Help yourself. Milk or sweet tea in the refrigerator!"

"Thanks!" Lucy yelled back. Grabbing five cookies and a tall glass of milk, she went upstairs to her room.

Before she ate the cookies or did anything else, she sat down at her desk, folded her hands, and began to pray. "Dear Lord, I am so sorry for lashing out at You. I know you understand my hunger—my need for a human friend. Granny is gone. Lenny is in a business relationship only as long as I bring him stories. Carl is an acquaintance I respect, but we are not close friends. You know I am afraid of being hurt. Please, give me the strength and the courage to move on and be patient until the time is right. Amen."

Lucy ate her cookies and milk, skipped her nighttime rituals, and went to bed. She had made her peace with God. She was exhausted and longed for sleep, but could not close her eyes. Every time she did, a thousand images from the day paraded across the stage within her mind. The voices were all clambering for her ears to hear: Alison, 'See ya, Lucy'. Maria, 'Ever milked a goat before, Lucy?' and Marcus, 'People are so unpredictable, Lucy'.

Then she remembered the old man at the lunch table, 'When you find the boy, look closely. He has a hole in his heart.' What did he mean, he has a hole in his heart? It was that voice that she kept hearing over and over until she finally drifted off to sleep.

Chapter 12

THE TINKERER

"Hey Luuucy!" came the voice from the bottom of the stairs. "Are you awake? You okay?"

It was Angela Robin's voice. "Oh my goodness, I must have forgotten to set my alarm last night," Lucy thought. She hopped out of bed and went to the bathroom mirror. *Yep, the eyes were still red but looking better than last night.* She grabbed her supplies, thanked Angela for the wake-up call, and headed out of the Nest.

She drove over to K's for a small bite of breakfast and two side orders of eavesdropping. If there was a secret government project going on in Welcome, she was convinced that K's would be the most likely place for loose lips to slip. After downing a Friday morning breakfast special, she headed over to Zack's place to spend the morning with the group's mechanical engineer.

Zack's place was on the west side of town, near an old-fashioned junkyard. For an engineer like Zack, its main attractions included older junked cars, trucks, farm equipment, and a good mix of industrial equipment. To him, it was like living near Treasure Island. Something interesting was always waiting to be explored.

His own personal property had been one of the last holdouts of the family-owned mechanic's garage and repair shops. As with most of these types of businesses, the service shop was on the street level, and the residence was on the second floor. Behind the residence and shop was a large vacant lot. It was there that all the cars would have been parked, either waiting for service or waiting to be stripped for parts.

Zack had redesigned the first floor area of the house as a bike repair and rental service. Behind, in the old vacant lot, he had erected a stand-alone building. It was a modern machine shop with all the tools and equipment of the digital age, plus some old vintage shop tools.

When Lucy arrived, she parked Max in one of the customer

parking spaces and got out. Beside the customer parking spaces were two bike racks with a variety of bike styles and sizes to be rented. The sign over the door read TINKER'S BIKE REPAIR AND RENTAL. Zack came out the front door.

"Good morning!" he said with a big smile from ear to ear.

"Good morning," Lucy said, and with one hand pointing up to the sign, she asked, "Are you Mr. Tinker?"

Zack laughed and said, "Tinker is not who I am; it is what I do. I tinker. Follow me, and I will show you the shop where I do my tinkering."

Lucy followed as he went around the bike shop toward the larger machine shop.

Inside the shop were all sorts of altered bikes now usable as one-of-a-kind human-powered pieces of equipment. There were pedal-powered grain shellers, grinders, generators, pumps, and a variety of shakers and sifters. Some of the drive wheels turned slowly, and some turned very fast. Some of them were weighted to become heavy flywheels with great potential power. Even though Lucy did not understand all the physics behind them or the laws of mechanical engineering that made them work, she was, indeed, very impressed. "I hope you have patents on these inventions of yours," Lucy remarked.

Zack shared that several of his prototypes were in use in third-world countries as part of the final stage of their research and development. "Also," he added, "Marcus and I are working together to adapt some of these human-powered pieces to be powered by his methane gas. It's really quite fun to try and merge the two passions and come up with something better than either of us has done by ourselves. But before I bore you to death with all this mechanical stuff, why don't we go look at the rabbits?"

Lucy had forgotten that he was the one talking about *bunny burgers* at the first meeting at Jenny's place. They walked toward a backyard storage shed tucked between two large trees.

"That's the rabbit shed over there," Zack said as he pointed.

"What kind of trees are those?" Lucy asked.

"Carpathian walnuts. In the grocery store, we know their nuts as English walnuts."

"I bet you get a lot of nuts off trees as big as those two are."

"No, not really," said Zack. "The squirrels usually get them all. It's a battle not worth fighting. Besides, two nut trees that big will support a lot of squirrels. Even though a single squirrel doesn't have all that much meat on him, he is still a crucial ingredient in making a meal of delicious biscuits and squirrel gravy," he said with a grin.

Why did I have to ask? Lucy thought and followed on. When they arrived at the cages, he opened one of the doors, pulled out one of the adult rabbits, and placed her on the cage's flat top. "There you are," he began, "one of the most efficient meat-producing animals in the world."

I was pretty sure I was about to get the Rabbit 101 class from the bunny burger man himself.

"Lucy," he began, "Just think of it: Two momma rabbits, just like Ruthy here, can produce enough offspring for six hundred pounds of meat in a single year. Compare that to a beef cow that has a calf. In that same twelve months, that calf will yield on average four hundred pounds of meat."

"Not only that, but the rabbits will have a feed-to-meat conversion rate of four pounds of feed to one pound of meat, while the beef will require seven pounds of feed for every pound of meat."

"That is amazing," Lucy remarked.

He continued, "Ruthy here has a lot more going for her than just meat."

Her manure is pre-pelletized and has very little odor. Even that small amount of odor can be eliminated if we add composting red worms in the manure beds beneath the rabbit cages. When the worms are harvested, they are a great source of protein for the chickens being raised over at Marcus' place."

Lucy was just about to ask why Ruthy and her little ones had not yet been on the cover of Time magazine when a truck pulled into the driveway. *Whew!* Lucy thought. *Saved by the FedEx truck.*

As they left the rabbit shed and walked back toward the shop, Lucy noticed that all three buildings had at least some solar panels. All buildings had rain gutters with downspouts that diverted the rainwater to rain barrels at the base of the downspouts. It also looked like those rain barrels had tubing running out of them and through the beds of fresh greens at the base of each building. These, no doubt, were some of Jenny's beds of greens she had talked about that first day at her place. Zack took care of his delivery, and we were ready to explore his bike rental and repair shop.

Lucy glanced down to look at her watch. Zack saw her check the time. "I wanted to show you the bike shop, but I know you have a full afternoon with Pete. Maybe you could come back after all the visits, and we could take the bikes out and tour the town of Welcome."

"I would love to do that." Lucy thanked Zack for an enlightening morning and headed back to K's for lunch. Arriving at the diner, she got out of the car and looked around. There were no school buses, no great noise coming from inside, and no old man with a white beard at the diner today. Taking a deep breath, Lucy said to herself, *It's okay, Lucy. You can do this. It's a new day.* She opened the door and went inside. *Ding-ding.*

Chapter 13

THE SWEET TOOTH

After lunch, Lucy drove over to Pete's house. His would be the last of the visits in what had been a whirlwind adventure. She pulled into the driveway and parked in front of the garage. The face of the property looked very much like all the rest of the houses on the street: average single-level ranch, modest, simple, and plain. As she started to get out of the car, a gate within the backyard privacy fence opened. Pete walked over to the car and said, "Good afternoon", and led her back through the gate.

The property may have looked modestly plain in the front, but as soon as Lucy walked through the gate, her jaw dropped. She had just stepped into a picturesque fairyland with blooming fruit trees and flowers. Between the trees were patches of raspberries, strawberries, and other perennial fruits and vegetables. Some were bushes, some were vines, and some were ground covers. All were artfully planted into a natural-looking landscape right out of a children's picture storybook.

It was all just as he had hinted on that first day at Jenny's house. There were several dwarf and semi-dwarf trees of apples, plums, pears, and peaches. There were strawberries, gooseberries, and blueberries. It was a living arboretum of fruit-bearing plants that made her mouth water as she scanned the large backyard. To complete the well-nurtured landscape was the essential beehive, tucked in beneath one of the trees and out of anyone's pathway.

She noticed that at the far back end of his lot was a tall chain-link fence. "Problem with the neighbors?" Lucy asked.

"Follow me," he said, and we walked toward the fence. He pointed through the fence. There was an elementary school. "I have about four hundred and fifty of the nicest neighbors anyone could ever ask for. We have a blessed relationship through a little thing I call *friendship farming*. When I have extra fruit or honey, I take it over and leave it in the teachers' lunchroom. They take turns sharing it with their students. In return, I receive thank-you notes from the kids as they learn to write. It's a win-win relationship; we all benefit from the trades."

Across the back of the house, facing south, Pete had constructed a lean-to greenhouse. Winter heat, as expected, largely came from circulating solar heat units mounted on the house roof. There were also black barrels of saline water used for solar heat storage within the greenhouse. After a quick tour and explanation of all things greenhouse, they went through the patio door and into the kitchen.

Pete then showed Lucy his seed-saving operation in the basement, where several racks of various-sized screens allowed him to sort, dry, and clean seeds to go into his built-in cold storage closet.

The canning section of the basement included a commercial restaurant gas stove. On it, all the canning and food processing took place to prepare and preserve a significant amount of winter-time food, including jellies, jams, and fruit preserves. The stove contained the magic oven from which Pete's famous pies and other sweet treats were cooked. The gas stove, of course, was fueled by a tank of methane gas, compliments of Marcus.

Pete continued to explain that he and Marcus were also responsible for the maple syrup and honey harvesting and processing. They did all of that over at Marcus' place in the barn beside the one that housed the digester and still. "Okay, Pete," Lucy said, "This may sound a little personal, but I have to ask. The other day, when Maria referred to you as *Sweet Pete*, was that a term of affection or one of team responsibility?"

Pete blushed and stammered just a little. "I am sure it was regarding responsibilities, I think. Yes, responsibilities." As he regained his composure, Pete said, "Let's go back upstairs and have an afternoon snack."

When we got back upstairs to the kitchen, Pete pulled out a delicious-looking strawberry-rhubarb pie and set it on the table. Then from the refrigerator-freezer, he brought out a plastic tub of homemade ice cream. He cut two pieces of pie and placed each on a plate. Then, looking up, he asked, "One scoop or two?"

Remembering that the ice cream would probably have been made from Maria's goat milk, she said, "One will be fine, thank you."

"You'll be sorry," he said. "Everyone takes at least two scoops." Pete suggested we go back outside and sit at the little table on the patio while we ate and talked. We stepped outside and sat down. Pete began, "We eat our pie and ice cream first. Then we talk."

"It's Aunt Millie's house rule number eighteen. She says, 'Words can never appreciate what the tongue can enjoy, and the tongue can never understand the meaning of words. So let each have their own time and purpose, and be blessed by both.'"

Lucy was thinking how fun it might be to interview this Aunt Millie person. "Who is Aunt Millie?" She asked.

"Oh, sorry. She's Caleb Burns' aunt. She and Uncle Joe live on a farm just outside Welcome. We all claim them as our own surrogate aunt and uncle. They are a couple of very special people to all of us."

Lucy put the first bite of pie and ice cream in her mouth. "Oh WOW!" Lucy started to mumble with her mouth full, but then realized she had just broken Aunt   Millie's house rule number eighteen. So she put her fingers over her mouth, gave Pete a big thumbs up with the other hand, and continued eating a very delicious piece of pie à la mode.

Moments later, Pete laid his fork down on an empty plate and wiped his mouth. "Well, Lucy, what do you think?"

"I think I should have asked for two scoops of ice cream." Her words were of true appreciation for yet another adventure into their homegrown food. "Actually, I do have a question. It has to do with the division of labor among the team. The strategy of how and why you work so closely together, yet no two of you seem to ever do the same thing."

Pete nodded and said, "The word is *synergy*. It's a concept that Marcus understands but has a hard time putting into an equation. That is because the mathematics of synergy don't seem to add up correctly. Some have defined it this way: *The sum of the whole is greater than the sum of the parts."*

Pete continued, "It's like this: if two companies merge, they can accomplish more together than each could ever do separately. One of them may have a strong research and development program, while the other may have a great marketing program. Each is currently generating X amount of income. They merge, recognizing and utilizing the unique strengths and knowledge of each team. They are now able to produce three or maybe even four times their original income thanks to the merger. The key to our success is just that simple—the whole is greater than the sum of our parts."

Lucy sat there for a moment, trying to internalize that thought—trying to understand why the concept of synergy in small-scale food production was not so obvious to all those would-be self-sufficient enthusiasts. Those who, at the end of the day, may have worked twice as hard but with less to show for their effort. We talked a little longer about the group, but only in generalities. It had been a full week, and Lucy was ready to get back to The Nest and *crash*.

Before she left, Pete directed her back through the patio door and into the kitchen. "Hang on just a minute," he said as he opened the refrigerator door and retrieved the strawberry-rhubarb pie. "Two pieces to go. One of these is for Ms. Robins." Smiling, he continued, "But I'll never ask her if she got any of it or not."

We both had a little laugh, and Lucy stepped out and walked toward Max. It was then she noticed a small yard sign by the drive: WHO PLANTS THE SEED BENEATH THE SOD AND WAITS, BELIEVES IN GOD. She smiled and thought, well, at least one of them is a believer.

****

Lucy swung by K's and got two dinner specials to go. Back at The Nest, Ms. Robins was in the kitchen. "I have dinner for two," Lucy told her.

"Let me guess", she said as she pretended to search the archives of her memory. "That would be roast beef hot-shot with gravy on a piece of sourdough bread and side orders of green beans and coleslaw."

"How did you know?" Lucy asked in true surprise.

"Same thing it has been every Friday evening for as many years as I can remember." Then Lucy reached in and pulled out the two pieces of pie. "Now we're talking," she said. "I'll get the plates and silverware."

They finished their meal, then Lucy mentioned she had a great many notes to organize and get into the tablet and journal before she went to bed. To that, Ms. Robins said, "Well, this must be your lucky night. It would appear that you did not bring an office with you from Chicago. In return for the pie, why don't you just spread your paperwork out right here on the kitchen table? I am going to be gone the rest of the evening and will not be back till very late. Our motto here at The Nest is *Never Hesitate to Accommodate.* I am also very mindful of the likes and dislikes of my house guests. To that end, you will also find in the refrigerator a Diet Coke and a few little bags of Cheetos in the cabinet over the stove. Help yourself."

"Ms. Robins, you're a lifesaver."

Ten minutes later, Ms. Robins was gone, and the kitchen table looked like a sorting station at a paper recycling center. Three hours later, Lucy had her notes copied and organized and her journal entries up to date.

As tired as her body was, her mind would not stop wrestling with Pete's comments about synergy: "The whole is greater than the sum of our parts." Was it possible that if a model could be duplicated enough times in enough towns and cities all over the country, it could possibly make a significant impact on local food security? The unanswered question remained: How could you get enough people or groups of people to actually buy into such a concept? Especially as both Lenny and Caleb Burns had stated, "Who cares, Lucy? As long as the shelves at the store are full, who really cares?"

Chapter 14

GIRLS' DAY OUT

Alison arrived at The Nest at eight o'clock on Saturday morning. She let herself in and walked past the parlor room and registration table. From there, it was a straight shot through the dining room into the kitchen. Without as much as a "Hello" or "Good morning," Alison just started talking. "I figured I'd find you two back here. None of my business, Angela, but you need to either fix your front door alarm or get yourself a dog. Cause if you don't, someday somebody is going to walk right in, bop you over the head, and try to steal your secret biscuit recipe."

Puzzled, Lucy turned to Ms. Robins and said, "You know her?"

With a feigned grimace, Ms. Robin said, "I'm afraid so. Alison comes over at least once a week and tries to recruit me to be the morning cook at K's diner."

Angela Robins then turned to face Alison and continued, "Alison, the answer today is the same as every other day; it isn't going to happen."

Alison chimed back, "Well, that is a shame, Angela, but I didn't come to recruit you anyway. I came to pick up Welcome's one and only foreign correspondent from Chicago, Ms. Lucy here. We are going shopping today and doing a little sightseeing. You know, girls' day out sort of thing. Bye."

A minute later, Angela watched as they got in the Jeep and drove off. *Okay, Alison, she's all yours.* Little did Lucy know that the gum-chewing waitress from K's diner was also part of the Welcome team. It was Alison whose job included interviewing and either approving or denying security clearances for all who would be on Team Welcome.

Alison had the day all planned out. They would first do a little sightseeing while the town was still waking up. They would hit the major points of interest and the places of seasonal and event celebrations, then it would be on to shopping. After a couple of department stores and the thrift store, they would get a quick lunch and then go back to shopping. It was a good plan. An hour and a half later, the two came out of the thrift store loaded down with bags and big smiles on their faces like two kids at a birthday party. Alison looked at Lucy and said, "Time to eat."

They threw their bags in the back of Alison's Jeep and drove a block to Welcome's downtown parking lot. For the girl from Chicago, it was a very strange sight. A few dozen cars and pickup trucks were all parked in rows on the same paved lot with no lift arms or payment stations. It was all so different from the city parking garages with the stacked layers of cars and pay-per-hour toll machines.

From there, they walked a few yards to one of the town's favorite lunchtime spots. Welcome's only outdoor hot dog stand was open from eleven to one o'clock only on Saturdays, during spring break, and when school was not in session. The proprietors were the children whose parents owned a small grocery store across the street. The menu selections consisted of hot dogs, hot dogs with barbecue, or barbecue sandwiches. Cold soda-pop was in the cooler, and you could make it a combo meal with a small bag of chips.

They each got a combo meal and sat down at one of the park's picnic tables. As they ate their lunches, they relaxed and talked. Lucy began by asking Alison, "If someone came into K's and asked you to tell them everything you could about Welcome, what would you say?"

"Well, let's see." Alison began. "Welcome is a quiet but growing city of about forty thousand nestled in the beautiful hill country of southern Indiana. We have a mayor and city council form of government. The school's football team does quite well in its Division 1 league contests. We have our share of parades with floats and bands and celebrations of all kinds. Welcome has a great park district, fire and police protection, and all those kinds of things."

"Lucy, are you here to write a story on Welcome for some travel magazine or social media website? If I knew the purpose of your questions, I could help you better with your research. What exactly is it that brings you to Welcome?"

Lucy once again began to tell her story of the possible secret government project. "Wow!" exclaimed Alison. "That sounds so exciting—writing about a secret government project. Maybe I could help you as an undercover agent and keep my ears open at the diner for any leads."

With a very despondent sound in her voice, Lucy said, "It's okay, Alison, I know you're just kidding. I guess the whole thing does sound a little far-fetched."

"No, Lucy. I really do think it would be exciting to be a writer and travel all over the country. I really do. Seriously, how is your research going so far?"

"Well, so far I have spent the most amazing week with those friends of Mr. Burns. I can't get over how much food they can produce on such a small amount of ground. I am not sure yet exactly how Mr. Burns fits into the equation, but I think it is significant. The group seems to respect him so much. I don't want to pry into their relationship and jeopardize any future help they might be willing to offer. So, maybe my favorite waitress, Alison, could give me a little of his background." Then Lucy quickly added, "Uh, for my research."

Alison came back with eyebrows up and a curious smile. "Sure, for your research." Alison continued. "As I hear it, Caleb Burns showed up in Welcome about four years ago, just a few months before I did. He has a military background, but he's not active now. He seems quiet and keeps to himself mostly. I think he has family members somewhere on a farm east of town—think maybe out on East Harvey Hill Road."

Lucy interjected, "I hear he's not married, right?"

Alison smiled again, "Your research is correct. But if you want me to try and fix you up, I'll see what I can do."

Lucy blushed. "Oh no," she said, "I was just curious, that's all."

Alison decided it was her time to ask the questions. "So you are a writer and you interview people all the time, right?"

"That's right," answered Lucy.

"Well, I interview people too, but then I'm just a waitress. Unfortunately, I never get past the small talk with the people that I interview. But my real dream is to someday be a writer and interview all those people and then write about their life stories."

"I think that is a great idea," said Lucy. "Alison, you can talk to anybody and everybody; that is obvious. Just sharpen your skills in listening and asking questions, and you will do amazingly well. Go ahead, ask me a couple of questions, and I'll show you what I mean."

In no time at all, Alison was asking a thousand questions for her first biography, *The Life and Times of Lucy Moore*. She was asking about everything: growing up, greatest accomplishments, love life or lack of it, religion, politics, and greatest fears and hopes for America. As Lucy answered her questions, Alison pretended she was writing it all down. They were like two schoolgirls playing a game. Lucy was actually having fun. Her professional defenses of getting personal and running the risk of getting hurt had melted away. It was as though someone actually cared about Lucy Moore. It had been a long time since she felt that way, not since Granny died.

About that time, the kids with the hot dog stand finished putting it all away. That meant it was past one o'clock, and the two gals in the park still had one more store and the mini-mart to check out.

On the way back to the parking lot, they walked on the other side of the city park, allowing for an informative stroll past other stores and businesses. Partway around the block, Lucy stopped in front of a vacant store that had a sign in the window. The sign simply said THE LORD'S CHURCH MEETS HERE EVERY SUNDAY AT 9:30 A.M. PLEASE COME AND JOIN US.

It had been a long time since Lucy had attended any formal church services. She read her Bible every day, said her prayers, and quite often had those conversations with God where she did all the talking and waited for Him to respond, in His own time. *I do miss going to church,* she thought to herself, remembering her childhood when Granny took her every Sunday. *Mr. Burns is not getting back till noon tomorrow. I might just check this little church out.*

By three o'clock, they had checked off another thrift store and stopped at the mini-mart. Lucy wanted to pick up a few staples and other items for the picnic. They got back in the truck. "Where to now?" Alison asked.

"Alison, I have had the most wonderful time today, but I really should be getting back to The Nest. I think I might visit that little church we passed in the morning. Mr Burns is back in town late tomorrow morning, so I need to prep some notes to go over with him and get our picnic lunch made."

As soon as the words were out of her mouth, she realized how it sounded. Alison's eyes got big, and a smile went from ear to ear. "Did you say that Caleb Burns is taking you on a picnic lunch tomorrow?"

"Oh, Alison. We are just reviewing the research notes from my visits this week. It's all business. I shouldn't have said it that way."

"Hey girl, whatever you say," Alison said, still grinning widely. "I just think it's about time some good lookin' girl like yourself is finally making some progress with Caleb Burns."

"I'm not trying to *make progress* with Mr. Burns," Lucy shot back, blushing again. "Like I said, it's business." Alison just pursed her lips and started whistling a little tune as though she hadn't heard a word Lucy just said. They both started laughing at each other. It had been a fun afternoon. That hard emotional wall she had built around her heart to protect her from getting hurt was starting to crack.

That evening as Lucy reviewed and updated her journal, she felt energized. With all that had happened, it seemed like she had been in Welcome for a month. The truth was, she had been in town less than a week. She had come looking for a secret government project but had gotten sidetracked by a bunch of locals.

They had captured her attention in a way so different than the corporate giants she was used to dealing with. They had taken in a stranger and made her feel at home. They had given their time and shared their passions and yet asked for nothing in return, but why?

One was no doubt a genius, another she considered to be the leader, and one was so sweet and endearing. They were all very different, yet there were a few things they did seem to have in common. None had regular full-time jobs, though they all seemed to have plenty of what they needed. None had a compelling schedule that dictated their place and time, except for maybe the one she called the leader. None were married. They were an intriguing bunch for sure.

Still, the question lingered: was there more to this group than first meets the eye? The investigating reporter inside Lucy's head kept asking the question, "Am I missing something here? Do they possibly know something about the secret government project but aren't ready to share?"

She got ready for bed and updated her notes and personal journal. She read her Bible, said her prayers, and went to sleep.

Chapter 15

On Sunday morning, Lucy woke up even earlier than usual. She never used Sunday as an excuse to sleep in, but this morning she had extra things to do early. There was a picnic lunch to prepare and a church service to get dressed for, all before nine-fifteen. As she began putting the lunch basket together, she was a little surprised at the detail to which she was making sure everything was just right. After all, it was just a little bite to eat as she and Caleb went over her notes from her visits, right? Still denying that the lunch was anything more than a business meeting, she continued to give it her very best efforts. Done with the lunch prep, she changed into some nice casual clothes and was out the door on her way to church.

It had been a long time since she had attended any structured worship service. As a child, her Granny would take Lucy to church every Sunday. They would walk the two blocks to the tall brick building with the white steeple on top. The organ would play, people would sing, and the preacher would preach. As Lucy got older and Granny could no longer walk the two blocks, they started staying at home and had their own Bible study and singing in Granny's apartment. Granny had always assured Lucy that God was wherever you are. 'He can hear you anywhere, and you can talk to Him anywhere,' she would say. And so they did. It was then that Lucy learned to talk to God, most often out loud. She had never stopped since that day.

Lucy parked Max in the parking lot where Alison had parked the day before. She got out of the car, picked up her Bible, and started walking the fifty yards toward the church. Approaching the entry, she saw several people greeting each other and going inside. She took a deep breath, exhaled slowly, and said to herself, *Here goes.* She walked in and was greeted by several friendly faces and warm welcomes. It was obvious they were about to start. There were thirty or forty people from varying social and economic backgrounds. To her surprise, she saw Pete sitting in a chair a few rows toward the front. *Of course*, she thought, remembering the little sign in his garden. Thinking it better not to surprise him with her presence, she quietly sat down in one of the back row chairs.

A man stood in front of the group and welcomed everyone. He announced the first song was number 136, "Christ Liveth in Me." There was no organ or band. It was just people singing with their voices and their hearts. It was both a beautiful sight and sound. After another song and a prayer, the song leader sat down, and another man stood up behind the lectern. He was dressed no differently than everyone else, but she thought maybe he was the preacher. As he stood up, there were young children who had left their seats and were finding their way to Sunday school classrooms off to the side of the main assembly room. As it turned out, the man at the lectern was a class discussion leader. The question of the morning was "Does God answer prayers?"

Lucy thought, well, that was a no-brainer. What would be the point of praying if He couldn't hear or wouldn't answer our prayers? There was considerable discussion with Biblical passages that affirmed that He did, indeed, hear and answer prayers. The debate mostly centered around the question of the speed at which prayers were answered. The discussion leader thanked everyone for their comments and then said, "Anyone else with a closing comment?" And then he looked right at Lucy and said, "How about our visitor today, we'd love to hear your thoughts as well".

There was a distinct gulp in Lucy's throat. She sure didn't see that one coming. "Well," said Lucy, "Just thinking off the top of my head, I'd say if a person prays to God without believing that He both hears and answers, then He might as well go over to K's diner and get themselves a big cheeseburger and pray to the cheeseburger. Then when you get done praying, you've at least got something to chew on."

Chuckles were heard throughout the room. The man up front then replied, "Thank you very much for such a candid response. I think you have given all of us some food for thought."

The group started to rearrange itself as the children returned from their classes. Lucy was trying to figure out if she had offended the group by her comment and whether she should stay or leave. She looked up and saw Pete waving for her to come and sit with him if she liked. Relieved, she went up and sat in the empty seat beside him. Moments later, the song leader returned, and a couple more songs were sung. He sat down, and another man got up—the preacher, who thanked everyone for coming and announced the sermon title, "Prosecutor or Messenger."

For whatever reason, Lucy had expected some kind of *Hellfire and brimstone* sermon. As it turned out, it wasn't that at all. The preacher spent his entire sermon making just two points. His first was that the children of God need to see themselves not as judges or prosecutors, but rather as messengers. "Our job is not to judge, but to share the story of Jesus. If we focus on that message, then we will have helped others on their journey to find their way, as together we all travel the pathway home."

After his sermon, the group took part in communion. Apparently, they did that every Sunday. There were closing comments, a prayer, and then the church service was over. Lucy thanked Pete for his hospitality in making her feel even more welcome. Then she told him she needed to hurry on because she had lunch plans, but would see him tomorrow at the farm.

****

At precisely one o'clock, Caleb arrived in a late-model, cab-and-a-half pickup truck. Lucy got in and immediately noticed the dog in the back of the cab. It was a shepherd mix with a twinkle in its eyes that belonged to a much younger dog. The dog looked at Lucy, then at Caleb, then back to Lucy. Lucy looked at Caleb as if to say, "Did I miss getting a memo?"

"Ah, yes, Ms. Moore, introductions: Ms. Moore, meet Sadie. Sadie, meet Ms. Moore."

Lucy climbed in, buckled up, and arranged the picnic basket in her lap. "Mr. Burns," Lucy began to ask, "Do you think it would be okay if Sadie called me Lucy instead of Ms. Moore?"

"Why not? Formal names are a little too traditional for such an up-to-date dog as Sadie."

"Well, in that case, would an up-to-date guy like Mr. Burns mind calling me Lucy as well?"

"Only if Lucy would consider calling Mr. Burns, 'Caleb,'" he said.

"Well, that takes care of that," said Lucy with a smirk. "Now everybody is all up-to-date, and the conversations between the three of us should flow much more smoothly."

"I hope you don't mind me bringing Sadie along," Caleb said. "She misses me when I go out of town and expects my full attention when I get back."

As they drove out into the countryside, every time Lucy turned to say something to Caleb, she found the head of a dog, stretching from back seat to front seat, staring intently into her face. When Caleb spoke, Sadie turned to face him, and when Lucy spoke, the dog turned back to face her. Like a bobble head on a dashboard, Sadie went from one to the other the entire time they were in the truck.

Oh well, thought Lucy, *we'll get to the picnic site, and then she'll run and chase chipmunks like any other good dog would do.* They drove on, Sadie listening to every word.

As they left the valley floor of Welcome, the road began to slope upward into the nearby hill country. Twenty minutes later, Caleb steered the truck off to the side of the road. There was a wide spot of flat ground with green grass, big shade trees, and a couple of old, broken-down picnic tables. Just beyond the grass area was the most breathtaking lookout point. It offered a view of Welcome in the near distance and the sprawling farm land beyond. It was a picture-perfect scene.

"What is this place?" wondered Lucy out loud. Caleb began to explain that a few generations ago, little places like this dotted roadsides all across America, wherever the roads went over and around the hills and mountains.

They were the travelers' rest spots and truckers' cooling stations. The trucks' cooling systems would overheat going up the hills, so they would pull over at a spot like this until the radiators cooled down. If they were going down the hills, the brakes would overheat with excessive use, so again the truckers would pull over and wait until the brakes cooled down.

"Back then, families traveled by car most often when they went on vacation. These little areas became familiar as unofficial rest spots. Families learned to count on them as a place to pull over and eat their lunch that had been packed that morning, since there were no fast-food places back then. The kids would get out and run and play, stretch their legs, and thirty minutes later everybody was back in the car and on their way again."

They got out of the truck, and Caleb retrieved the picnic basket and a blanket. After they walked toward a spot under one of the big shade trees, Caleb spread the blanket out on the ground. As soon as they had sat down and pulled out their lunch, a disturbance from the truck got their attention. It was Sadie. She had gone from the back seat to the front, out the open door, and was now quickly limping over to the two on the blanket. She nuzzled in between them and lay down. With her front feet now stretched out in front of her and her eyes closed, she had just given them permission as official chaperone to continue with their picnic.

After eating, they walked over to what had, no doubt, been the lookout spot for those traveling families. Sadie got up, limped over, and nudged in between as they looked out over the view.

Lucy took in the breathtaking view. "It truly is a beautiful sight," Lucy whispered. "It's so different from Chicago—so different from any place I've ever been. Do you like it here, Caleb?"

"I've lived all over the world, and I still travel a lot, but this is home for me. When I'm gone, I can't wait to get back. I live in an old farmhouse not far from here. It belongs to my Uncle Joe and Aunt Millie. When I got out of the service, I needed a place to live, and they needed someone to help with the upkeep of the place. It seemed like a good fit, so here I am."

Without warning, the sky began to darken. First lightning, then thunder rumbled from the fast-moving clouds. A summer downpour was coming through and began drenching them all. Lucy retrieved the basket and blanket as Caleb picked up Sadie and put her in behind their seats. As they closed the truck doors, soaked by the sudden rain, they turned and faced each other and immediately began laughing.

"What do you think? Maybe we can call it off for today?" Caleb laughed. "I'll pick you up in the morning for breakfast. Then the team can meet us at the farm, and we can all review your week together."

"Sounds good," she said as he started the truck and headed back to town. Lucy had always been the one to drive Lucy Moore wherever she went. Being a passenger was a new thing. She was not accustomed to being dependent on someone else to determine her path.

After a few minutes of quiet thought, she turned to Caleb and said, "Why don't I just meet you at K's for breakfast. Then I can follow you out to the farm. That way, you won't have to drive me back into town after the meeting?"

"Are you sure?" Caleb asked, sounding a little disappointed as he pulled to the curb at The Nest.

"I'm sure," she said. "I'll just meet you at K's, let's say, seven o'clock."

As Caleb drove away, Lucy couldn't help but reflect that he sounded a little disappointed at her suggestion to drive separately.

Chapter 16

Calm Before the Storm

They both pulled into K's about the same time—Caleb first, then Lucy. As Lucy approached Caleb, still standing beside the truck, she glanced in the back seat of the truck and said, "Where's Sadie?"

"She's back at the farm," he said. "She's sleeping in this morning. Sadie is getting on up in years. She's not the pup she used to be, but don't ever tell her that."

Ding-ding. Walking into K's together, they sat themselves in booth number seven. A moment later, Alison stepped over to greet them. "Good morning, Caleb. I hope your trip went well." Without giving him a chance to answer, she turned to Lucy and continued, "Hey girl, how's that research of yours coming?"

"Just fine, Alison, and thanks again for Saturday. Your personalized shopping tour was just what I needed."

"Sounds like you two have been getting to know each other while I was gone," said Caleb.

"You betcha," said Alison. "Like she said, we even went shopping. A girl has to help a girl whenever she can. Besides, this girl has been sitting in your booth every morning while you were gone."

Lucy blushed. "I thought someone should occupy it while you were gone so you wouldn't lose squatter's rights to your favorite booth."

"That was mighty kind of you, Ms. Moore, thank you."

"You're quite welcome, Mr. Burns."

Alison poured their coffee, took their orders, and left. Caleb scratched his head and said, "I thought I heard someone say that you didn't eat breakfast."

"That was before I spent a week in Welcome. This place has a way of giving a person a real appetite."

As they began to talk about the previous day's picnic, Lucy picked up her knife and put a pat of butter on her plate. She then poured the honey over it and began to swirl and stir just as Jenny had shown her. Caleb watched with intrigue. When she spread it on the biscuit and brought it up to her mouth, she took a bite. As she wiped her lips with her tongue, their eyes met, for a split second longer than either was comfortable with. She quickly put the biscuit down and, stammering just a little, said, "Boy, that's good honey! I'd like to take some back to Chicago when I go home. Remind me to ask Alison where they get it."

They soon finished breakfast and left the diner. Caleb took the lead, driving his truck, with Lucy driving Max following at a safe distance behind. At the edge of town, Caleb turned onto East Harvey Hill Road. Alone in the truck now, Caleb began to consider the morning ahead. Their meeting would be a turning point in the entire Welcome project. Would the writer from Chicago be able to accept the deception that had been laid upon her? Could she still trust the team enough to do what they needed her to do? Would she come on board and help the team launch the mission, or would the truth send her back to Chicago?

The team of five had decided that telling her the truth was worth the risk. They had so easily bonded with her in only a week. They truly wanted her as part of the secret government project in Welcome, Indiana. Caleb trusted the team's insights, their instincts, and judgments. He had turned the call over to them, to tell her the truth—or not. He knew he wanted her on board, but he was not ready to analyze his own motives as to why.

Behind the major's pickup, the girl in question was having a meeting within her own room of thoughts. There were so many questions. What was the greater purpose of the meeting this morning? She already had enough of her own notes and journal entries to write a good story. Their synergistic approach to growing local food was a tremendous idea with untold potential to put the power of sustainable food production into the hands of many. Her writer's gut, however, told her there was more to it—much more than meets the eye.

They all had accepted her, a stranger, into their little group. They seemed to be truly kind and considerate of her quest and were willing to help her in any way. So why shouldn't she be excited about this meeting? It seemed as though some piece of the puzzle was still missing and unknown. Why was part of her heart terrified of the morning that was about to unfold?

Ten minutes down the road, the major put on his right turn signal and slowed down his vehicle. It was then that Lucy saw the rusty old mailbox. White with red letters that looked like they had been painted twenty years ago. The two-inch letters said BURNS. Caleb turned the truck onto a gravel drive and continued with Lucy close behind.

The rough and rutted driveway continued another hundred yards. Briars and bushes encroached along the way until both vehicles came to rest in what appeared to be an old barnyard. To the left were two weathered barns with all their paint gone but still nicely maintained. To the right was a stately, old brick farmhouse set on a neatly mowed and manicured lawn. Flowerbeds full of spring-blooming flowers were scattered all around. Inside the old wrought-iron yard fence, a giant oak tree with limbs outstretched still secured a two-rope board swing. Lucy just sat there taking it all in.

"Come on, Lucy," Caleb said as he approached her, still sitting in her car. "Let's go inside. There is someone I want you to meet." She got out of the car and, looking around again, wondered if perhaps she had somehow become a character in an old Norman Rockwell painting.

They walked together toward the porch. From inside the house, they heard Sadie barking, and then they saw her as she pushed past the screen door. Down the porch she came and ran over, coming to a stop between them and licking Caleb's hand. "Yes, Sadie, I missed you too, but you were asleep when I left this morning, so don't be upset with me. Besides, look who I brought to see you."

Lucy was sure she saw Sadie roll her eyes as though to say, 'Good grief—not her again.' It was becoming obvious that if Lucy was going to stay another week in Welcome, she would need to make peace with Sadie.

As they stepped onto the porch, a voice called out, "In here, Caleb, in the kitchen." Inside, a tall, strong-framed woman in her eighties turned from the sink to say hello. "Hi there, I'm Aunt Millie," she said as she wiped her hands on her long kitchen apron and then stretched out one to welcome Lucy.

"Hi, I'm Lucy Moore, pleased to meet you, Aunt Millie."

"Your Uncle Joe went over to MacBurg this morning, Caleb. He needed to pick up some parts for the tractor. He'll be back by lunchtime. Oh, and Jenny is already here. She's out back cutting some flowers for the table. She said the others would be coming shortly. They all insisted on bringing something for lunch. Who was I to argue with a plan like that?" Aunt Millie smiled and winked at Lucy.

"Why don't I go out and help Jenny cut those flowers?" Lucy said. Lucy went out through the kitchen's back door. From the porch, she saw another enchanted world. Tall trees framed a large backyard. Fruit trees were scattered throughout. Flowering shrubs and small accent flower beds provided color that separated several raised beds of lush green vegetables, making their seasonal debut. Perhaps the thing that caught her attention the most was the scattered benches and swings strategically placed throughout the backyard. No matter the time of day or position of the sun, one could always find a place to sit in the shade and enjoy the view.

"Hi, Jenny!" Lucy yelled out once she saw where Jenny was working. "Need some help?"

"Of course, come on out. Aunt Millie likes lots of flowers in the house when she has company."

They talked while gathering the flowers, and then Jenny turned to Lucy and asked, "Is it true what a little birdie told me, that you and Caleb went on a picnic yesterday?"

"Yeah, but it was just time to catch up on what I did last week with all of you."

"I see", said Jenny, "then you won't mind if I ask you another little question?"

"Go ahead," said Lucy.

"Was it just the two of you, or was there another girl with him?"

"How did you know?" said Lucy.

"Oh, Lucy, don't take it personally. Sadie goes with Caleb every chance she gets. She's a very protective dog in case you haven't noticed."

"Oh, I noticed, alright," said Lucy. "Every time I got within three feet of Caleb, she limped over and squeezed in between us."

"That's our Sadie," laughed Jenny.

"So I have a question about Sadie," said Lucy. "Do you know why she limps the way she does?"

For a moment, Jenny just stared far out into the hayfield beyond. It was as though she hadn't heard the question. Then finally she said, "Yes, I do know why she limps. It all happened a few years ago when Caleb was stationed in Mozambique. This little starving mutt of a dog kept following him around. It was love at first sight. Caleb had just lost his wife. She had been killed in a head-on collision by a drunk driver. There was a really big hole in his life at that moment, and it seemed like he and the pup both needed each other."

"Sadie was never officially a military dog, but everyone on base treated her as though she was. One day while on patrol, Caleb's company was ambushed, and they ended up engaged in close-quarters combat. One of the rebels sighted in on Caleb, and before he knew what happened, Sadie had leaped through the air, knocking Caleb to the ground. In that split second, Sadie had taken the bullet intended for Caleb. Caleb got a medic to patch her up and save her life. But when the leg healed, it was never the same again."

"When Caleb came back to the states, a lot of rules were forgotten, heads turned the other way, and documents had coffee stains at the signature line. In the end of it all, Sadie and Caleb got off the plane and started a whole new life together here in Welcome. Sadie gets along just fine, but she is getting on up there in age, even for a dog. Some days I think that old war injury is starting to take its toll on her." Jenny said as her eyes finally met Lucy's.

"How do you know all of this story?" Lucy asked.

"Well, you might say that Sadie is a little bit of my story, too. You see, I was the nurse helping the medic put her back together that day in the field." Pointing back over her shoulder toward the house, Jenny said, "Both of those two in there have a very special place in my heart."

"So … how did you end up here in Welcome, here, with Caleb and Sadie?"

"The answer to that one is a little more complicated," Jenny said hesitantly.

At that moment, Caleb yelled from the back porch, "Come on in, you two. The rest of the group is here now!" Jenny and Lucy went inside, put the flowers in a bucket of water, and set them aside for Aunt

Millie to work with later.

Caleb spoke up, "Let's all go into the living room, and you can catch me up on what you did together while I was gone." Zack and Maria brought in a pitcher of iced tea and several bottles of water. Sadie went over and lay down by Caleb's chair.

Chapter 17

The Truth Comes Out

Lucy was asked to share her thoughts and reflections on the past week. She scooted forward on her chair and began.

"It's such an incredible, almost unbelievable story of what you few have been able to do. The possibilities for our country are huge. I want to write about it. I want to write a story that can actually make a difference in the lives of every American. Consider this: With the expansion of your model, it could become a valuable addition to supplement our existing high-input, large-scale farming practices. The possibilities are far-reaching for so many Americans."

Caleb interjected, "The problem, Lucy, is the same one I proposed the first day we met".

"And what was that, again?" Lucy asked.

"The question is: Who cares? Suppose you write your story or write a great book, and it's published. It is available in every bookstore and newsstand in America. Your publisher makes it available at a price everyone can afford. Will it motivate enough people actually to do what we are doing here in Welcome?"

Lucy said, "You sound just like my publisher. I know I'm not the only one in this room who sees a real sense of urgency. I've heard it in each of your stories this past week. You know the possibilities for a national crisis are real and grow stronger every day."

Caleb said, "Yes, Lucy, we do. We all do. That's why we invited you here."

"Excuse me?" Lucy said with a puzzled and frightened tone in her voice. "For a moment I thought you said, 'You invited me here.'"

"Well, we did—sort of," said Zack as he got back into the conversation.

"The anonymous phone tip to Lenny, your publisher, was from me."

"But why, Zack?" asked Lucy.

Maria leaned forward in her seat and began to answer. "Lucy, there is a story here to be written, but it is much, much bigger than anything you have seen so far. Our little project is just the tip of the iceberg. There is so much more to show you, but we had to be sure you would be the right one to tell that story to everyone else in America."

At this point, Caleb began to settle back in his chair. It was the team's turn to do all the talking. They were the ones that Lucy had spent time with and had gotten to know. They were the ones she needed to hear from to understand why she was brought here. They were the ones who would be able to justify the deception of omission. Only they could calm the storm that was obviously starting to rage inside her.

Jenny broke in, "We wanted to tell you from the very beginning. But we couldn't. We knew who you were as a writer. We have read every article, every extract, and every story you've ever written. We needed to get to know you as a person—to know your heart before we offered you the story we want you to tell.

In a shaky voice, Lucy said, "I don't know who you people really are. And I do not know what your real story is, but one thing I do know is that you have all deceived me. So I don't think I want to write your story. I think I need to leave, now—right now."

Pete quickly jumped up and said, "Lucy, wait. Wait a second. Just a minute ago, you said you wanted to write something that would make a real difference in people's lives. I know you talk to God every night. You probably read your Bible every day. Do you know the story of Esther and Mordecai, in II Kings Chapter Six?"

"Of course I do, Pete, but what does that have to do with all of this?"

"Remember in the story, Queen Esther had the opportunity to tell the story about her people to make a difference in the lives of all her people, a real life-and-death difference. She was afraid, though, because if she did what actually needed to be done, she could lose her own life as well. And what did her uncle Mordecai say?"

Lucy closed her eyes for a second. Then she opened them and said, "Mordecai asked Esther, 'How do you know that God has not put you here at this place and at this time to do His will?'"

Pete continued, "So my question to you, Lucy, is how do you

know that you are not here in this place at this time to make a very real difference in the lives of many, many people? Tonight, when you talk to God, ask Him to help you know for sure if the people in this room can be trusted, and if He has a work for you to do here in Welcome at this important time. Please, Lucy, ask Him."

Lucy looked around the room. Her gut wrenched inside like never before. Then she said, "Talks with God don't have to be at bedtime, Pete. I'll ask Him right now if Aunt Millie will loan me her backyard for a few minutes. I'd like to talk with Him out there, in the garden, if you don't mind, Aunt Millie."

"Go right ahead, child. Lots of folks find the garden a good place to talk to God. It's been a tradition that goes way back, at least a couple thousand years."

Lucy went out to the garden. Caleb stood at the window and watched her. Her lips were moving, and tears were flowing down her cheeks. As he watched, he remembered a time when he, too, had been close to God. It had been before his wife's death.

God had not saved her the night of the wreck. It was then that Caleb decided he could no longer trust God. Why hang around someone you can't trust? So Caleb had done what any angry child might have done—he turned his back on God. At that moment by the window, Caleb Burns was not only missing the closeness he had had with his wife, but he was also missing the close relationship he once had with God.

For the first time, he considered that the empty spot inside of himself that seemed so large and painful at times might in reality be two empty spots. He knew he couldn't do anything about the one caused by his wife's death. He also now realized that he was the only one who could do something about the other emptiness. Watching Lucy out there, she seemed to be talking to a dear old friend whom she truly counted on— someone she could trust. Maybe if she stayed and learned to trust the group, she could also help him relearn to trust God.

A few minutes later, she came back into the house. "I'll stay for now," she said, "but only until I get more answers from all of you about all of this. Besides, I have another reason for staying a little longer in Welcome, at least for now. It has nothing to do with any of you or your project. It's personal between me and an old man I met at lunch the other day."

"An old man at K's?" asked Pete.

"Yes," said Lucy, "Apparently, his boss has a son. I figure he meant grandson, but it was his story. Anyway, he has a son who is a runaway, and he was trying to find him. The last good information he had was that the boy was somewhere here, in the Welcome area. He seemed so personally torn up about the boy leaving and running away. My heart just ached listening to him. I told him I would do what I could, but I needed more information. After that, he said he would be around and in touch. Then he just got up and left the restaurant."

Caleb had been standing in the back of the room, near the window, but out of sight from the others. Through the kitchen doorway, Aunt Millie had been watching him watch Lucy as she had prayed in the garden. And just now, as Lucy mentioned the runaway, Aunt Millie was pretty sure that Major Burns had just wiped his red eyes. She looked to the kitchen ceiling and whispered, "Oh yes, Lord, yes. Thank you, dear God."

The room was quiet, but only for a moment. "All right, you people," said Aunt Millie, "You've got a big afternoon ahead of you, asking questions and answering questions. That kind of work can take a lot of energy, so whether you are hungry or not, you'd better get something to eat."

As they all walked toward the kitchen, they heard the sound of Uncle Joe's old pickup truck coming up the lane and stopping in the barn lot. When Uncle Joe came into the house, he sensed a chill in the air and started to retell a favorite old joke to try and break the tension.

Aunt Millie spoke out over Uncle Joe, "Come on in here, folks, and load up your plates, and then go sit down. I'll bring in the drinks in a minute. Remember Aunt Millie's house rule number eighteen: 'The Good Lord didn't make mealtimes so folks could talk business with their mouth full of food. Mealtime is time to enjoy the food, and to enjoy the company of folks with whom you are sharing the meal.'"

Since everyone had brought at least one dish for the potluck lunch, each took their turn around the table telling Lucy what they had made and what was special about it. They made jokes about each other's cooking skills and, with great fondness, talked about shared meals of the past. Soon, the tension was gone, and everyone was laughing. Lucy watched them. They were all so passionate about their food and the common bond they shared. They were like a family of brothers and sisters, all enjoying being together, like a family she had always dreamed of being a part of.

Lucy knew she wanted with all her heart to trust these people. The question was, was she willing to take the risk of getting hurt in exchange for the hope of receiving such love?

Uncle Joe stood up to announce that he needed to get back to work. He said he had lots to do and thanked everyone for bringing such a delicious lunch. As Uncle Joe left the dining room, the others began clearing the table. Aunt Millie insisted that everyone get out and that she would take care of the dishes.

They all went out to the porch and sat down. As they each found a place, Sadie ambled over to Lucy, took her shirt sleeve, and started tugging on her. She was pulling Lucy toward Caleb. "Well, will you look at that," said Jenny. "I think Sadie wants Caleb to start answering some of the thousand questions exploding inside Lucy's heart right about now."

Caleb stood, "You are absolutely right, Sadie. It is time. You lead the way." Sadie slowly made it down off the porch and walked straight to the old barn. She stopped and sat down in front of an old door hung on a rolling track. When the others got there, Caleb tapped an icon on his phone, and the door rolled open to one side. Behind that door was yet another door, but this one was made of heavy industrial plate steel. Another tap on Caleb's phone, and this one also rolled to the side, revealing a twelve-foot by twelve-foot carpeted room with an elevator door, just like in a hotel lobby. The elevator opened, revealing a spacious inside. Everyone stepped in, and Lucy followed. The door closed, and Caleb said, "B2". When the elevator stopped, the doors opened, and everyone stepped out.

Lucy took one look, and her jaw dropped in disbelief. Laid out in front of her was a sprawling, brightly lit workroom. Several people were moving from one workstation to another, walking between computer monitors and flat screens like a modern news studio. It reminded her of news reels she had seen from inside SpaceX launch sites.

"What is this place?" asked Lucy, as she tried to take it all in.

"This is Mother Hubbard's Central Command Center," Caleb began. From here, we constantly monitor a minimum of thirty-two global sites that in one way or the other have the potential of compromising the safety of the American food supply. Everyone who works in here lives in or around Welcome. They all hold down some kind of local involvement on a small scale, but this is everyone's true full-time work."

"Hey girl, good to see you," said a familiar-sounding voice from behind.

Lucy quickly turned to confirm the voice, and, seeing who she suspected, said, "Alison?"

"Of course, Lucy, who do you think interviewed you for your security clearance? And by the way, you passed, or you wouldn't even be down here. Well, got to go. See ya." With that, Alison and her tablet disappeared into the busy room.

Lucy just stood there, shaking her head in disbelief, trying to comprehend what was happening. "So, how many are in this project you call Mother Hubbard?"

"Officially, zero. But unofficially, forty-seven. We needed a sufficient number of people considered to be locals so that when we launch the mission, the support will seem to be from within the community, not from a bunch of outsiders."

"So whatever this Mother Hubbard mission is, you think you can pull it off with only forty-seven people?"

"No," said Caleb, "We needed forty-eight, including a very special forty-eighth person. That is why you are here."

"So I have been kidnapped to fill your team?"

"We'd rather you think of it as being recruited," said Caleb.

"What is to keep me from walking out of here and writing my own story with the information I have so far?" asked Lucy.

"Nothing is stopping you. You're free to go. But who was it that only a moment ago was talking about the great sense of urgency? Who was it that mentioned her publisher had doubts that such a story even needed to be published? And who was it that said she wanted a story that could really make a difference in the country's food security? Does that girl have all the resources needed to make that happen quickly?"

"Okay, okay," said Lucy, "but what about Lenny, my publisher? He thinks it was his tip that sent me here in the first place. I need to give him some kind of explanation if I end up staying long term."

"That's not a problem, Lucy. We know the one thing that will make Lenny very happy is for you to stay as long as necessary. We know that unless he quickly finds a significant increase in cash flow, Lenny Dekoskie will be bankrupt within months. You simply text him and let him know that the folks behind the Welcome project have very deep pockets. He has heard that before. They are willing to advance him a sizable amount of cash each month into his bank account. It will be considered an advance against any percentage of royalties that he would earn once the story breaks. If it never breaks, it is his money to keep—no strings attached. Tell him to expect the first bank deposit to be within ten days."

Lucy looked around the control center. All eyes were on her, watching and waiting for her response.

"You people are serious, aren't you?"

"We are, said Caleb. "The question is, are you?"

Lucy let out a long, slow breath. "So… when can you at least tell me what you expect me to write about?"

"I was hoping we could spend part of tomorrow going over the basics of what we want you to do. I think you've already had enough bombshells for one day."

Chapter 18

Dinner at Harry's

The next morning, Lucy left the Nest and arrived at the Burns' farm promptly at nine o'clock. She had just parked Max when Caleb greeted her and suggested they go into the house.

"I thought we might sit on the back porch for our discussions, but there are a few essentials for the meeting we need to pick up first." As it turned out, the essentials he had mentioned were just coming out of the oven as we stepped into his Aunt Millie's kitchen.

"Here you are," she said as she handed him a plate full of hot, homemade cinnamon rolls. "And what about drinks? Coffee, milk, or both?"

Caleb said, "Milk goes great with your rolls, and then maybe coffee a little later." Lucy knew she also wanted a glass of milk, but couldn't escape the memory of milking the goats a few days earlier. Caleb must have sensed her mental struggle and quickly added, "It's Kroger—two percent."

Feeling relieved, she answered, "I'll have the same."

Lucy & Caleb went through the kitchen's back door and onto the porch. Once again, she was taken by the beauty and serenity of the park-like landscape. Flowers, shrubs, and flowering trees were all exploding with their own individual announcements of spring. This time Lucy knew she had seen it before. It must have been on this very porch that Thomas Kincaid had sat and painted his famous work, *Springtime Memories*. It was all so beautiful! The trance was then broken when Caleb said, "We eat first, then talk."

"I know," Lucy said. "Aunt Millie's house rule number eighteen."

He blinked, intrigued by her response. "Right you are, Ms. Moore." He picked up a cinnamon roll, gestured a toast, and said, "Shall we eat?" For the next few minutes, they sat there together—strangers sharing the same beautiful space and time and wonderful food.

****

Caleb spent the morning and part of the afternoon briefing Lucy on the big picture of global events, but he omitted saying anything about the SEMP. He figured too much, too fast, was not a good thing right now. After a while, he concluded, "Your assignment, Lucy, is fairly simple. The execution of that assignment may seem impossible. You are here to help us, the team that you have spent the past week with, in figuring out how we can get a few million people to duplicate the same kind of model throughout communities all across America. You are the person of words, and you have a passion for the need."

"You can't be serious about expecting us to be able to pull that off," said Lucy.

"I am most serious about that," Caleb replied. "Besides, there's someone who wants to meet you at dinner tonight. It's someone who can bring some clarity and credibility to any doubts you may still have."

"So … I am going out to dinner tonight to meet someone I don't know. Can I at least ask who is taking me to dinner, and where it is that I am going, and what I should wear?"

"I'm afraid that you are still stuck with me for the first part."

"So long as I don't have to pay, I guess I can live with that part," said Lucy, smiling, "and the rest of it?"

Caleb continued, "When you get back to The Nest, just tell Ms. Robins you and I are going to Harry's place, and we will be meeting Ms. Janice. Ms. Robins can make some suggestions about what to wear and all that kind of girl stuff. I'll pick you up at six o'clock."

Still feeling a little unsure about the evening's arrangements, Lucy got in her little Mazda and headed back to town. Caleb stood in the barn lot and watched her drive down the long lane toward the mailbox. He was unable to take his eyes away, and, at that moment, he was unable to answer why.

****

Lucy got back to The Nest and found Ms. Robins in the kitchen. "Excuse me, Ms. Robins, but I just came from Mr. Burns' place, and he said to share with you that he and I will be meeting a Ms. Janice at Harry's tonight and that you could help me with what to …" Lucy stopped and looked right at Ms. Robins. "You're one of them too, aren't you?"

A big smile came over Ms. Robins' face as she said, "Come with me, Lucy".

They went upstairs to the room across the hall from Lucy's and went in. The room was not another guest room but was furnished as an office space. Ms. Robins walked Lucy over to the sliding closet doors. She opened them up and started fingering through several dresses. She pulled one out, held it up to Lucy, turned her toward the mirror, and said, "This one should work."

"It's a beautiful dress, but I can't wear it," said Lucy. "It probably won't fit, and it is not even my dress."

"Oh, I think it will fit you just fine, Lucy, and it is your dress. All of these are your clothes. This office space is yours as well."

Lucy shook her head again in disbelief. "Ms. Robins, if that is really your name, what else should I know about our arrangement—you know, you and me?"

Ms. Robins began, "Well, the short list goes something like this: The town of Welcome knows me simply as Ms. Robins, the sixties-something matron of a struggling B&B at the edge of town. I go to the First Baptist church on Sundays, volunteer at the local library two afternoons a week, and I let the local FFA chapter use my front porch as a pick-up point for their annual Christmas fruit sales."

"To you, Lucy Moore, I am special agent Angela Robins, your personal aide and concierge. I will be helping you in whatever way I am able: logistics, networking, appropriations, etc. But we can talk about all that later. Right now, you need to go get ready."

Promptly at six o'clock, Caleb's pickup pulled into the parking spot behind the B&B. He got out and went inside through the kitchen's back door.

Angela greeted him with an appraising look. "Well, look at you all dressed up like you are going to the prom or something. I'll tell your date that you're here."

Caleb cleared his throat and said, "Angela, you are having way too much fun with this. It is simply a business dinner with our recruit:

information sharing, logistics, plan of action, and meeting the boss. That sort of stuff."

"Mmhmm," said Angela with an approving grin on her face. "If you say so."

Caleb stepped into the living room while Angela went to get Lucy. A moment later, he heard a voice behind him, "Good evening, Mr. Burns."

Caleb turned and saw Lucy as he had never seen her before. Her usual shirt and jeans had been replaced with an evening gown, she wore high heels instead of sneakers, and she wore the makeup and jewelry of a model. She was beautiful.

"Good evening, Lucy. You look very, uh, very nice."

"As do you, Caleb."

With just a hint of stammer still in his voice, Caleb said, "Well, I guess we should be going. Our reservation is for eight." With that, he directed Lucy back toward the kitchen and then toward a door Lucy had never been through. "After you."

They stepped into an immaculate three-car garage. For a moment, Lucy thought she was in Bruce Wayne's bat cave. In the middle of the garage was a big, black luxury sedan and an amazing motorcycle, unlike any she had ever seen.

Caleb opened the car door for Lucy. She got in, and they drove out. A few miles out of town, they turned onto a country road, and within a few minutes, Lucy saw a large sign on a tall chain-link fence. The sign read U.S. ARMY RESERVES—INDIANA ARMY NATIONAL GUARD—ALL VISITORS CHECK IN AT SECURITY GATE.

Caleb pulled up to the gatehouse, and a young army reservist stepped up to the car, prompting Caleb to roll down the window. The recruit saw who it was and said, "Good evening, Major Burns. Your ride is ready for you in number four."

Major Burns' *ride*, as the young recruit had called it, was an Aerostar 601P. The plane was a twin piston aircraft that could comfortably fly at a speed of 250 mph. It was only half as fast as a personal jet the same size, perhaps, but requiring a much shorter runway. This allowed Burns to fly in and out of Welcome, switch to faster planes at other airports, and still maintain a low profile at home.

As they drove toward the hangar, Lucy looked over at Caleb and asked, "Are you really a major?"

"I was," said Caleb, "I'm a civilian now working for the Department of Defense. I am listed in the human resources department as Program Liaison—which means no one has a clue as to what I do, and I like it that way just fine."

The flight plan for the evening would have them landing at a small commercial airport outside Louisville, Kentucky, in forty minutes. From there, they would take a thirty-minute chauffeured ride to Fort Knox. Within ten minutes, they would be at Harry's, walking to their table, and being seated promptly at eight o'clock. Ms. Janice would be there by eight-fifteen.

Harry's was one of the Army's best-kept secrets. When Fort Knox was no longer needed to protect the gold that had historically backed U.S. currency, new uses were sought for the old maximum-security fort. It was the perfect place for a five-star restaurant where people protecting our country could go and get a bite to eat and not worry about someone overhearing their conversations.

When they arrived at Harry's, the chauffeur opened both car doors. They got out, and Caleb turned to Lucy. "Ms. Moore, would you allow me the honor of escorting you inside?"

"It would be my pleasure, Mr. Burns."

As they approached the restaurant's massive entryway, the doorman stepped forward and said, "Good evening, Major," and, turning to Lucy, he nodded, smiled, and added, "Ma'am."

They walked in and were greeted by the hostess, who showed them to their table. Once seated, Lucy looked to Caleb and said, "Tell me, Caleb, between the two, which is your favorite restaurant experience—K's diner on Market or Harry's place?"

Caleb rubbed his chin in a pensive, thoughtful expression and said, "My favorite dining experience is never determined by its location or by the food it serves, but rather by the company with whom I am sharing the food, the time, and the place."

Before Lucy could respond, Caleb abruptly stood up and addressed the woman now standing beside their table and said, "Good to see you again, Janice."

"Good to see you as well, Caleb." Turning to Lucy, she continued, "This must be our recruit, Lucy Moore. Hello, Lucy, I'm Janice Higgins."

Lucy couldn't believe her eyes or her ears. The woman who had just introduced herself was retired Rear Admiral Janice Higgins, currently serving as the nation's first Secretary of the Department of Provisions.

Lucy didn't know if she should nod her head or put out her hand, so she just said, "It's an honor to meet you, Madam Secretary."

Higgins continued, "I wanted to personally meet you to assure you that what you have been hit with over the last several hours is real. The people are real, the project is real, and we consider your assignment within the project to be most sincerely real and urgent."

A few minutes later, a waiter took their orders, and Higgins began the discussion again. "I was born and raised in a little town in Kansas. I was the only child of Tom and Louise Hubbard. With a name like Hubbard, you might guess that, as a young schoolgirl, I was teased a lot about whether or not our cupboard was bare. I never gave it much thought until I was assigned as an admiral on a nuclear submarine that would go out to sea for three months at a time. It was then that I took the ownership and responsibility of making sure that the cupboard on board was never bare."

"When I retired from the Navy, I served as Undersecretary for the Department of Defense for a while. It was there that I saw how millions of dollars could be so easily redirected into any pet project that those at the top were supporting. When I was asked by the president to serve as Secretary for Homeland Preparedness, my passion for a full and secure cupboard came to life again. This time it was not about the cupboard in my home or on a submarine—but the cupboard of the United States of America."

"For years, I had been concerned about the safety, sustainability, and availability of our food supply. Issues of disease outbreaks, transportation, crop failures, and power outages could all bring our country to its knees overnight. I started looking around for other like-minded people who I thought might be willing to do something about it. The criteria were simple: being passionate about the problem, having a security clearance of at least level eight, willing to be creative with their existing budgets, and, of course, an unquestioning love for their country."

"When my last sub command, the Oklahoma, came into dry-dock for three days, I arranged a visit of significant political leaders for a sightseeing tour of the Oklahoma. Her new commander, an old friend of mine, was most cooperative and gave us full access to the sub. The conference room had been equipped with a very special, simple toggle switch—a switch known only to each successive commander. With the flip of that little switch, all recording devices in the room were inoperable."

"Soon after that meeting, project Mother Hubbard was born. Our mission was simple: To develop a food production model that could be replicated repeatedly. The model was never intended to replace our massive agricultural production system but rather to provide a safety net. A safety net that would be needed if, for some reason, any part of our national food system should become jeopardized. The Welcome Model has shown us that with training, a sustainable, small-scale effort can produce great amounts of fresh, safe, local food. If there are enough of those models already in place in a community, then that community will at least have a chance of survival."

"We are now ready for phase II of the Mother Hubbard Mission, and that's where you come in, Lucy. That is why I personally picked you for this assignment. Caleb will explain the specifics and your assignment within this new phase." Higgins rose from her chair and stretched out her hand to shake Lucy's. "Welcome aboard," she said, and excused herself from the table.

****

The ride back to the airport was quiet, with neither Caleb nor Lucy feeling the need to talk; they just enjoyed the night sights along the way. At one point, Caleb turned and saw Lucy looking out the window. It was now too dark to focus on any of the outside sights. Instead, in her mind, she was watching an instant replay of the unbelievable events that had happened over the past fourteen hours. Five minutes later, Caleb was confident that she had closed her eyes and fallen asleep.

She has to be exhausted, he thought to himself. A minute later, he glanced her way again and contemplated how beautiful she was. Startled by what he was thinking, he realized he had not looked at a woman with those thoughts for years— especially not someone he would be working with on a very close and intensive pace.

When they arrived in Louisville, Lucy turned to face Caleb. "Oh, you're still here," she said.

With a quizzical expression, Caleb said, "Was I supposed to go somewhere?"

"No. I just meant, it's not a dream, is it? It is all very real, isn't it?"

They boarded the plane, and forty-five minutes later, Caleb was driving her to The Robins' Nest. Back through the garage and into the kitchen, they said their good nights. Caleb then got in his truck and drove back to the farm.

As Lucy got ready for bed, she put on her pajamas and started to hang up the dress. She paused, looked at the dress, and said softly, "This was already my dress. How did they know I would say yes?" Sitting down in the chair with the dress in her lap, she started to recount all that had happened. She considered what Zack had said about God possibly having a job for her here in Welcome just as He had had a job for Queen Esther.

As Lucy sat, she wondered whether her trip to Welcome had been one of chance or of Providence. As she began to consider the possibilities, she promptly
fell asleep.

Chapter 19   It Just Might Work

It was seven-thirty the next morning when Lucy finally woke up. She was still in the chair with the dress in her lap.

There was a text message from Caleb. "I have a meeting in D.C. for the next couple of days. Take the time off and do nothing with Mother Hubbard. Try to rest and relax. See you in a couple of days."

When she came down the stairs, Angela had already started breakfast. That suited Lucy just fine. For some unexplainable reason, she had very little interest in going to K's for breakfast, at least not without Caleb Burns. She wasn't sure why those feelings were there, but they were there just the same.

Lucy told Angela that Caleb said she was to take a couple of days off to rest and relax. She told her it was obvious that he didn't know her very well yet, suggesting such a silly thing as rest and relaxation. Lucy was hoping that Angela could help her with what she needed to do to get settled in. She wanted to get started on whatever it was that she was supposed to do."

"All in due time," Angela said. "Let me catch you up to speed on what has already been done for you."

"First, you have a personal bank account set up here in town with Welcome First National Bank. Your first month's pay is already deposited. With that account comes a bank credit card and a debit card. All of this is for your personal use. After we finish breakfast, we can go back upstairs to your office. I will show you a few other things that will help with your work."

The rest of the morning was like the first day on a new job. Angela went over the basics of Lucy's new computer, printer, and cellphone. All of these came with a security sophistication she had never imagined. The phone was like having her very own personal secretary all the time. Ask it whatever, and instantly it had the answers she would need. AI had certainly come a long way in just the past few years—maybe a bit too far, too fast. As Lucy continued in-service on the equipment, she also made a few notes of things to pick up to give the office a more personal touch.

That afternoon, she visited the local library to get a sense of the town's history and also to do a little people watching. She had always thought you could tell a lot about a community just by going to its library and watching its people. While at the library, Lucy found notes on the town's founding fathers, its former and current businesses and industries, and she obtained a healthy perspective on local politics.

She also found a section displaying local events, including upcoming garage sales. Lucy had never been to a garage sale in Chicago. Such a thing was unheard of in her neighborhood. She found a couple of garage sales that might have a few things for her office, so she jotted down times and addresses for those. Now all that she needed was a local street map. Max had been updated with a good navigation program, but Lucy wanted to experience the treasure hunt as perhaps Granny would have in her time. The library did not disappoint. She found a free Welcome city map, a county road map, and even some township road maps provided by the local farm agencies.

****

On Thursday morning, Lucy headed out in Max for some of that downtime that Caleb had insisted she take. Visiting garage sales turned out to be a fun and exciting adventure. Having some newly acquired spending money made it even more fun.

Lucy took the next two days and continued to explore not only Welcome but also the countryside. It was just the two of them, her and Max, having a little quality time together.

On Sunday, Lucy went back to the storefront church. The experience there was so different; there wasn't all the pomp and circumstance like you find in most big churches. It was more like a family getting together to talk and search the Bible for ways to live their lives in a way pleasing to God. They spoke of ways to humbly thank Him for all the blessings they enjoyed and for His great love. As she sat there beside Pete, she wondered if she might not also someday become a part of this little church family.

After church services, she drove out to the Dairy Queen and got a coney dog and an ice cream cone. A few minutes later, it was back to The Nest and some overdue writing in her journal.

****

The next morning, Lucy came down the stairs and went straight to the kitchen. She and Angela had started eating breakfast together as a simple way to brainstorm and go over plans for the day ahead. As Lucy stepped over to the stove to get some more biscuits, she heard Angela say, "Well, I'll be! Will you look at this?" She was holding up the Welcome morning paper and had zeroed in on a photo on the front page.

"What is it, Angela?"

"It's my FFA kids I told you about. The ones that sell their fruit off my front porch at Christmastime. They just won first place in two state contests and will be competing at the national convention next fall. I tell you, that bunch of kids is something else. Just last week, they asked to put a poster up in the library. It was to let folks know about their new podcast for employers to connect kids with summer jobs. You could access it through either their FFA website, their Facebook page, or their Instagram account."

"Wait a minute," said Lucy. "Are we talking about high school kids doing all this?"

"Absolutely, yes," responded Angela. "It's all part of their Agricultural Communications class with Miss Spargo. Ag Communications was one of the contests they just won first place in. The other one was Ag Engineering. The contests they compete in are a direct reflection of what they are learning in the classroom."

Angela continued, "It's no different than when all the students are required to take physical education. Those who excel in those classes are often the ones who are on sports teams. Sport teams like football, basketball, and gymnastics compete with other school teams until there are local, regional, and state winners.

"Angela," said Lucy, "You seem to know a lot about these FFA kids who sell fruit off your front porch—"

Angela interrupted, "Did I tell you they wrote a feature article on The Robins' Nest on their web page last winter?"

"You have now," said Lucy, starting to speak very rapidly. "Angela, I need you to focus. Do you know any more of the class subject areas other than Communications and Engineering?"

"Well, let's see," said Angela. "I know some of them. There is Horticulture, where they grow flowers and vegetable plants, and have a big plant sale in the spring. There's one called Small Engines, where they work on mowers and garden tillers. I think there's one called Agronomy, which is about soils, insects, and diseases. There are probably more, but that's all I can think of right now."

Suddenly, Lucy got a faraway look on her face. She jumped up, ran around to the other side of the table, and gave Angela a big shoulder hug. "Angela, you are a genius!"

"I am?" she questioned. Then she quickly said, "Of course I am, but what was it I just said that let you in on that little secret?"

Lucy faced her and said, "The parts about competition and social media and Ag Communications…. don't you see Angela? It just might work!"

Lucy's mind was exploding in a hundred different directions. She had started conceptualizing a framework to get the Mother Hubbard food production project put into a competitive challenge for FFA members all over the country. The big difference would be instead of single skill competitions, the teams would be collaborative in their approach—combining skill sets from a variety of Ag Ed programs. The result would be potentially having many synergistic youth groups, just like the Welcome team, all over the country.

As Lucy thought out loud, Angela chimed in, "It says here in the newspaper that there are now over nine thousand five hundred FFA chapters in America. If your job is to get the word out as fast as you can to as many as you can, this may have some real possibilities."

"Who's in charge of the Ag Education and FFA programs at Welcome High School?" Lucy asked.

"Hannah Spargo. She's the Ag Department supervisor, and she also teaches the Ag Communications class."

Lucy hurriedly said, "Can you get me her contact info so I can try to talk with her?"

"Slow down, Lucy," Angela replied, "I know her well. I'll call her, set up the meeting, and while I'm at it, gently drop the thought that the meeting could eventually put her class and Welcome FFA in a national spotlight for the foreseeable future. She'll like that."

Two days later, with Caleb still out of town, Lucy met Hannah Spargo at the school. She was happy to give Lucy a tour of the facility, including the labs, shops, and greenhouses. She was very excited to share about the school's Agricultural Education academic offerings, plus their long history of FFA skills competitions.

Lucy then began to explain to Miss Spargo the idea of a hybrid contest. The contest structure must first include a combination of current skills contests, and secondly, a website and social media presence to share the ongoing efforts of the team.

Through social media platforms, other FFA groups across the country would be challenged to join in the competition within their own communities. Miss Spargo liked the idea very much. Her only concern was that if it really took off and turned out to be a potential contest for all schools, she wanted to run it past the national FFA executives in Indianapolis. "Not to worry, Lucy." She said. "I am sure they will love it and support it. Either way, count us in."

When Lucy got back to The Nest, she updated Angela on all that had happened. Angela said, "Good. Caleb's flight comes into the airbase at ten o'clock tonight. I sent him word to stop by The Nest on his way home and pick up a package for Aunt Millie. You can fill him in then."

"What was Aunt Millie needing that couldn't wait until tomorrow, if you don't mind my asking?"

"Oh, I don't know yet," said Angela. "I'll think of something. Maybe I will box up some old books. I'll tell him it's a surprise." Lucy looked at Angela with a questioning frown on her face. "Oh, it's okay," said Angela. "It's part of my duties as your liaison."

"Liaison?" questioned Lucy.

"Well, of course," Angela continued. "I serve as your official liaison when you need to connect in person with Caleb Burns. He's a man who would never consider stopping in at a young lady's place at this late hour of the night, even though he is most anxious to find out everything that has happened over the last few days. You, on the other hand, would never be so bold as to invite a man such as Caleb to your place this late at night. You are also very excited to tell him about what you have come up with as a real game-changer for the project's mission. So, you go do whatever you need to do." She said with a knowing grin. "I need to find some books to box up."

It was ten-forty when Lucy heard the back door of the kitchen open. Caleb had not expected to see anyone still awake. Startled at first, he was surprised to see Lucy going over her notes that were spread out on the dining room table. "Looks like you've been busy while I was in D.C.," Caleb said.

"I have been," Lucy said, "and I can't wait to go over all of it with you tomorrow after you've rested up."

To that, Caleb said, "Actually, I slept the whole flight coming back. Maybe, if you're not too tired, we could hit some of the high points of your progress."

It was after midnight when they finally began to slow down. The adrenaline was still there, but they both knew they would be worthless the next day if they didn't get some rest.

"What time did you say we are to meet with Miss Spargo tomorrow?"

"Ten sharp." They stood and walked away from the table and toward the kitchen. "I think the box over there on the counter is for Aunt Millie."

"Thanks, Lucy, I almost forgot why I stopped. One other thing, Ms. Lucy Moore." He put his hands on her shoulders and looked sternly into her eyes. "The next time I tell you to take a few days off and do nothing, I expect …" And then his stern expression changed to one big smile. "I expect you to do what you do best. Secretary Higgins was right. You are the best."

Then, without thinking, he put his arms around her, pulled her in close, and said, "I am so proud of you." Immediately, they were both keenly aware of the close embrace they were sharing. Was it awkward? Yes. But neither seemed to be in a panic to separate. Caleb and his team were a family—close and physical in their celebrations. She was new to the team and unaware of such a relationship. Had he, in his excitement, become too forward in his celebration? Had he just jeopardized a future working relationship with a new team member?

"Just doing my job, Mr. Burns," she said. They stepped back from each other, and Caleb picked up the box off the counter. As Caleb walked toward the back door, he heard a soft voice say, "See you in the morning. Be careful driving home."

Chapter 20

A Plan Comes Together

The next day, Lucy, Caleb, and the team of five met Hannah Spargo at the school to begin planning the logistics of the competition. Lucy emphasized that the financial backers would provide all supplies and materials needed, but the identity of the backers must remain anonymous. The Welcome Ag Program would get full credit for everything, and the sponsors would get what they need.

The group then did a little brainstorming session to devise what an ideal site would look like. It would need to have one or more small buildings to serve as shelter. It needed to be convenient, but at the same time appear isolated. Basic utilities like water and electricity would be nice, but not critical. The quality of soil would determine, to some degree, the size and scope of the overall endeavor.

Lucy then asked Miss Spargo how she envisioned the size and structure of the student team. "Well, we have five different Ag Programs: horticulture, mechanics, animal care, food science and technology, and communications. If we figure two students from each program, that would mean ten students. It would give a good mix of basic skills for a hybrid contest. If we had ten involved, then I could petition the school board to treat the program as a summer school class. That way, the kids could pick up some extra credits toward graduation. The only thing the Board of Education might balk at would be paying me as an un-budgeted summer school teacher."

"Not to worry," Caleb quickly responded. "I am sure that the sponsors of the project will be happy to contribute more than enough to cover your salary and benefits."

Spargo shook her head. "These sponsors of yours are serious about this project, aren't they?"

"Indeed, they are."

"Have you given any thought to the student recruitment

process?" asked Lucy.

Spargo responded, "I don't want to open this up to volunteers. I will hand-pick the students, and I also know their parents. At some point, parental support will be a critical resource to have."

"Can you pull together a meeting of those students and their parents to discuss all the particulars?"

"Sure, that shouldn't be a problem."

****

The meeting took place at Welcome High School three days later. Parents, students, and the Welcome team were all present. Hannah Spargo chaired the meeting that began with an introduction of the Welcome team and the writer from Chicago. She described the project in question as this year's community service project. It would be a project to address growing concerns for local food availability and affordability in both good times and in times of crisis.

A professional social media group from out of state would work with the students to advance their ag communication skills. The plan was that within two weeks, a new project website and multiple social media platforms would come online. Each would document the progress throughout the summer, starting with the site's present status, and then post ongoing developments throughout the summer. Unlike Welcome's FFA community service projects of the past, this one would have national exposure.

At that point, one of the parents asked, "Why the sense of urgency to put skills that traditionally have been taught in the classroom into yet another social media game?"

Hannah acknowledged that there is a growing national concern about our food: where the food comes from, its purity, its availability, and its cost. She reminded them that when they were young and the pandemic hit, grocery store shelves emptied overnight. "We are a nation that specializes in just-in-time delivery systems, but when that supply chain is interrupted or stopped, we quickly run out of food. The goal of our service project would be to demonstrate and offer a plan to avoid that dependency on such a fragile system."

One parent spoke up. "I still don't see how the social media part helps solve that problem."

Spargo continued, "In the late 1900s, there lived a man by the name of Buckminster Fuller." All of a sudden, Marcus sat on the edge of his chair and began listening even more intently to what she was saying. "He was a genius, an inventor, and a futurist. One of his most profound contributions to social change was about getting people to change their way of thinking. Bucky, as he was often referred to, said that if you want people to think differently, don't try to teach the new concepts to them. Instead, give them a tool or a game that, in the process of using or playing, will change their way of thinking."

"This has never been clearer than with the introduction of the personal computer and other digital devices. Kids did not learn how to use technology in the classroom—they learned it from each other, playing games on their computers and smartphones and on other digital tools with games." As a result, a whole generation of young people quickly learned the basics of digital technology—a completely new way of thinking.

"Our goal is to document the experience of young people learning to grow their own food, then take that experience and infuse it within an online challenge. The postings would be a record of daily successes and failures by which everyone could learn. Social media platforms are hungry for young people to share in positive and wholesome interactions. We hope to invite and engage other FFA chapters all across the country to join in a competitive challenge to do the same thing in their communities. It would be a new way of thinking about their food—a paradigm shift in the value of local food production."

At this point, Marcus was totally engaged. Bucky Fuller had been one of his favorite heroes from childhood. Marcus had used this very same principle to triple the student sign-up numbers for the Chemistry 101 class at the university. His success with the enrollment numbers and the proficiency of the students' scores came as a surprise to the university, but not to Marcus.

His tactic had been a simple one. He had changed the name of the class from Chemistry 101 to Basic Winemaking. The students needed to learn all the basics of chemistry to meet their goal of making a bottle of fine wine. The notoriety of the class improved even more with a wine making competition and celebration at the end of the semester. Marcus was awake and listening to every word Hannah Spargo was saying.

The meeting continued with expected concerns and comments of support. Finally, only one question remained. "Where is all this going to take place?" asked the parents.

"We were hoping you might have some ideas," Hannah said. She explained the criteria needed for the site. It seemed like the group was at a loss.

Lucy had been watching Marcus since midway through the meeting. He had been intent on watching and listening to Hannah. Lucy looked over to Marcus. "Got any ideas, Marcus?"

Marcus looked at Lucy, then to Hannah, then back to Lucy. He took a deep breath. "Yes, I do." He said matter-of-factly. "I know where there's an old 4-H camp with ten cabins." He told the group. "It would be convenient to get to, yet quite isolated from the public eye. Yes, I know a place we can get."

He looked over to Lucy for approval. She smiled and mouthed a silent, "*Thank you.*"

Conversation became more animated. Uncle Joe chimed in. "I can bring the tractor in and start bush hogging to clear off some of the grounds."

"Great idea, Uncle Joe, but better wait till we get some good pictures and video of the site first to compare progress throughout the summer."

Everyone continued asking questions. The students had as many questions as their parents. The Welcome team each identified their training specialties. Each of the five team members would partner with two students, based on the students' special interests and training. Each of those teams of three would have two cabins to use as their base of operation. The result would be a duplication of what the Welcome team had been doing for the past four years, but this time, all five would be located in the same physical location.

There would be a mechanical trio. Another group would be in

charge of vegetable production, and another would be responsible for small animal production and care. One would be responsible for fruit production, and one would be in charge of food processing. There would be areas of overlap and shared duties, just as the Welcome team had so successfully been doing.

Hannah Spargo walked in and out of the clusters of conversation. She was so excited for her students. They, together with their parents and their new outside mentors, were actively engaged as equal partners in what might just well become an experience of a lifetime.

Chapter 21

Who We Become

It was the last week in May. Angela had located a young social media agency that had done federal security work before. She booked their services and reserved their rooms in a hotel within a reasonable driving distance. The senior students were now out of school, while the younger students' classes were still in session, but they only had final exams left to take. When they weren't at school, the students were at the campsite.

The social media group established an area in the camp dining hall as their base of operation. Marcus had given everyone a quick, cursory tour of the camp. They were all taking photos and videos of the entire camp to establish the point of beginning. It was a rough, abandoned site that would need a lot of work to be transformed into the envisioned oasis of production.

The early days were full of collaborative planning to establish an initial plan to get things started. Uncle Joe would bring in a tractor and bush hog to do the initial land clearing. Once that was done, he would bring other implements like a plow and rotary tiller to prep the garden growing beds. Pete and his students would then mark out where the main garden beds should go.

Marcus would work inside the dining hall, prepping it as a command center and a place for meetings, logistics, and a staging area for the AV people.

Maria would select which cabins would fit best for what animals and where accessory structures like greenhouses or animal runs should be placed.

Zack would be looking at the best places to apply retrofittings for collecting rainwater and places for the application of solar panels. His crew would also look at converting the implement shed into a workable shop with on-site tools.

Zack and Marcus would work together with electricians from the Hubbard group to install a buried electrical line for temporary service running from Marcus' house to the mess hall.

Jenny would make sure that all the health and hygiene concerns were met.

Aunt Millie would be the motor pool acquisitions person who would run errands with the pickup truck to get whatever was not on site.

Back at the high school, Ms. Spargo's horticulture students had the basic vegetable starter plants. These would go to the campsite as soon as the garden beds were ready. Students would also start new seedlings in the greenhouse to have plants suitable for mid- and late-summer planting.

That evening, as Lucy was doing her journal entry, she wrote, *"Seeds and ideas are very much alike. When a vision's ideas begin to sprout, there's no telling how big and beautiful the vision will grow."*

****

By next week, the social media group had enough material to begin an internet push-out for the following week.

Jenny determined that all health and hygiene considerations were being integrated throughout the campsite.

Some of the younger students were still going into school for make-up exams. Once they finished, they stayed and worked in the ag workshop. There they were constructing a very nice billboard to install at the entrance of the camp. It would identify the site as the FFA's community-service project. Materials for renovation on several of the cabins were brought on-site. At least three cabins would be modified to house chickens, goats, and rabbits.

Things were coming together amazingly well. Then the project hit a snag. Hannah Spargo was sitting at a small, round table at the end of the dining hall porch. Lucy was inside the building getting things ready for an all-hands meeting in the afternoon. She was about to leave when she glanced out one of the windows and saw all the students marching toward Ms. Spargo. Lucy stepped back and stood out of sight, waiting to hear if there was bad news or good news.

The group of ten was led by the youngest and smallest member of the team. She was a spunky, freckled-faced, skinny little girl named Rachel. They arrived at the steps of the porch and stopped. Sensing something amiss. Hannah said in a cheerful voice, "Well, good morning, everyone, what's up?"

Rachel then stepped up onto the porch and walked directly to their teacher. She stopped in front of her and, with arms crossed, stated bluntly, "Ms. Spargo, we have a problem."

In a very assuring voice, Hannah said, "Well, I am so glad you brought this problem to me instead of keeping it all bundled up inside. Let's see if we can all work together to find a solution, okay?"

"It's our friends," said Rachel, as the rest of the team stepped up onto the porch, closer to their teacher. "They think we don't like them anymore because we won't tell them what we are doing or where we are spending the day. They think we are just avoiding them, and they know we aren't working part-time jobs where they all work. We are afraid that this will not only affect our friendships this summer, but when we go back to school this fall, we're worried they will ditch us."

"Wow, we do seem to have a problem here, don't we?" Spargo asked the rest of the kids to come closer and all be a part of the conversation. "Now let's see," she began. "I think we have a two-part problem. First, I think I heard that your friends want to know what you are doing. That one has a quick and easy answer. By this time next week, all your friends will know exactly what you are doing. The social media crew tells me that next week you are going online with your new website and other social media possibilities. Your friends still won't know where you are, but that will be explained through the digital launch. They will know exactly what you are doing and will no doubt wish that they were part of such a cool experience as well."

"Now, the second part of the problem is that you want to know what you're getting out of the experience other than a few summer school credits. That has the best answer of all. Instead of asking 'What do we get?' you need to ask, 'Who do we become?'"

"When this summer is over, your friends will have experienced the very same thing that a few hundred thousand other teens will have experienced this summer: flipping burgers at a fast-food place, mowing grass for a lawn-care company, or stocking items on the shelves in the grocery store. Those are all good jobs, and the extra money in their pockets is nice, too. However, when school starts back in the fall, they will basically pick up right where they left off a couple of weeks ago. On the other hand, none of you will be the same person who left the classroom. You will have changed."

"What do you mean, Miss Spargo?" asked one of the students.

Spargo then asked him to repeat the FFA motto. With an assured confidence, he said, "**Learning to do, doing to earn, earning to live, living to serve**.*"

"Very good," she said. "You know it well."

"Here's the deal. By the end of this summer, all of you will have *learned* to grow and preserve your own food. That is a skill and confidence level that less than one-half of one percent of the people in the whole world have. In *doing* that and sharing those skills with thousands of other people, you will have *earned* the admiration and respect of all who follow your work. With that respect, you will come to *live* a quality of life that no amount of money can ever buy. With that quality of life, your individual lives will become *lives of service* to those within your families, your community, and your country. That, my young friends, is what you will earn and who you will become by the end of this summer. Any questions?"

Rachel turned and faced her classmates. "You heard the teacher. Let's get back to work."

Chapter 22

Departures and Arrivals

It was a Saturday morning like any other June morning in Welcome. The sun was up, the birds were singing, and people were enjoying breakfast just a little bit later than usual. Lucy was sitting cross-legged in the porch swing, reviewing her journal notes from the night before, when her phone chirped. It was Jenny calling.

"Hey, good morning, Jenny. What's up?"

"Lucy," she said, "I've got some bad news. Sadie died in her sleep last night. Can you come out to the farm? All of us are going out as soon as we can."

With a numbness of disbelief in her voice, Lucy said, "On my way."

A few minutes later, she parked Max in the middle of the barn lot. Uncle Joe was coming through the backyard gate and leaned his shovel against the side of the house. Lucy then saw Aunt Millie standing there alone, between the house and the barn, watching and waiting for her. Lucy quickly got out of the car and hugged her with a tearful embrace. "Where's Caleb?" she asked.

"He's in the barn with the others," Millie sadly responded.

Uncle Joe reached over and put his hand on her shoulder and said, "Lucy, Caleb has known for days that Sadie's discharge papers had already been signed. He's been making a burying box for over a week now. I thought yesterday he was probably about done. He put the carrying handles on it and painted it army green. It looks like a military ammunition box."

About that time, the barn door opened, and Zack, Pete, and Marcus walked out carrying the coffin—one holding each side and one holding the balance handle at the back. Jenny and Maria followed after them, followed by Caleb. They had started walking toward the others when a black Suburban with U.S. Government tags drove up to the group and stopped. Uncle Joe leaned over to Aunt Millie and whispered,

"They made it."

Uncle Joe walked around the car to the passenger door and opened it. A white-haired man wearing a full dress military uniform got out. "I hope we're not too late, Joe," he said.

"Just in time, Tom. Glad you made it."

General Tom Tipton had gotten a call at midnight when Uncle Joe found Sadie. She was already gone, so there was no reason to wake the others. Tipton had been Caleb's commanding officer while stationed in Africa. He had also been the one most responsible for ensuring Sadie returned to the States and was discharged to Major Caleb Burns. General Tipton had scrambled an honor guard, chartered a private flight to the National Guard Base outside Welcome, and picked up the Suburban from the motor pool in less than ten hours.

The General walked over to Caleb, who automatically saluted the man standing before him. "At ease, major," Tipton continued. "She was a fine soldier, Caleb —a mighty fine soldier." He then reached inside his uniform and pulled out a small box and handed it to Caleb.

Inside the box, Caleb found a silver medallion of a shepherd dog. It was attached to a Purple Heart pendant, like those awarded to soldiers wounded in action. "Thank you, Sir." The two men embraced each other, not as soldiers, but as two friends—one grieving and the other giving comfort.

Those carrying Sadie's coffin led the way through the gate and into Aunt Millie's beautiful backyard garden. They continued to walk toward the gravesite that Uncle Joe had finished digging only moments earlier. Caleb walked closest to the open grave. The others all stood behind him. Sensing the pain he must be experiencing, Lucy got Jenny's attention and motioned for her to step up and stand by Caleb. Jenny shook her head "No" and pointed to Lucy and then to Caleb.

Lucy gave Jenny an "Are you sure?" look, and Jenny reaffirmed by again pointing to Lucy and then to Caleb. Lucy stepped forward and stood by Caleb.

The four other servicemen who had come to serve as the honor guard had already positioned themselves several yards away from the group. A minute or two passed before one of the guards shouted out, "Ready, FIRE!" The quiet country air exploded with the sound of three rifles firing in unison. Then a second "Ready, FIRE!" A sound like lightning again split the air apart. Then the third and last "Ready, FIRE!"

When the final vibrations from the rifle fire subsided, a new sound began to fill the air. It was the sound of a bugle playing Taps. As the bugle played its comforting sounds, Lucy's hand found its way to the hand of the man standing beside her. She took it and held it within her. She held it with no intention of letting go. She stood there, realizing how the lives shared by these few people, even during a time of so much hurt, had brought out so much love. Most of all, within that shared love was the shared hope of a better tomorrow.

Her mind then flashed back to that first morning when she walked into K's diner and saw Caleb Burns in booth number seven. Inside her mind, where no one could see, she saw herself, Lucy Moore from Chicago, with a smile on her face.

In that moment, she heard a voice whispering in her mind. *'See what I told you, Lucy child?'* It was Granny again. *'So long as you have your memories, you still have your yesterdays. I mean, that was a good memory you just had, wasn't it? So now it's time you start figuring out what it is you want to be hoping for, so you can really look forward to some great tomorrows. Then, while you are at it, start soaking up some of their love that these people all around you are willing to share. Accept it, enjoy it, and be warmed by it. Then tonight when you say your prayers, you can thank the Good Lord for your very own beautiful day.'*

Lucy blinked. She shook her head, realizing the bugle had stopped. She turned and looked at Caleb. With a big smile, he said, "For a Chicago girl, you have a good grip."

Lucy blushed and quickly pulled her hand away from his. He smiled softly, "I shouldn't have said it that way. Here, let me show you how I've seen it done in Welcome." He gently took her hand into his and, walking very close to each other, they proceeded to join the others at the house.

****

Lucy left The Nest early the next morning before breakfast. It would no doubt be a day of mourning for the family at the farm, and she did not consider herself family, nor did she want to seem intrusive during such a sensitive time. She ate breakfast at K's and then went out to the campsite.

The work there continued and was going smoothly. Caleb stopped by midmorning and told the team he needed to go to D.C. "I should be back in three days. Stay in touch if you need anything." He looked around at all the activity. "I can't believe it's all falling into place as fast as it has."

As he was leaving the campsite, he turned back to look at the activity once more. *Is it possible?* he thought to himself as he left. *Is it possible that this unlikely bunch of young people is about to pull off one of the greatest national security missions of our lifetime?* He turned to look toward the road ahead. "Yeah, I think they just might do it."

Lunchtime came, and Jenny and Lucy took their break sitting on the porch of cabin number six. After a bit of small talk, Jenny put her sandwich down and turned to face Lucy. "You know, Lucy, Aunt Millie, Angela, and I were talking the other day, and we were thinking with all you've got going on now, you may want to think about consolidating your workspaces."

Lucy looked at her and said, "And I suppose you three have given thought as to how I ought to do that?"

"Well, yes," Jenny continued. "Aunt Millie thought, since she still has four big, empty rooms in that huge, old farmhouse of theirs, you could have two of them—one for your living quarters and one for your office. That way, you and Caleb could work on things together more easily and efficiently. Aunt Millie said she could help out with your laundry, shopping, and things like that, which would give you more time for … whatever."

"And I suppose you three have already figured out what the whatever might be?"

"Ah, come on, Lucy," Jenny said with a big smile. "Stop fighting it. You know as well as we all do that you have feelings for Caleb. It's okay. You two need each other more than ever to get this project done, and fighting your feelings just complicates it that much more."

Lucy looked at Jenny and said, "But what about you and Caleb? I know you love him, too."

Jenny took her by the hand and said, "Let me try to explain. Our relationship is that of brother and sister—always there for each other. Perhaps it's a carryover from serving together in Africa. War has a way of doing that, bonding people for a lifetime. Some events are hard to forget, and memories that rip at your heart—memories that only someone else who knows the same pain can help calm the rage when it surfaces inside your heart. We have allowed ourselves to be there for each other when the heart comes under attack. It is a deep and abiding love, but I guarantee you, it is a love void of any romance." Jenny continued, "As tough as Caleb appears on the outside, he is very tender and compassionate on the inside."

"When his wife, Susan, died, he first blamed himself for not being there for her, with her. Then, he blamed the army for having him stationed so far away. Then, he blamed God. Finally, he ran out of people to blame. He was in total meltdown mode one day when a little, scrawny pup came wandering through the camp. Tail wagging and nose sniffing for food, she just happened to stop at the feet of a grieving soldier who was sitting on the steps of the mess hall."

"His affection for Sadie was never more than a bandage over open wounds that could never heal on their own. It would take a very special person to reconnect him to God. It will take a very, very special person to give him the courage to experience love again. You, Lucy Moore from Chicago, are the only person I dare trust to help him do that."

Jenny stood up, and Lucy threw her arms around her as the tears flowed down the cheeks of both of them. Jenny had just granted her permission to follow her heart, and Lucy had just lifted a heavy load that Jenny had graciously carried for a friend.

"Okay," said Jenny, "Here's the plan. Caleb left town this morning and won't be back in town till tomorrow evening. That gives us the rest of today and all day tomorrow. I will help you move to the farm tomorrow morning. The crew can finish up here today. You go on over to the Nest now and start packing. I will go out to the farm and help Aunt Millie finish getting things ready for her new boarder. Oh, by the way, I'm not the only one who has to sign off on turning Caleb over to you. Aunt Millie would be most happy to have you keep an eye on her

126

beloved Caleb."

The next morning, Jenny helped Lucy get her few things loaded into her truck and hauled them to the farm. The goal was to get Lucy settled in before Caleb made it back from D.C. Uncle Joe suggested to Lucy, "Why don't you park that little car of yours behind the tractor barn this evening. No need to worry, Caleb, if he gets in late tonight and sees your car sitting in the barn lot. Besides, I want to see the expression on his face in the morning when he realizes Millie has taken in boarders.

That evening after dinner, Aunt Millie said to Lucy, "I'm sure you want to go do a little personalizing of your new room, so don't think you have to be social with a couple of old-timers like us. We're not the most exciting people to be around in the evening anyway. And Lucy, just so you know, we are both very happy you took us up on the offer to stay with us."

Lucy went to her new room down the hallway that connected the kitchen and dining room to the rest of the house. The room reminded her a lot of her childhood room, the one she had while growing up in Granny's old house. The walls were tall and plaster-hard. A flower garden wallpaper covered two walls, with the other two painted a soft, sky blue. A nice, large desk with empty shelves above it would work nicely for her office space. Yes, indeed. She was already starting to feel at home.

She heard a knock at her door. It was Aunt Millie holding a window fan in her hand. "Almost forgot," she said. "Usually, this room is quite comfortable at night, but if you get too warm, this little fan will cool things down. Oh, and the little bathroom next door is for guests. Toss your used towels in the hamper, and I'll get them later."

Alone again, Lucy made a few entries in her daily notes and then picked up her Bible. Perhaps it was the room that took her back to her childhood home. Perhaps it was the sense of a relationship growing with Aunt Millie, a woman more than old enough to be her mother, if she had still had one. For whatever reason, Lucy soon found herself reading from the book of Ruth. She began reading in chapter 1 of the young woman living in exile away from home.

She had come to be with her aging mother-in-law, Naomi, but was being encouraged to return to her former, familiar way of life. Then in verse six, Lucy read aloud, *"And Ruth said, entreat me not to leave you nor from following after you. For where thou goest I will go. Where thou lodges, I will lodge. Your people shall be my people and your God will be my God. And where you are buried, there will I be buried also."*

Of course, Aunt Millie was neither her aunt nor her mother-in-law as Naomi was to Ruth. Yet, in the few short weeks that Lucy had been in Welcome, Aunt Millie, a total stranger, had treated her with kindness and affection. She had been so understanding when Lucy wanted to use her garden to talk to God. Millie had welcomed her to share the family's house of mourning when Sadie died. Tonight, she was sharing her home unconditionally with Lucy Moore, the girl from Chicago.

There was one thing she was sure of. She knew that when the time came for her to return to Chicago, when her work here would be done, she would never forget Aunt Millie.

Chapter 23

Breakfast with a Bark

By six-thirty the next morning, the big pot of coffee had filled the house with its familiar aroma. The front porch door was open, and the warm morning sunshine was coming through the screen door. The major was headed for the kitchen for his cup of coffee.

"Good morning, Caleb," said Aunt Millie as he stood in the kitchen doorway. How was your trip?"

"Okay," he said, "I've got a lot of updates to go over with Lucy this morning. I sent her a message last night about meeting for breakfast, so you don't need to fix me any. I'll just run on in to K's, and we'll talk there."

Aunt Millie crossed her arms and said, "Caleb Burns, you spend entirely too much time always going or coming instead of staying put. There has to be a better way for you two to communicate. Why don't you call her and tell her whatever you need to say to her?"

Caleb frowned at Millie. "You know it doesn't work that way, Aunt Millie."

"Well, when have you ever tried calling her instead of driving into town?" Aunt Millie retorted.

Caleb was confused and started to get a little irritated. "What are you trying to say, Aunt Millie?"

She put her hands on her hips and, with feigned exasperation, said, "Good grief, Caleb. Just put your hands up to your mouth like this, and call her." With that, Aunt Millie yelled, "Lucy! Oh, Lucy!"

Caleb heard footsteps behind him, and a soft, sleepy voice said, "Did someone call me?"

Caleb turned so fast he almost lost his balance. "Where did you come from?" he asked, completely confused.

Lucy smiled, "From Chicago. I thought I told you that the first time we met."

"I mean, right now."

At that, Aunt Millie decided the surprise had gone far enough. "We decided that since you two need this ongoing, close contact with the project right now, it only made sense for Lucy to move here. Besides, Angela said she could use the empty rooms at The Nest for the folks helping with the filming and social media segments." Aunt Millie looked at everyone, smiled, and said, "Now that that's settled, let's eat breakfast before the food gets cold."

Caleb just stood there. The major, who was used to being in charge of operations, had just found himself outside of the need-to-know group. On the other hand, he was quite happy that someone else had decided for him.

The first thing Lucy noticed when she got to camp that morning was a new sign. It was designed to resemble a state park sign, with five brown boards and gold lettering. It must have been installed after Lucy and Jenny had left camp. Posted at the gate entrance, the sign looked very official, plus it was accentuated with nice landscaping and mulch. WELCOME FFA: Learning to Do– Doing to Earn – Earning to Live – Living to Serve. It was the FFA motto. It would be a sign they would see every day when the crew came to work— a sign to remind them not only of who they were and what they were doing, but also who they were becoming.

****

The next morning, back at the Burns' farm, Aunt Millie had made ham and eggs, hash browns, and of course, a batch of hot biscuits. Joe and Millie were eating their breakfast and seemed deeply engaged in their own conversation with strongly opposing views.

Caleb turned to Lucy, "Lucy, who was it that taught you the proper way to mix my honey for your biscuit?" Joe and Millie were still involved in their own debate.

Lucy quietly said, "You mean like this?" Once again, she blended the butter and honey in a swirling motion with her knife. In that short moment of blending, she heard a voice inside her head. It was Jenny. *Now Lucy—Now. Go for it.* Once again, she put it on a half biscuit, put it to her mouth, and took a bite. But this time she looked him straight in the eyes and very, very slowly licked the honey off her lips. Caleb dropped his fork. Uncle Joe had caught it all out of the corner of his eye and thought to himself, *That a girl! Now you're talkin'*!

The table was cleared moments later. As everyone started to engage in the day ahead, they heard a vehicle in the barn lot. Uncle Joe got up, went to the screen door, and peered out. "You all better come take a look," he said. "Looks like we have us an official U.S. Army jeep that may have run out of gas." Aunt Millie wiped her hands on her apron and quickly caught up with the others.

They approached a young sergeant standing by his jeep. "Good morning, folks. Sorry to bother you so early in the morning. I'll get right to the point. I am here on behalf of General Tipton's family."

"Oh no!" gasped Aunt Millie. "He was just here a couple of weeks ago. What happened?"

"Oh, the General is fine, Ma'am. It's his grandson, and the general was hoping maybe you folks could help."

"What's wrong with the boy?" Uncle Joe said. "Tom knows very well we'll do anything we can."

The young sergeant scratched his head and said, "Best I start all over at the beginning. Last week, the canine unit on base got a new batch of pups to start their training. One little pooch was outperforming all the rest—except for one thing. The pup was allergic to gunpowder or any kind of explosives. The little guy would start rolling over and sneezing his little head off. No matter how good he was in all his other training, this one thing meant an automatic discharge from the unit."

"When the General heard what a lovable, smart pup he was and that he was getting discharged, he decided it might be the perfect pup for his grandson. The paperwork was completed, and he gave the pup to the boy. Two days later, they found out that the grandson, the youngest granddaughter, and the boy's mother were all highly allergic to the dog. The General knew you folks had just lost yours, so he was hoping you might be able to help him out by taking this little guy. If not, at least keep him for a few days till you can find him a forever home."

Uncle Joe looked at Aunt Millie and said, "How can we say no to Tom after all he did for Sadie?"

Caleb seemed reluctant until Lucy said, "I've never had a pet before, but if you teach me what to do, I will be happy to help take care of him."

Caleb countered, "It's a big commitment."

To that, she replied, "I hear that is the case with most any worthwhile relationship." They all looked at each other.

Uncle Joe said, "Sergeant, tell the General the pup has a new home." The young soldier nodded his appreciation and handed Uncle Joe the pup's leash. He then got back in the jeep and drove out of the barn lot.

"Well, well, well, Millie Burns," said Uncle Joe. "Looks like we have gone and taken in another boarder." Everyone walked back to the porch and sat down.

Caleb stood and said, "I just remembered, I have a meeting with the mayor and some city council members shortly, so I need to be going. Sorry, I can't help with the pup this morning."

Joe chimed in, "I need to get over to MacBurg this morning and pick up some parts for that old John Deere disc. They need it at camp ASAP."

Millie turned to Lucy and said, "Lucy, as you can see, the heavy lifting is left to those who can do it. If you can spare a few minutes before you head out, I would appreciate the help of another heavy lifter."

"Of course, Aunt Millie."

As Joe and Caleb were walking away from the porch with their hands in the air, waving bye, they both said, "Thanks, Ladies."

Aunt Millie said, "Don't you two worry yourselves. We can put an ad in the Welcome paper: 'Adorable pup looking for a forever home.' We can do that first thing this morning." Joe and Caleb stopped in their tracks and turned to face the three on the porch. Millie stood stiff, with arms crossed. Lucy was holding the pup in her arms. Head bent down, she was dabbing her eyes with her shirt sleeve—appearing to be wiping away tears.

"No, that's okay, Millie, no need to spend your morning with that. Maybe we should all discuss how to deal with the problem after supper tonight."

"If you say so, Joe. You two go on now, and get out of here." As soon as the two were driving down the lane, Millie turned and faced Lucy. "You are good, young lady. You learn fast and on the spot."

Lucy smiled, not a real tear in sight. "That was fun, but I have no experience in the finer arts of deceptive persuasion."

"No need to worry. Your Aunt Millie will share her notes with you on how to *survive* with those we love."

Taking the pup inside, Millie said, "I'll give him treats, and you can play with him on the floor. Let's get this little fellow to know and love us before he finds out he is one of them."

They all got acquainted over the next several minutes, then the pup settled down into Lucy's lap. She continued to gently rub the pup's head and ears until he soon closed his eyes and fell asleep. After a minute of rubbing the pup without talking, Lucy said in a very soft voice, "I'm scared, Aunt Millie."

"I know you are, Lucy," Millie replied in a most understanding way. "And I know he is too. You both are scared in your own and different ways. You're walking side by side on a path that seems full of potholes and puddles filled with the scary unknown."

"What should we do?" Lucy asked.

Aunt Millie replied, "Keep walking—side by side for now. If it's meant to be, the day will come when you decide that you're both better together than you ever were alone. At that point, most of those potholes will vanish. For the few that remain, you'll learn to either walk around them or help each other out of them if you do fall in."

Millie continued, "You know our friend Pete says that one of his favorite verses from his namesake is 1 Peter 5:7. It says, '*Cast all your cares on Him, for He cares for you.*' He was with you in Chicago. He is with you here, in Welcome. He will always be with you wherever you go."

Real tears were now running down Lucy's cheeks as she wiped her eyes with her sleeve. "You know, Aunt Millie, on the way down to Welcome, I was in a rest area. I was doing some people-watching. At one point, I started crying because I thought I might never find love. Now I am crying because I think I have found it, and I don't know what to do with it."

"All in due time, child. All in due time."

Chapter 24

Lucy and Milly finished getting the pup settled in and made a list of things Millie would pick up at the store for the new boarder.

Twenty minutes later, Lucy turned Max onto Bickett Road and headed toward the camp entrance. She planned to hide in the dining hall and get caught up on what she called her recreational writing. It was a manuscript that had nothing to do with the Welcome project. It was her first attempt to write a novel, but the time dedicated to it had recently diminished. She had just concluded that the hours she felt behind on the manuscript were probably in direct proportion to the time she had been spending on the couch with a new friend. *Not to worry, Lucy*, she had been telling herself. *Manuscripts come and go. Major friendships, on the other hand, are perhaps once in a lifetime.*

She found a secluded space, pulled out her laptop, and began pecking away on the keyboard. Two hours later, her back was aching, and her neck was making funny cracking noises. She needed a break, so she stepped out of the dining hall and down off the porch. Scanning her options, she decided to walk back up Bickett Road to Mulberry, then turn around and come back to the dining hall. That should make her body feel better, and the exercise app on her phone could stop scolding her for sitting too long.

After turning around, Lucy had passed Marcus' house and was several yards closer to camp when a pure white pigeon flew past—only a few feet above her head. She turned to see why the bird was flying so low and where it might have been headed. It was then she spotted the pigeon perched on an outside rail of a tall, enclosed cage. The cage was attached to the north end of Marcus's carport. Marcus was opening a small door near the rail, and the bird hopped into the cage. She walked back up to where Marcus was now putting food and fresh water in the cage for the bird that had just arrived.

Fearful of another confusing conversation, Lucy took a chance, "Do you two happen to know each other?"

Marcus grinned and said, "Lucy, this is Avogadro. He is one of the most predictable and dependable beings that I have ever met."

Lucy asked, "Do you know his motives for being so predictable and dependable?"

"I do," said Marcus, "Two things: good food and fresh water. He never asks for more nor expects anything less." Then, as though he had made a social blunder, Marcus said, "Oh, I'm sorry, Avogadro, this is Lucy Moore from Chicago".

"Pleased to meet you, Avogadro." Then, looking down and whispering very softly under her breath, she said, "*I can't believe I'm still talking to pigeons.*"

With her head still lowered, she spotted a small sign at the corner of the cage. In bold print, the sign said "Avogadro 6.022x10^23. Bickett Rd". Lucy asked, "Is this his official address?"

"No," replied Marcus. With a twinkle in his eye, he said, "It's Avogadro's number. It's not a secret. A lot of people go online to look him up."

Afraid to ask for an explanation, she said, "Well, I'd better get moving on into camp. See you later." Lucy waved bye to Marcus and walked down the road toward the campground. As she continued along, she felt pretty sure she had just been the tail end of a private joke between Marcus and Avogadro.

When she got back to the dining hall, she resumed work on the manuscript for another hour and then quit. It was almost time for lunch when she walked out of the dining hall and onto the porch. She noticed that Marcus had walked down to camp and was leaning against one of the porch posts. He was gazing out over the activities that were underway all over the campground. She also noticed he seemed to be especially focused in the direction of where Hannah Spargo was working with three of her young people. Lucy quietly walked up to the next nearest porch post and took up her own watching position. They both stood there leaning against the posts—just watching. She was starting to question whether Marcus was focused on the group or on their teacher as she worked with the crew in a number of different activities.

Hannah Spargo was dressed in farmer jeans, a short-sleeved work blouse, and a John Deere ball cap. Lucy approached Marcus and stood on the other side of his post. Finally, Marcus said in a low, almost whisper, as though talking to himself, "Amazing. Just flat-out wonderfully amazing."

Lucy then turned to face Marcus. "You know, none of this would be happening had you not offered the campground. I must admit I was a little surprised when you offered it. The last thing I remembered hearing was that you liked your privacy. You said something about 'not being comfortable with those unpredictable relationships of people and all their complex motives.'"

Marcus shrugged his shoulders and said, "Well, this is different. This is all about the kids."

She gave him a teasing little smile and added, "All about the kids and nothing about their teacher?"

Ignoring her jab, he went on, "It's just the way she handles those kids. For instance, she never praises their accomplishments because they're smart. She praises them for their effort. They have no control over their IQ, Lucy, but they each have total control over their personal efforts. That puts them all on equal footing to try to achieve and to excel regardless of their IQ. Most teachers don't get that, but she does, and the kids love her for it."

"I agree, Marcus. There is, as our project theme would suggest, a synergy of sorts with the students and Hannah. All of them are working together as one to get this project pulled off. So Marcus, how do you read Hannah as a potential member of the Mother Hubbard team?"

Lucy was surprised when he made no effort to avoid the question. "Well," he began, "She has a very interesting background. After growing up on a grain, grass, and livestock farm in the hill country of Iowa, she graduated summa cum laude from Purdue with a major in agronomy. Then, she went on to get a dual master's degree from Ohio State in crop genetics and molecular biology."

"Cornell University in New York offered her a doctoral fellowship, but she turned it down. Then, she did nothing at all for three years. It was as though she had been abducted by aliens from outer space. There was nothing, Lucy! Nothing at all on the whereabouts of

Hannah Spargo."

"And then?" she asked.

"And then, she shows up in Welcome, Indiana, teaching a bunch of kids in a high school. She could have gotten a corporate job paying three or four times what a school teacher makes. So why here? Why here in Welcome?"

"Does it matter, Marcus?" Lucy asked.

Sensing that he may have revealed too much curiosity about the ag teacher, he said, "I guess not. I'm just intrigued as to why someone that smart would seem to be sufficiently satisfied teaching in a high school instead of teaching doctoral candidates in grad school or doing research in a corporate setting. What do you think?"

Lucy smiled and said, "Marcus, this is what I think. I think Miss Hannah might be just as intrigued as to why a young genius is content to teach a couple of entry-level chemistry classes, and in his spare time, dabble in making methane gas and alcohol from barnyard manure and food waste."

She looked at him and said, "Marcus, a new friend of mine very recently told me that people's behaviors are most often determined by their motives. It's hard to know why they do what they do without knowing their true motives."

Marcus replied, "So what are you trying to say, Lucy? What do you really think about Hannah?"

Again, she smiled and said, "I think the same exciting thoughts for her as I do for you, Marcus."

With a frown on his face, "What's that supposed to mean?"

"What I mean is that I think it is special that you each have a marvelous puzzle on your hands. I am quite sure you both can have a wonderful time sorting out the pieces while helping each other discover the beautiful images found in both puzzles."

****

Over the next few days, the campsite continued coming together as they constructed animal quarters in one of the cabins and added lean-to sheds for rabbit cages and chicken cages in another cabin. Marcus had been right; Hannah and her crew were unstoppable.

The garden beds were taking shape with early greens, peas, and some perennials. Rhubarb and asparagus were getting transplanted from some of the Welcome team's own gardens. They even planted three dwarf fruit trees.

The roofs of the cabins were getting retrofitted with gutters, downspouts, and rain barrels to collect summer rainwater for irrigation purposes. Maria had donated some of her Tilapia to live in the rain barrels until they had time to start a real fish production program. The crew had been using their own cameras and phones to video and take pictures from day one for their own FFA scrapbook.

By week three, the online viewership caught the attention of nearly seven thousand local FFA chapters across America. With the potential of Welcome's model becoming a national skills contest, the interest was exceedingly high. Students in the thousands were logging on to follow, and several were asking about their own local FFA clubs joining in. Some would have plenty of growing season left, while others wanted to start the process and be ready for next spring.

The project had achieved engaging a whole new generation of young people to have conversations about real hands-on experiences— not virtual, about real things in the natural world—not AI-generated topics. They were learning new information, not just for the sake of information, as they could get that anytime from a chatbot. These young people were learning new information to own and to keep for a lifetime. It was not just information, but knowledge—with all the rights of ownership that went with that newfound knowledge.

****

A few weeks into the project, Lucy asked Hannah to call her team together for a quick meeting. Acknowledging the impact the social media challenge was having within the FFA organization, she suggested that they offer other youth groups to join in as well. After all, if it was a good thing for their group, would the others not benefit as well? The invitation went out to leaders within the Scouts, 4-H, and the Boys and Girls Clubs of America. They were all encouraged to join in. It would be an opportunity for the youth of America to make a real contribution.

With the social media reach exploding, the industry was quick to get involved. They became eager to offer sponsorship to local efforts. Companies from all segments of the food industry were helping to increase consumer awareness of their particular products: garden seeds, equipment, tools, and processing and preserving supplies. Companies all wanted to have their names attached to the movement.

The Hubbard team continued to be the mentors, but when it came to the public eye, they stayed out of the picture. It was all about Welcome's FFA and the growing movement of young people across the American landscape.

Chapter 25

Let the Games Begin

The last of the young crew had just left the campground and was headed home. It had been another productive day of work. The team gathered in the dining hall as they did on most days to discuss how the day had gone. Caleb began, "Anyone see any problems today that we need to address first thing in the morning?" Everyone considered their progress and concluded that everything seemed to be going great. "Good," said Caleb. "I have an idea that I want to run past you and get your thoughts on it."

"These kids have been showing up every day since school let out and have been working their tails off. What would you think of taking tomorrow off from work? Let them experience some of the fun and games that might have taken place in this old 4-H campground several generations ago?" Everyone looked at each other and then back at Caleb.

Jenny was the first to speak up. "As the official nurse for this group, do you think I should take his temperature and see if he has a fever?"

Pete quickly spoke up, "I'll get a picnic lunch organized and on location."

Maria chimed in, "I will make sure we have some young people's music."

Zack said he would text all the crew and let them know that tomorrow would officially be a play and party day at the campground.

Then Hannah, knowing that Marcus was standing behind her, spoke out. "Marcus and I will organize a bunch of classic outdoor games." A little startled by this announcement, Marcus stepped around to face her.

Hannah looked him in the eyes, and with her fingers gave him the *it's okay* sign.

For the first time ever, Marcus thought to himself, *Maybe being unpredictable might have its benefits.*

When the young crew arrived the next morning, they were still a little confused and apprehensive as to why a play day. Hannah tried to set their minds at ease. "Here's the deal. Take notes if you like. Learning is a lifelong adventure. From now on, work will also be a lifelong adventure. But during all those years of learning and working, it is equally important to find pleasure in play. You must never forget how to play and have fun."

"For the past several weeks, you've been showing other young people all over the country a new way of thinking about growing their own food. Today can be an opportunity for you to show those same young people a new way of thinking about their free time and play."

"Many years ago, this campsite was the home of a 4-H camp. I assure you that when the young campers had free time to play, they did not pull out their phones or tablets or some other digital device to have fun. They interacted with their friends. They were very physical in their play. They were in constant conversation in their play. They were building and growing relationships with other young friends that would last a lifetime. They were truly becoming connected. Mr. Burns suggested that our games today should be the same or similar to games that would have been played here when he might have been a camper."

"EXCUSE ME!" Caleb's loud voice interjected. "Those would be the games that perhaps my grandfather would have played. How old do you think I am anyway?" The kids all laughed. Caleb continued, "I talked to the production crew last evening, and they loved the idea of taking clips of you guys playing. They would use them as funny or intriguing outtakes at the end of some of your regular postings. They assured me it could be a real fun addition to your posts."

Hannah led the crew to where Marcus was looking very official, standing behind a card table covered in a variety of items. Marcus began, "Welcome to the games, young people. As would be expected, these people-type games will no doubt have unpredictable outcomes since your skill levels are also very unpredictable."

Hannah, standing behind her students, gave Marcus the silent *cut it* signal as she quickly crossed her throat with an outstretched finger. Marcus got her message. "Uh, so Ms. Spargo will now explain the games to you."

"We have a variety of games that I think you will enjoy. Raise your hands if any of these are familiar to you. How about a three-legged race or Dizzy-Izzy?" No one raised their hand. "Okay, what about Andy Over, or an egg-on-a-spoon relay race, or tug-of-war?" Her list went on, but with no hands in the air. "I have more, but I think we will just start with these. However, before we start, the video crew wants a minute of your time."

One of the production crew members came over and asked for a few actors for an upcoming shoot. Hands went up in the air. "That's great," she said. "This here is the basket you all drop your phones into each morning when you arrive. If you will each pick out your phone and open it up, please." They all looked at each other, totally confused as to what was about to happen.

"Now, each of you can either sit in a chair, on the ground, or at a picnic table—wherever you feel relaxed. I just need a few clips of all of you taking a break and having fun on your phones." Very quickly, they were all on their phones. Silent, and with no interaction between each other. Each one was in the presence of wherever their phone screens had taken them.

When they had finished recording the clip, they returned to start the games. With each new game, Marcus and Hannah would demonstrate how it was played, and then the crew would try it. After all the games had been demonstrated and attempted, they paired off into five teams. Each game was a timed relay race. As the games began, crew members were soon laughing at and with each other. They were booing and cheering, rolling around, egging each other on, and a host of other things that young people might naturally do if they didn't have a phone in their hands.

In what felt like no time, the morning games were over. The film crew had plenty of great footage of the games and of phone time. They would splice these into a video collage, add a few graphics, and then add them to some of the online postings when a little laughter might be appropriate. It would be a hard sell, but they might even get some of their followers to consider not only a new way of thinking about growing food, but possibly even a new way of thinking about play and having fun.

Soon, everyone was occupied by the deep and burning question,

"What's for lunch?" As they began to walk up the incline to the dining hall, they heard the sound of Uncle Joe's old truck coming through the campground's open gates. Upon seeing the truck, the crew all shared a combined expression of happy anticipation. As soon as the truck came to rest, Aunt Millie started to open the door on her side.

Before it was half opened, out jumped Pup and, as fast as he could, he took off running toward his young friends.

From a short distance away, Caleb watched the activity being played out in front of him. They all seemed so happy and carefree as they ate and talked of the morning games and took their turn playing with Pup. Along with all those good feelings, he could not shake the thought that their sole purpose for being here, at this place, at this time, was a purpose with an ominous, dark cloud that would silently strike with lightning speed and change their lives forever.

Lunchtime was soon over. Hannah and Marcus took the teams back out into the open space surrounded by the ten cabins. There was only one game for the afternoon—the treasure hunt. They would be divided into two teams. One team would have five, and the other would have five plus Pup. Even the picking of teams was an old version of selection: '*Apples, peaches, pears, and plums, tell me when your birthday comes....*' As the different jingles were recited in full, the two teams soon emerged.

The map to the treasure was five pages long. It held many clues that were cloaked in obscure hints, symbolic directions, and some that would challenge the crew's mastery of academic skills learned back in the classroom. It would be a game of *Synergy of the Minds*. Could it be that even in thinking, in brainstorming, that the whole game is greater than the sum of its parts? Hannah and Marcus both thought that Buckminster Fuller would be pleased with the challenging game they had given the crew.

The hunt lasted just over an hour and a half, until the treasure was claimed by five young crewmates and one exhausted little pup.

Chapter 26

Home of the Brave

I t was the last week of June, and Secretary Janice Higgins from the U.S. Department of Provisions was coming to town. She was coming to acknowledge and to thank a few of Welcome's young people who had captured the attention of the entire nation. Their accomplishments in creating a massive movement to help prepare American communities regarding local food security were unmatched. They had done in only a few weeks what no bureaucratic group had been able to do through years of effort.

When the Welcome City government heard that Higgins would be in town on the first of July, they came up with an idea to create an *Independence Week of Celebration*. The Secretary could be the guest of honor to start off the week. From year to year, July Fourth might be at the beginning of the week, in the middle, or at the end of the week. This week-long celebration would allow families and friends to celebrate on the days that best met their work and travel schedules. The traditional picnicking, parades, and fireworks would be spread throughout the week. Hopefully, the citizens will like the new arrangement. Hopefully, the citizens would also give the mayor and council members credit for bringing the Secretary to town, especially when it came time to vote in the fall.

Today was the day. The city workers and volunteers started getting the city park ready early in the morning. Chairs were being set up in the center of the park. The stage was a pair of semi-truck flatbed trailers parked side by side and covered with connecting sheets of plywood, which were then covered with rolls of artificial grass. The entire stage front and sides were decorated with red, white, and blue streamers and other decorations. The outside perimeter of the park's open space was lined with commercial vendors. They represented all facets of the local foods initiative. Some vendors sold seeds or equipment, some were selling chickens, goats, or rabbits, and yet others represented tools and equipment for either growing or processing.

Secretary Higgins was scheduled to start the celebration by addressing the crowd at eleven o'clock. The air was filled with anticipation and excitement as the time grew closer. Hannah and her crew of young people would be seated in the front row of chairs—along with a few local and state dignitaries and the Secretary and CEO of the National FFA Organization.

The crew was out mingling with friends and families throughout the crowd. Rachel, however, was sitting by herself on a park bench under a nearby tree. She was going over in her mind the speech she had prepared the night before. She started scanning the activity all around her and noticed the great number of people moving in all directions along with the increased number of local police and state troopers.

The noise of it all seemed to be getting louder and louder. Her heart started racing. A new and unfamiliar feeling started to wash over the small teenager. She didn't like the feeling, so she crossed her arms to make it go away, but it didn't. She pulled her feet up on the bench and put her arms around her legs, putting herself into a fetal position.

Spargo looked over and spotted her. Rachel sat there alone and felt so small. She closed her eyes and started rocking ever so slightly. Then, a hand touched her shoulder and a familiar voice said, "Is everything alright, Rachel?"

Rachel opened her eyes as she turned toward the familiar voice and threw her arms around Hannah Spargo. "I'm scared, Ms. Spargo", she said as she embraced her teacher. "I think you should pick someone else to be the student speaker today."

Hannah faced Rachel directly and calmly said, "Being brave does not mean that we are never scared. It just means that when we do get scared, we go ahead and do whatever needs to be done anyway." She continued to talk as the rest of the crew was approaching from behind. "Rachel, you have always been my bravest young leader. You can do this."

Knowing the crew was now standing behind her, Hannah looked Rachel in the eyes and winked. She then turned around to face her crew. "The last thing I want to say to all of you is just how proud I am of every one of you for all the efforts you have put forth. Today, let's just relax and enjoy the moment. I'll meet you in the front row in a minute."

Spargo went back to her chair and watched them as they moved out. After a few steps, Rachel turned around and quickly came back. She stepped up very close to her teacher, crossed her arms, looked her straight in the eyes—and winked. Turning back around, she yelled, "Hey, wait for me!" as she ran to catch up with the others.

The noise in the park continued for a short time, and then it suddenly grew quiet. People with their hands shading their eyes were looking up and pointing into the air. Suddenly, everyone started cheering. The large tan helicopter from the National Guard Base began to descend and hover over the north side of the park.

As the aircraft gently landed, four black SUVs drove onto the grounds and parked—two on each side of the chopper. The Secret Service got out of their cars and stood at the ready. The mayor and Hannah Spargo went over to welcome the lady who was exiting the helicopter.

Moments later, the designated speakers were all on stage—each with their own handheld microphone. The mayor gave his *Welcome to Welcome* speech. One by one, the others made their brief comments. Then a small, young girl with reddish hair and freckles stood up to speak. Hers was the shortest of all the speeches, but she captured the audience with her unwritten, unrehearsed speech about what it means to be brave.

She spoke of the brave Americans she had learned about in school, who had fought to gain and to keep America's independence— the independence that everyone would be celebrating in the days to come. Then she challenged all American communities to try to duplicate what her little group was doing in Welcome—what her little group had the opportunity and the freedom to try. She said, "And if you are afraid you might fail, then you should try it anyway. You are, after all, free to try. That's what brave Americans do. They do what needs to be done, even if they are afraid. That's why they call us the land of the free and the home of the brave." She sat back down as the crowd exploded with applause.

As Secretary Higgins rose to speak, she encouraged the crowd to continue their appreciation for Rachel's short speech. As the applause subsided, Higgins said, "Wow! I know a few people in Washington who could use that young lady as their speechwriter, right?" She then continued with praise and gratitude for the unbelievable grassroots movement that had so greatly impacted Americans in just a few short weeks. She spoke of the power and potential of young people to solve problems that the adult world had not yet shown the genius or the will to solve. "The can-do spirit of America is alive and well in Welcome, Indiana, and is starting to spread across America once again. This synergistic approach they talk about shows us that as a country we are stronger when we work together, each doing what we do best, for the good of all."

"Next week, America celebrates the Fourth of July, our Independence Day. This project, led by young people in blue jackets all across our great country, is giving hope to millions of people. It is the hope that they can have access to fresh, nutritious food, independent of whatever calamity might come one's way. It is a hope of a homeland that is prepared."

When the clapping and cheering subsided and everyone was off the stage, the crowds began to disperse. Some went on their way, while some remained and continued discussions in small groups throughout the park. Caleb had gathered with the team to confirm activities for the rest of the day. Lucy noticed Janice Higgins was facing Caleb while walking toward the group from behind.

Out of the corner of her eye, Lucy saw Higgins silently mouth the words, "*Walk with me*". She saw Caleb excuse himself from the group and walk over to Higgins and the Secret Service folks who stood not too far off. "You throw a great party, Caleb," she said with a smile.

He returned the compliment with "Well, it is easy to do when you invite the right people."

"I'll get to the point. Have you told Miss Moore the reason for the timing and urgency of her recruitment? Have you told her about the solar activity and the projected SEMPS?"

Caleb shook his head. "No, not yet. I wanted to wait as long as possible. I wanted to make sure the project was well on its way and working."

Higgins retorted, "Caleb, it has a life of its own now! She has far exceeded my hopes for a magic pill to do exactly what we wanted. She has done that and more. Her focus now needs to be the same as yours. Her sense of urgency now needs to be the same as yours. From this point on, I want both you and her to focus on an exit strategy."

"Based on yesterday's intel updates, I want you and your team to be ready to leave Welcome at a moment's notice and transition to the valley. Does Lucy even know about the valley?"

"No, not yet".

Higgins exhaled a long and slow breath. "Caleb, it is time. Tell her!" Then sensing she may have just come across as a critical parent, she said, "By the way, Major, I just want to say I am so unbelievably proud of you and your team. You may even get a rank promotion out of this."

"Janice, I'm a civilian now."

"Small details, Caleb. I'll see what I can do." With that, she put her cheek to his and whispered in his ear, "Take care, my friend." She turned and began walking away.

As Higgins headed back to the chopper, she hesitated, then turned to one of the Secret Service agents and said, "Go back and ask Miss Spargo to step over and join me before we take off."

Hannah came over and walked up to Janice Higgins. "Yes, Ma'am, you wanted to see me?"

Higgins looked her over, smiled, and said, "Correct me if I'm mistaken, but I believe we have met before. We have possibly even served together."

Hannah returned the smile and said, "Yes, Ma'am, aboard the Missouri three years ago. I was at Intel Security. Our paths rarely crossed, but it was a pleasure to serve under you."

"And what was it that all the guys on board called you when not on duty?"

"Farm Girl, Ma'am, and I was proud of it."

Higgins replied, "As I am likewise proud of you today, Hannah Spargo." They saluted each other, Higgins boarded the chopper, and it lifted off.

Chapter 27

The Red Rope Inn

Caleb and Lucy were starting to spend more time together in the evenings. It was agreed that couch-talk was not to be work-talk; it was personal and family time together. Often, they would sit on the couch with Pup at their feet. A big pan of stovetop popcorn was becoming the snack of choice. An occasional movie or a ball game could fill the time as well. Increasingly, though, Caleb was asking Lucy to help him with Bible study.

One night, they were studying the missionary travels of the apostle Paul, and there was a passage in the book of Acts, chapter 27, verse 8, about their boat putting into harbor at a place called Fair Haven to sit out the storm that was raging on the Mediterranean Sea. "The world could use a few places like that right now," Lucy said.

Caleb asked, "If you could have such a place to call home, what would it be like?"

Lucy thought a moment and then said. "It's hard to put into words. Yeah, I know, me the writer, having a hard time finding the words to express my secret place."

Then Caleb suggested a little game that he played as a child that might help.

"I would close my eyes and block out everything, and then start looking around in the dark. Sometimes we have to look in the dark to find the things we can't find in the light. So close your eyes. No peeking. Now, one by one, tell me what you see when you get to Fair Haven."

Lucy started to put together her imaginary hideaway. "I see green rolling hills, just like here, around Welcome. I'm standing in a valley, and in the distance, there is a small town. There is a road going into the town, but I see no cars or trucks on the road. Everything is so quiet and peaceful. There are no planes in the sky, just a few birds flying overhead. The sky is so blue with a few fluffy white clouds. A meadow stretches out in front of me, filled with patches of wildflowers."

"Sounds like a wonderful place," responded Caleb, "but what would you be willing to give up to live in such a place?"

"What do you mean, Caleb?"

Caleb continued, "It sounds a little primitive compared to our lives today. Does your Fair Haven have high-speed internet service, movies on demand, cell phones, state-of-the-art medical care, or service shops for little sports cars? The obvious question is: In which place would you rather live, Ms. Moore?"

"Well, Mr. Burns, not long ago I asked a friend a very similar question. Would he rather eat in a very plain and simple little diner or at a five-star restaurant?"

"And what was his reply?"

"He said it wasn't about the food he ate, or the ambiance of the place, but rather about the person with whom he was sharing the meal. I think that would be a good answer to your question as well. It's all about who I am sharing the time and the place with."

"Sounds like my kind of guy," said Caleb.

"He is indeed," she said. "He is indeed."

****

The morning breeze was sneaking through the window screens. It was an early morning ritual in Lucy's room. First, the breeze would move the soft, sheer curtains just enough to let the sun in and fill the room. This would be followed by a full chorus of birds singing a medley of familiar tunes. The concert would often end with a few bars of music from the tinkling bell section. It was the sound of the bells that Lucy now used as her official wake-up call. The sounds were all so different than Chicago's garbage trucks, and the *tap-tap-tap* of the pigeons on the windowsill.

Lucy rolled out of bed just as Pup jumped to the floor. She walked over to the window and pulled back the curtains to get a better view. "Good morning," she said to a pair of donkeys standing on the pasture side of the backyard fence. The larger, slightly heavier of the pair wore a collar with three small bells attached. The other donkey had no collar. The one with the collar always stood closest to the fence, with the other one slightly behind. The one with the collar was always the lead donkey, and the other, the follower. Was this some kind of donkey patriarchy, Lucy wondered. *So much to learn about farm life,* she thought as she began to dress for the day.

Pup had been patiently waiting for his orders. As he looked up to Lucy with his little tail wagging, she said, "Let's go help Millie." Pup bolted through the door and down the hallway, heading for the kitchen.

Entering the kitchen, Aunt Millie said, "Pour yourself a cup of coffee while we wait on the others. When we're about ready, we'll send Pup to get them. He's getting pretty good at fetching folks when needed. If he keeps it up, we may have to promote him to corporal before long. I just don't want him fetching and bringing critters in from outside." They both laughed at the prospects of what that might look like.

"Speaking of outside critters," Lucy began, "I do have a question about the two donkeys that showed up at the backyard fence every morning."

"Those aren't donkeys," said Millie. "Those are burros. They are sort of like cousins to donkeys—a little smaller and a little more nimble with their feet, but they pretty much serve the same use as pack animals. Their names are Jasper and Marigold. There's a man up the hillside road who borrows them on occasion, but for the most part, they are retired. So, what was your question?"

"It's just an observation," Lucy began, "but it seems like Jasper is the one always in charge. He stands in front, and she stands behind him. He's always the one who leads, and she always follows."

Aunt Millie stirred the scrambled eggs and turned to face Lucy. "That's not all that different than some couples I know," said Aunt Millie. "She trusts him and blindly follows along wherever he goes. Different couples have different kinds of relationships. It's not my place to judge one way or the other, so long as it works for them." She turned to Pup and said, "Okay. Pup, go get them." The little dog took off so fast he lost most of his traction at first—his tiny paws skidding on the smooth, hard floor. Soon Joe, Caleb, and Pup were all in the kitchen and ready for breakfast.

Shortly after breakfast, Caleb and Lucy headed out to the campsite together. The team and their young apprentices were already hard at work. Some were working the gardens, while some were retrofitting one of the cabins with new solar panels and other structural changes to accommodate its new intended use. Maria and her young ward were working with two new goats that would be the future dairy component. Working together, they were transforming the old campground into a new and lively little community all its own.

By midmorning, Caleb had decided it was time to tell Lucy everything—just as Secretary Higgins had insisted.

"Lucy?"

"Yes, Caleb?"

"I still owe you a picnic lunch. The last time I took you on a picnic, we got rained out. I was hoping you might be willing to give me another chance?"

"Well, that depends. Is this time for business or for pleasure?"

The question threw Caleb off guard, "Well, uh, I guess it's a little bit of both."

"Well then," said Lucy, "I guess it's worth the gamble."

A very confused Caleb scratched his head and said, "I'll get the truck.

They left the campground and headed back up the road toward the farm. "Are we eating in that beautiful park known as the Burns' backyard or somewhere else?"

"Somewhere else," he replied. "I was thinking maybe a famous old inn, very close to your imaginary Fair Haven valley." Moments later, the truck turned into the Burns' driveway.

They found Aunt Millie working in the kitchen. "What brings you two back so early?" she asked.

With obvious excitement in her voice, Lucy said, "We're going on a picnic!"

"Do I know the picnic place?" asked Aunt Millie, as she watched them putting their lunch together and placing it in a picnic basket.

"The Red Rope Inn," replied Caleb.

"Oh dear, do be careful, you two. I don't think anyone has picnicked there for nearly two hundred years."

Lucy's eyes opened up wide as golf balls. "Don't listen to her," said Caleb. "I'm sure all the rumors about the old inn being haunted are greatly exaggerated."

They drove up Harvey Hill Road a few miles to where the pavement seemed to level off. Caleb pulled over and parked along the side of the road. Before they got out of the truck, he said, "Lucy, I don't even know where to begin, but I brought you here to share so much more than a picnic. There have been days I wanted to tell you things about the project, but didn't. I told myself it was to protect you, but I realize now that Lucy Moore needs no protection from the truth. This picnic is my attempt to be completely honest with you in all matters from this day forward. I thought here, at the Red Rope Inn, could be the right place to start over." Lucy wasn't sure where this conversation was headed, but she did like the idea of no more secrets.

They got out of the truck and walked another hundred feet and around a slight bend in the road. Suddenly, Lucy gasped and grabbed hold of Caleb by the arm. "Look, up ahead!" she said in a startled voice. "It looks like some homeless drunk is sleeping it off at the base of that big tree."

"So it does," whispered Caleb. Putting his finger up to his pursed lips, he said, "Shhh. Just be really quiet, and we can go around him."

They walked in a wide circle around him and headed on toward the inn when suddenly they heard. "HEY!" The drunk yelled in a slurred-sounding voice, "You don't wanna go up there. I done checked it out!"

Caleb quietly said, "Look straight ahead, and just keep walking."

The homeless man roused a little as the two continued. "Nothin' up there but an old run-down inn. I done checked it out," he said again in a slightly slurred voice.

Caleb stopped and turned to face Lucy. "I promised you a few minutes ago, no more secrets, so here is my first proof of promise." He took her by the hand, turned around, and started walking back toward the man under the tree. As they approached the man still on the ground, Caleb yelled out, "Good morning, Truman!"

The man quickly stood up, brushed himself off, and said, "Morning, Major."

"Truman, I'd like to introduce you to Ms. Lucy Moore."

"Pleased to meet you, Ms. Lucy. I've heard a lot of wonderful things about you."

Lucy turned to face Caleb and, with a glare and a jaw set hard, said, "You just promised no more secrets, and yet you didn't tell me who Truman was until he scared the wits out of me."

Truman quickly came to Caleb's defense. "Please don't be mad at him, Ms. Lucy. He knows I need all the practice I can get. This is the most boring job you could ever imagine. The apology is on me, ma'am. I should be thanking you for even stopping by. Sorry about the scare. I guess I should go back to work. You two have a great afternoon." With that said, Truman slid back down on the ground, pulled the hat over his eyes, and started snoring. Caleb and Lucy turned and continued walking back up the hill.

"You're awful, you know," Lucy said as she continued walking a few feet behind him. A vision of Jasper and Marigold flashed before her. She quickly picked up her pace and began walking beside Caleb. Smiling, she said, "Awful! But I forgive you anyway."

Chapter 28

GHOST ON THE GROUNDS

After another eighty feet or so, Caleb slowed his walk and pointed to the right. "We turn in here," he said as he moved two small cedar trees. Both trees had been cut, and now, with the brown needles of dead trees, they had been piled across the path. Once they were removed, another trail became visible. After another hundred feet through brush and vines, the path entered an area of tall trees with very little vegetation on the forest floor. Lucy spotted what appeared to be a chain-link fence.

As they approached the fence, she quickly saw its height to be nearly twelve feet high. The fence itself extended as far as she could see both to the right and to the left. Attached to the fence every hundred feet or so were old metal signs, rusted, but the red letters were still legible: STOP. DO NOT ENTER. U.S. GOVERNMENT TOXIC WASTE DUMP SITE.

Caleb picked up the picnic basket and walked closer to the fence. "Caleb! The sign says, 'Do Not Enter!'"

"I know," he responded, "The owner of the land knows I come and go through here regularly. Our picnic spot is just a few yards on the other side. There's a spot over here where we can go through. Follow me." They continued through the fence, and after another eighty feet, they came to a clearing in the woods.

Stretched out in front of them was a grassy area of about three acres. At the edge of the grassy area, she saw a flagstone-paved circular driveway. From that driveway was another wide stone walkway that led to steps up to the porch of a three-story high stone building. Lucy stood there gazing all around, taking it all in. "What is this place, Caleb?"

"It was once known as The Red Rope Inn. A real go-to place for the rich and famous and for those who were seeking help with all kinds of health problems. Today, the vegetation near the road hides it from the view of anyone driving along the road." Lucy had to admit, as she stood there in what would have been the inn's front lawn, the old place was amazingly impressive.

"What do you think, Lucy?" She turned to face Caleb. He continued, "I mean, a little imagination, and this place could really come alive, right?"

Lucy rolled her eyes. "Please don't take this wrong, Caleb, but my imagination has been working overtime just to follow you this far."

Caleb said, "How's that? If you don't mind me asking?"

"Well, to start with, when you pulled the truck off the road and parked, I was sure there was going to be a bright flash of light. Your pickup truck should have become a shiny golden carriage pulled by two black horses—you know, a Cinderella moment. Then we saw the homeless man under the tree, who scared me to death. So I imagined another *poof!* He was transformed into our coachman. He wore a bright red suit and tall, shiny, black boots. Then he led us to the Inn's front porch. There, Alison, dressed in a long, flowing white dress, escorted us into the inn and seated us at our table. Maria was our waitress. Of course, Angela, the proprietor of the inn, came to our table to make sure everything was to our liking."

"About that time, three young troubadours who looked a lot like Marcus, Zack, and Pete came by our table playing the most beautiful music. Then you, Caleb Burns, pushed your chair back. You stood and took my hand. You looked me in the eyes and said, Ms. Lucy, would you like to dance?" Lucy took a deep breath and continued, "How's that, Caleb, for a little imagination?"

Caleb smiled, "Remind me to never again question the imagination of a writer."

****

They spread the picnic blanket over the grass and began taking their lunch out of the basket. Lucy looked around, piecing together part of a puzzle in her mind. How is it possible that the grass in this lawn area is as short as it is? It looks like it's been mowed not too long ago.

Raising his eyebrows, Caleb said, "You might not like my answer."

"Try me," she said.

He had to think fast. He couldn't let her imagination out imagine his. "Well," he said, still formulating an answer, "The legend goes that many years ago, an old shepherd found this place and managed to get a section of the fence open. He moved into the old inn and brought his flock of sheep with him. The sheep stayed in the animal quarters behind the inn. Each day, he would pasture his sheep on the front lawn. They all got their drinking water from the spring house behind the inn. Over time, the toxins from the radiation buried below ground finally gave them radiation poisoning, and they all died."

"According to the legend, on nice summer days like today, his ghost still brings his phantom flock out to pasture, right here, on the inn's front lawn. There's no need to worry, though. If you do see the grass moving by itself, it's probably just a mouse." Caleb continued as Lucy listened warily.

"I have heard, though, that some have claimed to have actually seen the phantom sheep. Apparently, they are rather tall for sheep, very skinny, and the wool hangs from their bony frames almost to the ground. Their eye sockets are dark and empty. They will silently walk up right beside you, and with grass still stuck in their front teeth, they will just stare at you." Lucy was painting the terrifying image in her mind when, in mid-sentence, Caleb yelled, "WATCH OUT, LUCY!"

She screamed and leaped across the blanket. Then, realizing she had been tricked, she started playfully pounding on Caleb. His legs were crossed in front of him as he sat on the blanket. "You are horrible, Caleb Burns, trying to scare me like that. Just horrible."

As she continued punching, Caleb lost his balance and ended up flat on his back. Lucy landed on top of him… and froze. They silently stared into each other's eyes. The scuffle had them both breathing hard. Neither was able to speak. Neither knew what to do next.

"Now what?" said Lucy.

"Honestly," Caleb said, "Honestly, the Major is a little scared."

Lucy softly replied, "Honestly, Major, so is the writer from Chicago."

Caleb then said, "I think the rules of engagement say that in such a case, both sides should consider a ceasefire."

"Agreed," said Lucy, as they both awkwardly tried to untangle themselves. Back on the blanket, they sat and ate their lunch. As they ate, they faced the collapsing spa that looked like it could be the centerpiece of an old horror movie. "What was it like here at the Red Rope Inn?" asked Lucy.

Caleb began, "The real story goes back to the early 1800s. It was a very popular resort and health spa. The trains were starting to come west, but they were still few and far between. People from miles away would take the train as close as they could, then they traveled by stagecoach the rest of the way. This was a place for the rich and famous to indulge in fine food and to soak in the mineral springs that are abundant in these parts of Indiana.

In peak tourist months, the inn's rooms would be filled with guests—all except the corner room right up there on the third floor. The real legend had it that that room was the only room with a permanent resident. You could know you had arrived at the Red Rope Inn by looking up to her corner room. Out of that window would always be dangling a thick red rope. It was called the Rope of Hope.

"People would come to soak in the springs in the hope that the mineral water would heal them of their ailments and afflictions. Barren wives would soak in the hope that they would afterwards conceive and have a child. Those who were distressed over heartache and grief would soak in hope of finding peace.

Perhaps the most hopeful of all were the slaves in the South who had heard that if they made it to the Red Rope Inn, there would be a secret passageway. Hiding on the grounds of the inn, it could get them safely onto a trail headed north and on to freedom. All this hope was from a simple red rope hanging from a corner window on the third floor."

"Did this mysterious woman have a name?" asked Lucy.

Caleb replied, "Her name was Rahab."

"But Rahab was a Bible character in the Old Testament. She lived a few thousand years ago."

Caleb nodded and asked, "And what was she famous for?"

Lucy considered her answer. "For her hope and faith. Her faith was that if she tied a red rope on the bars of her window, she and her family would be spared when Jericho would be destroyed. I see what you mean—a window of hope."

Caleb nodded.

They finished their lunch, folded up the blanket, and retrieved the picnic basket. "Lucy," Caleb said in a tone that required her attention.

She turned to face him. "Yes, Caleb, what is it?"

"There is something else about this place. I told you this morning that our picnic spot would be near your elusive Fair Haven. When the slaves made it to the Red Rope Inn, they too were looking for a port in the storm, a Fair Haven for their lives. Because it was a secret passageway, the exact location was never written down, never recorded for fear it might be exposed."

"Do you think this passage is more than a legend?" Lucy asked, "Does it really exist?"

Caleb answered, "I do."

"And do you know where it is?"

"I do."

"And all of this has something to do with the Welcome project?"

"It does."

"Three days before Lenny Dekoskie got his phone call about a secret government project, I had been in a meeting with Secretary Higgins at Camp David. At that meeting, all of the Mother Hubbard project leaders were informed about a possible and increasingly probable solar electronic magnetic pulse, a SEMP. You have shared with everyone here your own concerns about certain what-ifs. The Welcome Project has been going on for about four years, preparing for the what-ifs and how we can give hope to people when such a crisis occurs."

"A SEMP has always been a possibility, but recently our intel has confirmed that the *possible* has changed to a *probable*. At that time, Secretary Higgins wanted you on board with the rest of the team. Just last week, the *probable* escalated to *likely*. There are only two more steps, *very likely* and then *imminent*.

He took her by both hands and brought her close to him. "Lucy, I don't want anything to ever, ever happen to you. If and when the *imminent* comes, if by any chance we are not together, you must promise me you will do whatever is necessary to come here. It is from here that you will find Fair Haven. Truman will be watching for you, and he will make sure your passage is possible."

When they relaxed their hold on each other, he tilted his head down slightly and kissed her on the forehead. Then he said, "I guess we'd better get back to camp, or someone might wonder what happened to us."

Lucy's little silent inside voice said, *"Well, yes, Mr. Burns. I was just thinking that very same thing. What just happened to us?"* The ride back to town was quiet, neither knowing just what to say. Both, however, were quite sure that their relationship had just made a significant paradigm shift.

Chapter 29

Puzzles and Picnics

The next few days involved very little work on the project. There was plenty of social media material already finished and ready to post. Everyone needed a little downtime to prepare for and enjoy the holiday. It was the evening of July third, and supper was over. Joe and Caleb had gone out to the barn, and Lucy was helping Millie clear the table. "How is your office space working out for you?" asked Aunt Millie. "Do you need any other furniture or things like that?"

"Everything is great," replied Lucy. "I do have a question, though, if you don't mind answering. I have noticed that on one of the bookcase shelves, there are more than a few puzzle boxes. I was just curious as to who might be the puzzle master in the Burns family?"

Aunt Millie wiped her hands on a dishtowel and said, "The menfolk just went to the barn. The answer to your question is more like a short story. I think we may need a second piece of pie and a cup of coffee to get us through it." They got their dessert and sat back down at the table.

Aunt Millie began, "Ever since Caleb was a little boy, even before starting school, he loved jigsaw puzzles. He was fascinated by their shapes, colors, and patterns, and that each piece had its own uniqueness. He would turn all the pieces over and view their faces, then, looking at the picture on the puzzle box cover, he would, in amazingly fast time, have the puzzle completely assembled. He continued to sharpen his skills as he went from simple puzzles to ones that had hundreds of tiny pieces. It was then that Uncle Joe stepped in and made a change to the process.

Every year from then on, Joe would buy two 1,000-piece puzzles for Caleb, one for Christmas and the other for his birthday. The difference now was that Joe would cover and tape over any picture on the box that revealed what the puzzle would look like when all the pieces were finally put in place. He would then write a letter to Caleb regarding the picture and a few life lessons to be found within the completed puzzle. The letter was always taped on the box top with the words on the envelope, '*To Caleb. Do not open this letter until you have completed the puzzle. Love, Uncle Joe.*'"

"But why would Uncle Joe make it so hard for Caleb?" Lucy asked.

Millie smiled in reflecting on the times and said, "Neither of them considered it as a burden, but as a challenge. Uncle Joe knew Caleb had an exceptionally bright mind. Early on, he was able to look at a situation and conceptualize the pieces and parts of a problem, and, quicker than most, arrive at a good solution."

"To answer your question about the puzzle boxes on the bookshelf, those are all Caleb's. There are sixteen boxes of difficult puzzles that he quickly claimed victory over. There are two for each year from the time he was twelve until he turned twenty."

"Why did he stop?" Lucy asked.

Millie looked down on her empty plate, swallowed hard, wiped her eyes, and said, "He went to war."

Lucy reached over and put her hand on top of Millie's. Another wipe and deep breath, and Millie continued. "It was then that Caleb had been given two puzzles of life, whose pieces had been mixed. One was of home and one was of war. While he was sorting out the pieces of the war at hand, the pieces of the home picture were being ripped out and destroyed."

"They had been married only three years when the war in Africa broke out. He didn't have to go, but he knew it would mean an increase in rank and better pay for them. Susan asked him not to go. He promised her he would make it back. Fifteen months later, she was killed in a horrific car crash. He blamed himself for not being there, for picking the wrong puzzle to focus on. Caleb has not set foot in that room since he came back. Maybe someday he will. With the right motivation, he just might."

****

162

It was the Fourth of July, and on the Burns' farm, it was always a very special time for family. It was one of two occasions when everyone there might not wear the name of Burns, but everyone there was certainly considered family. This year's attendees included all those on the Welcome team. The team had grown by two with the addition of Lucy and Hannah. There was another special guest this year; Maria had brought her two-year-old nephew, Diego.

The long dining table was brought out of the house and set under one of the shade trees in the backyard. Everyone had brought more than enough food to fill it. For each one gathered there, it was more than just a meal. It was a time to celebrate the uniqueness of America. Some of those sitting at the table had served in the military, some had come to America as emigrants, some had their roots in the big city, and others had roots in the deep soil of farm country. Today, they were all fellow Americans.

Mealtime began with a substantial prayer from Uncle Joe, who was not known for long prayers. Food was passed, and the conversations began.

It was truly a remarkable sight. Once again, Lucy saw herself as one little character in a most beautiful Norman Rockwell painting of a time in the past. Dessert would be served after other activities. Of course, the traditional dessert would be hand-cranked ice cream, homemade in partnership with Maria's goats, Angelina and Bonita. Fresh fruit from Pete's garden would serve as toppings.

Soon the table was cleared, and the younger folks were picking out croquet mallets, horseshoes, or a variety of other options to earn bragging rights until the next year's Fourth of July picnic.

Maria's little guest was being a bit fussy, so she was hanging back from joining in the fun of the games. Uncle Joe was watching the drama unfold when Aunt Millie said, "What are you waiting for, Joe? You've been wanting to hold the little fella in your lap all morning. Just call Maria over and volunteer to be the nap sitter."

He hesitated for just a second, and then Millie shouted out, "Hey Maria, bring Diego over here. Uncle Joe needs someone to rock him to sleep."

Maria came over with Diego in tow and said, "Are you sure,

Uncle Joe?"

"Of course," he said, reaching out to take the little guy to settle him in on his lap. "Now scoot on out there with the rest of them and enjoy yourself. We got this."

Soon, the little boy was all nestled in and beginning his much-needed nap. Millie glanced over at them. "Well, will you look at you? You haven't lost your touch at all." The two rocked back and forth now—not as two, but as one. A moment later, Millie looked and noticed that Uncle Joe's eyes were damp.

"I know, Joe", Millie said. "Seems like only yesterday that you had John in your lap. You two were such a sight as father and son. He grew up, got married, and we soon became grandparents. Everything was right and beautiful in the world. Then the phone rang." The words caught in her throat. "Our John was dead, but the good Lord had spared Linda and little Caleb in the crash."

"I suppose God knew that they would help us to heal from our own broken hearts. That little Caleb was a lapful, but by then, your lap had increased enough to accommodate a little boy who often needed to be rocked. Do you remember the day he started calling you Uncle Joe instead of Grandfather, and you asked him why?"

Joe said, "Yes, I remember. He said the one whom he had always called father died when the car rolled down the hill. He didn't want to ever call anyone father or even grandfather for fear their car might roll down the hill too. I think little ones
have a sixth sense, an empathic sense that lets them know when older folks are hurting or lonely inside. I think it's not so much about us holding them, but maybe them holding us, and rocking us until we feel better."

"Oh Joe, where has the time gone?" Millie asked. "With all the tragedies in our family, it would have been easy to feel like Job in the Bible. We lost our John, then Linda. When Caleb grew up and married Susan, you were so looking forward to another little Burns to rock in your lap. Then Susan was killed in a car crash. Caleb was all that we had left, and we were afraid that the war might take him. But it didn't. And like Job in the Bible, after all that was lost, he was blessed with an even larger family than before, because he never turned his back on God.

Look out there in the yard right now, Joe. We have a family bigger than ever before."

"Blessed we are, my sweet Millie. Blessed we are."

Soon, the games were over, and everyone was ready for ice cream with fresh berries from the garden. To make the ice cream, they used a vintage White Mountain crank freezer, and everyone took a turn at the handle. They all agreed, "It doesn't get any better than this."

Soon the table was cleared, and all the chairs were carried back into the house. They said their goodbyes, and all the guests left.

Inside the Burns' farmhouse, they put the last few things away, then went to their respective rooms. Lying in bed, Joe and Millie continued to talk of yet another great family reunion. Finally, Millie said, "The weather folks say we may get some rain tomorrow."

Uncle Joe replied, "Now that the picnic is over, that would be mighty good. We could use some rain. Things are getting a little dry around here."

"Good night, Millie."

"Good night, Joe."

Chapter 30

GOING HOME TO CHICAGO

The crack of gunfire split the air. Immediately, the loud booming sounds of the big trucks rumbled off into the night. It was a familiar sound that lasted only seconds, but it was long enough to startle her awake. Sitting up in bed, Lucy quickly realized she was not in her apartment in Chicago. She was, after all, in the comfort and safety of the Burns' farmhouse in Welcome, Indiana.

It had not been a street fight, as the dream had suggested. Instead, she had been woken by the sounds of a full-fledged July downpour. This one came complete with all the special effects of crashing thunder and close-your-eyes lightning. At least the storm had waited until after the picnic, but barely. Lucy got out of bed and stepped to the window. She pulled back the curtains as she reached for a nearby rocking chair. Lucy Moore was not about to miss God's latest production, complete with surround sound and a cast of Creation's greatest performers.

She then considered that the theater's lobby might still be open for self-serve. She very quietly slipped out of her room and tiptoed to the kitchen. "*Yes,*" She said very softly to herself. She reached for some of the leftover cookies from the picnic, poured a glass of milk, and headed back to her room. Settling back into the rocker, she placed her feet on an old hassock-style footstool. She was now ready as the show continued.

With each bolt of lightning and clap of thunder, scenes from the past few weeks flashed before her. Then, a flash of lightning was so close and so bright that it forced her to close her eyes. She left them closed and listened, intent only on the sounds of the storm as it slowly passed through. With eyes still closed, fog seemed to be setting in over the dark backyard. As the fog got denser, Lucy's hand holding the last cookie went to the side of the rocker. Ever so slowly, her fingers lessened their grip … until finally the cookie dropped. Once again, Lucy was sound asleep.

A few short hours later, the smell of coffee permeated the air. Uncle Joe, Caleb, and Pup all made their way to the kitchen. Last to arrive was Lucy, looking like she could have slept a little longer had it not been for the morning sunshine coming through her window. Aunt Millie poured the coffee and then started setting breakfast on the table. "Fine bunch of picnickers you all make", she said in her typical Aunt Millie teasing tone. "Had to send Pup back to Caleb's room three times before we got a successful retrieval." Caleb began to protest, but Millie smiled, winked, and said, "What's on everyone's agenda for today?"

Uncle Joe was working at the campsite. He had equipment to service and maintenance to do. He wanted to share those skills with some of the crew who seemed especially interested in the equipment. Caleb would be down in the Hubbard Command Center all day in virtual meetings with Secretary Higgins and the other team leaders.

It was Lucy's turn to complete the day's agenda. "I've been thinking I need to get back up to Chicago for a couple of days. My apartment there has always been a home office, but lately, Welcome has felt a lot more like home than Chicago. If I could close down my apartment in Chicago, maybe the Burns' could let me continue here for a while longer until …"

Aunt Millie put her arms around Lucy and said, "You go do whatever you need to do in Chicago, and hurry back as soon as you can." They all continued eating their breakfast until Aunt Millie finally broke her silence and said, "Not that anyone asked, but while you three are out saving the world, Aunt Millie will be right here doing her thing."

"Which is what?" asked Uncle Joe, then thinking he had just got himself into serious trouble for asking.

With a *do you really want to know look*, Aunt Millie said, "Oh Joe, surely you have known for a long time. *Wonder Woman* here, cleverly disguised as an old farmwife, will continue doing her housework and mundane chores, running errands, and such, until the rest of you need me to swing into action and save the day."

To that, Uncle Joe said, "Well, Millie Burns, I don't know what to say except, can I have your autograph?"

Aunt Millie picked up a dish towel and started swatting at Uncle

Joe and said, "You all get on out of here. *Wonder Woman* has work to do."

Everyone laughed as they scrambled out of the kitchen, saying, "We love you, *Wonder Woman*. We love you!" Soon, the kitchen was cleared, leaving Aunt Millie standing by the stove with her arms crossed and the dish towel in her hands. "Thank you, Lord," she said, "for all the joy and happiness that has found its way back into this old house."

Lucy went to her room and began getting a few things together for her trip back to Chicago. An hour later, she was on I-65 heading north.

Along the way, she talked with God as she always did while traveling long distances. She was pretty sure He already knew what she was going to say before she said it. Even so, she would tell Him herself.

Lucy told Him about all the transformations in her life over the past two months. That conversation also served to reaffirm to her that it had, indeed, all happened. She spoke of things like being alone to now having a family, from freelancing for Lenny to now working for one of the President's Cabinet
Secretaries.

She had gone from being afraid of getting emotionally hurt to being emotionally hopeful of being loved. She asked God to help her navigate through the uncharted world in front of her. Most important in her mind, she asked Him to help her always make choices that would please Him.

After talking with God, Lucy's thoughts turned to an action plan for when she got back to Chicago. This would be her last trip to her old apartment, for she had a new home now with a new job in a new town. She would pay rent two months ahead on the apartment and would need to connect with Carl. Everything remaining in the apartment would be left for Carl, as she planned to take very little back to Welcome. He could take it and use it, or sell it and keep the cash to help his family. With two months' rent paid up front, Carl could take his time in doing whatever he wanted to do with all that she left. He might have some early costs in getting help to do the work, so she would leave an envelope with a few hundred dollars in his mailbox.

There were two things she had committed not to do when she got there. First, she would not contact Lenny, and, second, she would not go by Granny's old house where she had grown up. Sometimes things are best remembered as the way they were—not the way they might have become.

Lucy made good time driving back to Chicago. She had been trying to wean herself off of Cheetos, so she brought with her some fresh fruit and a few healthy sandwiches. It was time she practiced what she preached. If fresh, nutritious food were important for the masses, it ought to be a priority for Lucy Moore as well. This allowed her to gas up at the highway service centers but avoid lingering in the food section.

By early afternoon, she was pulling into spot number nine in her apartment's parking garage. Carrying up the first load of things she had brought with her, she turned the door key with one hand and kicked the door open with her foot. She found a pizza in the freezer, an unopened bag of chips in the kitchen cabinet, and an unopened can of fruit cocktail still on the counter. There was a frozen dessert in the freezer with an expiration date that had passed a few weeks ago. It was then that Lucy had her first encounter with feeling homesick for the team back in Welcome. They had indeed spoiled her to fresh food, void of all the extra ingredients in the processed food she was about to eat.

The rest of the evening was spent sorting and deciding what few things she would keep and take back to Welcome, and what things would be left for Carl to deal with. She went through boxes filled with the past. There were personal items of Granny's and some items of Lucy's that Granny had saved as she went through her school years. There were even a few things of her mom and dad's from their early years together, and some from when Lucy was born. Her family was all gone now, and she started to feel very alone here in Chicago. There would be no sitting on the couch with Caleb tonight.

She was definitely feeling lonely now, so she got up and opened the bedroom closet. She found a little step stool, and standing on the second step, she reached high into a box on the top shelf. "YES!" shouted Lucy, as her hand retrieved a single party-size bag of Cheetos.

She looked at the expiration date on the package; it was still good. As she headed back into the other room, she walked by a full-length wall mirror. Catching her own reflection in the mirror, she suddenly stopped. She turned and saw Lucy Moore looking right back at her, holding a bag of her favorite go-to treat for when she was lonely or sad.

A voice from somewhere in the mirror came without warning. 'And just what do you have there in your hands, Lucy child?' It was Granny. Lucy quickly put the bag behind her, out of sight. The voice continued. 'You've been clean for three weeks. No orange fingers. No little orange crumbs on the floor or between the cushions on the couch. No amount of Cheetos will ever substitute for his affection. You can eat that whole bag, and all you will have then is an upset stomach to go with a lonely heart. Why not just write him a letter to say what's in your heart? If you never send it or give it to him, you will at least have had an honest conversation with yourself about your feelings for the man.'

Lucy went to her little kitchen table and began to write. It was a slow process. This was not a paper for a journalism class. This type of personal writing was all so new to her, with all the feelings she was trying to put on paper. When she was done, she simply signed it, Lucy. Then beneath her name, she printed three letters ILY. The fantasy of him reading the letter and trying to figure out what ILY meant was enough to get her back on track with her sorting and boxing.

****

The next morning, Lucy was still in bed when she heard it. *Tap-tap-tap. Tap-tap-tap.* She rolled over, faced the window, and waved at her old friends. She spent the rest of the morning dealing with the utilities and rental office regarding closing out the rental agreement in two months. After making a couple of trips, taking things down to Max, she felt good about the closure on the apartment and her plans for what she left Carl to deal with it. At lunchtime, Lucy pulled the other half of the pizza out of the refrigerator, heated it, and finished off the bag of chips. She was ready to head out for the last time. When she went over to pick up her purse, she saw the bag of Cheetos she had tossed aside the night before.

A deep sigh. "Yes, Lord, You are right. If I need comfort and love, I should turn to You, and not these." With that, she tossed the bag in the trash can and walked out of the apartment for the last time.

When she got down to ground level of the parking garage, she looked around for Carl. He was not in his booth, nor was he anywhere to be seen. When she reached Max, she stopped and scanned once more to see if she could see Carl. "Can I help you?" came a voice from behind. She had not seen the man, so his deep voice startled her.

Lucy said, "I was looking for Carl, the garage attendant."

"Carl is not here today. I'm his friend Gabe." The man looked over at Max. "Spot number nine," he said, "So that must be Max, and you must be Miss Lucy," the man said with a warm and welcoming smile. "Yes, Miss Lucy, Carl really is my friend, a very close friend. His wife has been having some medical problems, and Carl needed to take her to the clinic today. I told him I'd cover for him so he wouldn't lose a day's pay. Extra medical expenses are the last thing Carl needs right now."

The man continued. "I've known Carl since he was a young man. Then, when he went and married Ms. Cynthia, I was right there beside him. Over the years, as those three boys came along, I spent many an evening with Carl listening to him talk about those boys."

"Okay," Lucy said, "You convinced me. You do know Carl." She explained what she had in mind regarding Carl and cleaning out the apartment.

Gabe nodded his head in agreement and said to Lucy, "That's a mighty neighborly thing to do, Miss Lucy."

In that moment, she thought to herself, *Where have I just heard someone say the same thing recently?* She finished up the details with Gabe and headed out. The trip home seemed exhilarating with Chicago in her rearview mirror and things to look forward to in Welcome. Perhaps the thing she anticipated most was being back together with Caleb.

Lucy felt as though her life had changed more in the past few months than it had over the past several years. The whole relationship thing with Caleb was all so new. What were the rules? Dare she trespass into his past, or pull the curtain back and peek into his hopes and dreams for the future? She settled on a plan. She would seek such counseling from none other than Wonder Woman, aka Aunt Millie Burns.

A few hours later, Lucy pulled into the Burns' barn lot and parked. She got out of Max, grabbed just a few things, and very quickly and quietly went into the house. She would unload the car tomorrow.

It was still raining, and she was tired. She went to her room, got ready for bed, and said her prayers. When she had finished, there was a little tap on her door. It was Aunt Millie. "Just wanting to say, glad to see you made it back okay."

Lucy looked at her and thought of Granny, who would wait up for her when she got old enough to be out on her own and get in late. "Thanks, Aunt Millie." And sensing there might be more, she added, "Anything else, Aunt Millie?"

Millie hesitated and then said, "I don't want you to think I listen, because I don't, but I do love to hear the sound of your voice saying your prayers at night. It sounds as though you are talking to God while He's sitting right there in the rocking chair just listening to everything you say."

"Well, I think He is," said Lucy. "We're pretty good friends, God and me, so we just talk with each other whenever we need to." Aunt Millie hesitated again. "What is it, Aunt Millie?"

"Well, I was wondering if maybe sometime, if you didn't mind, and if you think He wouldn't mind, maybe I could share some of that time with the two of you. It's been a long time since I did much serious praying to God, and I'd sure like to learn how to again."

Lucy put her arms around Aunt Millie and said, "I love you, Aunt Millie, and I know God does too. So, yes, of course."

The two continued to talk for a little longer, then Lucy turned to Millie and said, "Aunt Millie, I need to ask a big favor of you."

"Of course, Lucy, what is it?"

"I need you to arrange a counseling session for me with Wonder Woman. I need her to advise me on some personal things."

Chapter 31

Synergy for All

The social media spots had been online for a full month now, and the executives at the National FFA Headquarters in Indianapolis had been watching with great interest. In the short time that Welcome's FFA had been online, they had gained more than ten thousand followers. Although some were from the two hundred FFA clubs in Indiana, most were not.

Two years earlier, the total enrollment and membership in the FFA exceeded the one million mark. The national leadership in Indianapolis sent out their *heads-up* post to all nine thousand chapters to take a look at what was happening in Welcome. They were all being encouraged to get involved in what would likely be the model for a new national skills competition. Two weeks after the alert went out, tens of thousands of new viewers all across the country were signing on and accepting the challenge to do the same in their local communities. As word of the project spread, more and more parents started following along. The parents told their friends, who told their friends, and the attention to the Welcome's FFA site exploded overnight.

It was as though the youth, who had been growing up on digital screens playing fantasy games with virtual characters, had found something new. It was a passion for gaming with real problems and working with real people. It was about the players acquiring real skills—important life skills that had been lost over the past few generations. It was about the expression of a new adolescent independence that was not based on rebellion against the present, but rather on embracing skills and values of the past. All of this paradigm shift was in the hands of several thousand school-aged kids. Kids who were, in their own right, becoming national leaders.

It was truly as Bucky Fuller had advocated: 'If you want to get people to change their way of thinking, don't try to teach them the new way of thinking. Instead, give them a tool or a game, the use of which will require them to learn the skills needed to use the tool or to play the game.' That had been true of learning digital technology. It was now true once again as people were learning to grow, process, and preserve their own food.

****

It was now the second full week in July, and another big rainstorm came through. Everyone was to take the end of the week off, get some rest, and let the kids have a few normal summer days.

That evening, the Burns' household thought they should set the example. Uncle Joe was the first to claim the kitchen. He was developing a real interest in becoming a cookie chef. Aunt Millie thought herself to be magnanimous to let him use her kitchen, so long as he put everything back in its proper place.

Aunt Millie loved to read. It was a pastime she rarely gave herself, but since the R & R was mandated, she would obligingly follow orders. As she picked up a book she had started reading a month earlier, she noticed that neither Lucy nor Caleb had figured out what to do.

"If you two can't come up with anything to do, may I suggest you finish my jigsaw puzzle." It wasn't a question.

Caleb was very hesitant, but then asked, "Are all the pieces there?"

"I think so. It might be missing one or two. In either case, you'll still be able to get the picture. Sometimes you just have to use your imagination to fill in the space and create your own vision of what the missing piece might look like."

As Caleb and Lucy worked on the puzzle, Lucy said, "A few minutes ago, Millie said something about a missing piece to the puzzle. I need to ask—is there still a missing piece in the Welcome puzzle? The piece where I see if we stay in Welcome when the SEMP hits, or do we find ourselves in a completely different puzzle—a picture where it is safe and not affected by the SEMP?"

Caleb responded, "You mean a place like your imaginary Fair Haven, the port in the storm? The answer is *yes*, and as I hinted last week, when that time comes, we all go to the Red Rope Inn. We'll leave from

174

there, not to find the last piece of the Welcome puzzle, but rather the first piece of Fair Haven."

****

Friday morning was still an official day off for the project. Marcus thought it might be a good time to do the unpredictable thing and invite Hannah over to his house. He had a surprise for her and was excited to share it. His hesitation to call her, no doubt, had its origin deep within his motives for the surprise. Marcus could talk about other people's motives but still had a hard time understanding his own. Finally, courage won out over fear, and he made the call. She accepted the invitation.

When she arrived, she had the same apprehensions that Lucy had had before going into the apparently neglected house. And just like Lucy, when she stepped in, she could not believe her eyes.

First, the AI assistant greeted her, and then Marcus spoke. "I have a little surprise," he said.

"No", said Hannah, "You had a big surprise. I see it with my own eyes, and I can't believe it."

"Actually, this is not the surprise," Marcus gestured to the house. "There is something else I want to show you, and I hope I don't offend you when I do. In no way do I want you to feel that what I want to share with you is in any way suggestive of compromising our relationship. Relationships can be very complicated, you know, so, well—"

Hannah interrupted him and said, "Marcus, it's okay. I know you wouldn't do anything to hurt my feelings, so just show me, and don't worry about it."

Marcus led her over to a full-length mirror on the wall. Standing in front of the mirror, he spoke to Julie, his AI assistant. "Julie, second floor, please." The mirror slid to the right-revealing an open elevator. Marcus motioned for Hannah to step in. The door closed, and seconds later it opened on the second floor of his house.

"If you will follow me, Hannah, what I want to show you is right this way." He led her to the last door on the left and opened it. They both stepped into the large, unfurnished room. He led her to what appeared

175

to be a window on the west wall and said, "Julie, open the southwest window on the second floor." The plasma screen came alive with a view that truly startled Hannah. It was a view from Hannah's own bedroom in the house she had grown up in back in Iowa. It was as though she had been transported to a time and place of her childhood.

"What is all this?" she asked. "How did you do this?"

"It was really quite easy. I just asked Julie to search the internet for information about the time you were growing up in Iowa. I had her search the location of your family farm and capture aerial images of crops in the fields and animals in the pastures outside the house for all four sides during all four seasons. So no matter which room up here you go into, you should get the real view of what was going on outside your home back then in Iowa."

He continued, "If you would rather have other views, it's no big deal. Julie can do it all quite quickly, and she does like to stay busy. There's really not much for her to do here. She would like very much to have other house chores to do regularly."

Hannah could not believe what had just happened. "Why, Marcus? Why all this?"

"Well, I was thinking you are here at the camp almost every day. It is several miles that you drive to either school or to here. I just thought I might offer another option. A place to stay over, on occasion, without having to drive so far back home, or to school."

A big smile came over her face.

"So you like it?" he asked.

"I love it, Marcus! You are so thoughtful and kind to have done all this." She continued, "Now I have just one favor to ask," she said as she turned and stood in front of him.

"Okay, sure, what is it?" asked Marcus.

"You have to close your eyes," urged Hannah.

"Okay, now what?"

Hannah leaned in a little closer and kissed Marcus on his cheek and said, "Thank you, Marcus."

Chapter 32

Back to School

The rest of the summer at the campground was taken up with picking and processing fruits and vegetables. The social media posts of the crew harvesting and extracting the honey from the beehives were a big hit. On the other hand, the posts of filleting fish, processing a meat chicken, and butchering a meat rabbit were met with mixed reviews.

Toward the end of August, most of the harvest was coming to an end. The crew began looking forward to going back to school and starting their new classes.

On the last Sunday before Labor Day, Hannah Spargo was throwing a party for the crew and all their families. She was calling it a *Super Sunday Send-off Luncheon*. Hannah had rented a banquet meeting room in one of Welcome's older office buildings. There would be buffet-style food with sandwiches, drinks, and desserts. She wanted to give her personal and private *thank you* to all the parents, the crew, and the crew's siblings who had also made many concessions on their behalf.

It was yet another time of bonding together for this very special group of people. As they snacked, they began to play a game of reflection. It was a simple little game called, *Remember When. Remember that day when …* or *What about that time that …* Everyone had a memory to share. Crew members, parents, and younger brothers and sisters all joined in the game. As Hannah watched them enjoying the time together, she smiled and silently thought to herself, *These are my people, my one and only family. Could this possibly be the first of many family reunions to be shared? I hope so.*

An hour later, Hannah raised her hand in the air, and the room got quiet. *Works every time,* she thought and smiled to herself. She paused and then said, "Thanks for your attention. There is one more thing I wanted to share with you today. Last week, I got a phone call from the National FFA headquarters in Indianapolis. It seems that they, too, wanted to express their appreciation for all that you have done. So, on the last Wednesday in October, a fifteen-passenger van and driver will be coming down to Welcome. The purpose of the van is to take all of you to the National FFA Convention. Along with the ride comes an all-expenses-paid stay, including motel, food, and a little spending money. There will be two extra empty seats, so if a couple of parents would like to go along as chaperones, that would be great as well.

The crew exploded with excitement. They were jumping and hugging each other as they were comprehending what she had just said. It would, indeed, be four days that they would never forget.

Hannah started to raise her hand again. "Oh yes, I almost forgot. They also want to honor all of you by asking one of you to speak at the convention. It would be at one of the open sessions. They said something about it being on the topic of encouraging all the other members there to be brave, and even if they felt scared, to go ahead and accept the challenges that come their way." The crew all turned to Rachel, and, pointing to her in agreement, said that she should be the speaker.

Rachel looked up to her teacher and asked, "How many will be there?"

Spargo smiled and said, "Usually, a little over seventy thousand in total, but in any one session, probably no more than ten or twelve thousand. Why?"

The color drained out of Rachel's face as she said, "I think I'd better sit down."

****

As the summer was coming to an end, there was a growing concern about the exposure of the camp's secret location. Before long all the trees and other vegetation near the entrance of the campsite would lose their leaves. At that point, it might be possible to see some of the buildings from the street and recognize them. Hardly anyone ever came down Mulberry Street as far as Marcus' property, but no one, especially Marcus, wanted to take the chance.

There was a tall, rusted, old chain-link fence that separated his property from that of the abandoned manufacturing buildings next door.

The team would have contractors come in and create a buffer zone of trees and shrubs. The plan was to come in from Mulberry Street about seventy-five feet and connect to the existing property line fence. From there, a new but also rusty-looking fence would head east toward Bickett Road. At the Bickett driveway, a similar looking sliding security gate would be installed. On the other side of Bickett, the fence and the buffer vegetation strip would continue all the way to the guard rail and dead-end sign at the end of Mulberry. The gate would be covered with vintage signs like KEEP OUT, and PRIVATE PROPERTY—TRESPASSERS WILL BE PROSECUTED. With multiple signs on the gate, visibility down Bickett would be nearly impossible. Once the fence was up and the buffer vegetation was planted, another row of evergreen pine trees would be planted on the inside of the new property fence.

Both Marcus' property and the camp's entrance were now practically impossible to see by anyone lost, looking, or just driving down Mulberry Street. Everyone who had a reason to access the campsite was given their own phone security code which automatically opened or closed the sliding gate.

****

It was the first day back to school. The day began with students going to their homerooms for attendance and morning announcements. It was also there that all students secured their cellphones into designated personal cellphone cubbies. It had been three years since the school policy had been introduced that all cellphones were left in homeroom during the school day. If parents had an emergency, they simply called the school's Children Services Office, and the message would be relayed to the student. Over the past three years, the number of parental *emergencies* had dropped by nearly seventy percent. School officials had noted that with those fewer disruptions, combined with the lack of student access to their phones during instruction, overall academic achievement had improved on average by one-and-a-half letter grades.

On this first day, the students would follow a very abbreviated schedule to meet their new teachers and pick up their textbooks and personal computers. After that, it would be lunchtime. Following lunch, the all-school assembly would include introductions of the administration and all support staff, highlights of the coming year, and encouragement for students to go over the student handbook with their parents.

The assembly began promptly at twelve-thirty. The principal did his *Welcome Back* speech with a special welcome to the new incoming freshman class. Counselors, cafeteria, janitorial, and other support staff were introduced, each with their own comments. The principal continued, "At this time, I would like to ask Ms. Spargo and her summer crew of agriculture students to come to the stage."

The crew all looked at Spargo as if to ask, 'What's going on?' She encouraged them to stand and follow her. She then motioned for them to join the principal on the stage. As they were doing that, Robert, who had been a crew member all summer, came from behind the stage curtains and also joined them.

Once they were all on stage, the principal looked out over his audience and continued, "If you are a student of Welcome High School, then you have, no doubt, been following the adventures of these classmates over the summer. Their social media platforms have captured the minds and hearts of perhaps millions of people across America. A year ago, they all sat where you sit today. One of them, Robert Robins here, had just graduated and had decided on a career goal. He wanted to become an ag teacher, like the ones he had enjoyed while attending here at Welcome High School. He would have to find a summer job and save every penny if he had any hope of pursuing his college dream. Then Ms. Spargo offered him a summer opportunity, along with the others standing with him here today. The opportunity was to share with others a new way of personal food independence.

The downside was that there would be no pay for any of them for the many hours of hard work that this particular job would require. I asked Robert this morning to share with everyone here today why he still did it—even if he knew he wasn't going to get paid.

Robert faced the crowd of students. "Ms. Spargo told us that often it's not about what you get from a job, but rather it's about who you become by taking the job. I think she was right. I don't think I'm the same person today, that I was four months ago."

"Well Robert," the principal continued, "There are some other people that agree with you on that point, and one of them is here today to offer you yet another opportunity. So, at this time, let's all give a big Welcome High School welcome to Dr. James Whitaker, Dean of the College of Agriculture Education at The Ohio State University."

Everyone began to clap as the dean stepped onto the stage and walked up to Robert and the others. Shaking hands with Robert, he began, "Good afternoon, Robert. You know, America is always in need of good teachers who have a passion such as yours to share, even sometimes in a new and perhaps unconventional way, the story of America's bountiful, safe, and affordable food. We at Ohio State have been watching you and the entire crew ever since you went online this past summer. Let me say congratulations to all of you on such a phenomenal accomplishment."

He continued, "Now, I know that I'm in Indiana, but Ohio State is not shy about crossing state lines to encourage and draft the leaders of tomorrow. I am here today to offer you and your team a token of our appreciation and confidence in all of you. Robert, on behalf of Ohio State's College of Agriculture Education, I have for you a full scholarship covering room and board and all instructional fees for your first year. It is renewable each year thereafter as long as you maintain certain standards of progress. The same scholarship has been set aside for each of your teammates— who upon high school graduation might choose to select and pursue a study from any of our program offerings."

The whole student body stood with thunderous cheers and applause. The crew was ecstatic. They all hurried over to their teacher. The girls embraced her, and the guys high-fived her. Tears ran down her face as she took hold of their hands and raised them high in the air as a sign of victory.

****

With each passing week, the camp was changing its wardrobe. The dark green leaves of summer were turning to light green and yellow— then to orange with a little red. Autumn was well on its way.

With each week, the Northern Lights continued to fade as their travel schedule of performances took them more and more to the southern hemisphere.

Chapter 33

FESTIVALS AND CONVENTIONS

I
t was early October in southern Indiana. Cooler nights and warm, sunny days brought on the season of festivals. Every festival had its own focus, but regardless of the focus, they all had one thing in common— food. There were apple festivals and honey festivals, pumpkin and squash festivals, sorghum and popcorn festivals, and the local walnut harvest. There seemed to be no end of selections to choose from.

Each event always had a good variety of food trucks, but this year, a different kind of food truck was finding great sales success. Instead of offering food, these trucks sold the equipment to process and preserve the harvested food. Food prices at the stores had not come down as fast as people had hoped. There had also been a growing concern regarding the over-processing and additives that more and more people were finding objectionable. People were starting to seriously look for alternatives.

The festivals were sensing this shift in consumer attitudes and tried to accommodate. Tree nurseries were offering young fruit trees for small spaces. Apples, peaches, cherries, and plums were just a few of the kinds being offered. Some savvy vendors clustered together to show the whole picture. There would be a nursery selling small fruit trees along with a bushel of their potential apples. Alongside that vendor would be a different one selling hot apple pies or half-moon pies of different varieties of fresh fruit fillings. Next to the pie maker would be the vendor who offered the equipment to process, cook, or store the delicious autumn treats. In this arrangement, potential buyers could see themselves engaged in all three segments. *If I had a tree like that one, then I could make some pies like those, using equipment like that. Why not?* At the end of the day, there might even be some trading among the vendors of their unsold surplus. It was a win-win situation for all involved.

With the camp harvest nearly completed, only a few things

remained to be done. Seed saving from a few of the garden plants was very important. The cooler weather was also a good time to *harvest* more of the meat chickens and young rabbits.

By the third week in October, the camp had been put to bed. The goats and remaining rabbits and chickens were returned to the team members' homes for their winter care. Plans were developed for regular social media posting throughout the school year to stay connected to the crew's devoted followers. The mission of preparation would continue for as long as time would allow.

****

THE NATIONAL CONVENTION

It was now the last week in October. The school parking lot had just cleared from afternoon dismissal traffic when a long blue and gold van pulled in. The driver got out and walked up to his prospective passengers. "Good afternoon, folks. My name is Josh. I'll be your driver on behalf of the FFA Foundation. I know you were expecting one of our fifteen-passenger vans. Sorry, somehow things got mixed up, and yours went somewhere else and hadn't returned in time. The boss said, 'Take whatever is left.' That means you guys and gals are stuck with this one. It's our new Mercedes, high-roof Sprinter van. You can take a peek inside and see if you think it will do."

Inside, it was like a limo with luxurious, individual seats. It had overhead storage compartments just like in a jet airliner. There was so much space! They were going in style! Ten teenagers, all wearing their official blue FFA jackets, posed alongside the van as pictures were taken. The drive time from Welcome to Indianapolis should take just under three hours. That would give them plenty of time to check into the motel, get something to eat, and make plans as they looked through the handbook of scheduled events.

The FFA National Convention was a big deal by any convention standards. Over nine thousand high schools across the nation offered agriculture education classes, which included the FFA leadership component. Any students enrolled in those programs were entitled to attend. They came from all fifty states, Puerto Rico, and the U.S. Virgin Islands. Attendance at the convention over the past few years had exceeded seventy-four thousand members annually. That was a huge number, but not surprising. They were representing the largest youth organization in the U.S.A. The student numbers were now well over the one million mark.

For the crew from Welcome, Indiana, it was, indeed, a big deal. Every day went by so fast. Every hour was filled with activities about leadership, community, overcoming obstacles, and excelling in things that matter. Every moment was a time of having *seeds* planted in their hearts. These *seeds* would sprout, become rooted, and grow from within for the rest of their lives. They heard it all from the best speakers who had walked the walk and knew how to connect with these young, future leaders of America.

It was on the last day, during the morning session, that the final awards and recognitions were taking place. The convention hall was packed with a sea of blue jackets. Each jacket told a story. On the back was embroidered the official FFA seal.
Above that emblem was the state from which that person came. Below was the school or chapter the student represented. On the front was their personal name and the year they would graduate.

This year, among the more than seventy thousand blue jackets that were worn to the convention, ten from Welcome, Indiana, were now on the stage.

The new national president stepped to the front of the stage and began to speak. "In just a few minutes, I'll share a few closing comments, and the convention will officially be over. But before I do, I want to take this opportunity to introduce to you, in person today, ten of your fellow FFA members. Most of you have already met them virtually. Last summer, you invited them into your lives and connected with them through their BOAC community service project. BOAC, as you all know, stands for Building Our American Community. However, this group seems to have been so busy working on their project that they didn't take the time to fill out and submit their own application. We all know that sometimes things have a way of working out anyway. At this time, I'd like to ask Ms. Spargo, their advisor, to come forward."

Hannah stepped over to the young man holding the microphone. He continued, "I understand, Ms. Spargo, that you are the ag department's supervisor, one of the FFA advisors at Welcome, and have taught each of these ten members sometime during their classroom experience." Hannah nodded in agreement. "Well, Ms. Spargo, I have here for you a very special recognition from a friend of the FFA. She is someone who is also very interested in building and strengthening every American community. If I may?"

He was handed a framed document which he began to read. *"Presented to Hannah Spargo: Thank you for your generous commitment of time, support, and inspiration in helping America's Communities to be better prepared to meet their future needs of available food and nutrition. With sincere respect and appreciation, signed, Janice Hubbard Higgins, Secretary, U.S. Department of Provisions, United States of America."*

"Congratulations, Ms. Spargo, to you and your winning team from Welcome. At this time, we have for each of your team an identical document with their name appropriately in its place." Another national officer approached the crew and began giving them their personal documents. Everyone in the arena, a sea of seventy thousand blue jackets, gave the Welcome team a standing ovation. The team and Hannah all returned to their seats on the stage.

The young man with the mic continued. "There is one more thing from these awesome members behind me that I want to ask one of them to do. At this time, I would like Rachel Sullivan to come forward and say a few words."

As Rachel stepped to the front of the stage, a mic stand was set up, lowered, and the hand mic inserted. Rachel walked up to the mic and crossed her arms in traditional Rachel style. She began to scan the crowd. In the sea of thousands of faces, she settled on one. It was no doubt a teacher, and at that distance, her resemblance would do just fine as a Spargo look-alike. With arms still crossed, she took a deep breath and began, "People, we need to talk."

Five minutes later, Rachel finished her speech on what it means to be brave. The arena once again exploded with applause. Rachel bowed, then turned. With shoulders straight and head held high, she felt a little taller. The tears advancing down her cheeks were not those of a scared girl, but of a young woman who was enjoying the taste of victory over her own defeated fears.

****

By four o'clock, the van was loaded and ready to return to Welcome. The ride would not be a quiet one. There was still too much unused adrenaline flowing—too much excitement from the morning's stage experience. They talked of the speakers they had heard and the things they had learned. They talked and joked and poked fun at each other.

The van rolled down I-65 south, toward Welcome. Three hours later, it pulled into the school parking lot and stopped. Everyone grabbed their luggage and stood by the van for more pictures. Suddenly, Rachel broke ranks, stepped over to Josh, the driver, and asked him to join them in the picture. "You did such a great job driving for us; we all want you to be a part of our memories."

"Wow," he said, "No one has ever before asked me to be a part of their memories. You guys know how to make a driver feel special." Rachel looked over to her teacher and smiled. Spargo returned the smile, winked, and gave a big thumbs up.

Chapter 34

November came in with a big one-two punch. First, the lower Midwest was hit with a once-in-a-century ice storm. There were multiple power outages spread over several states. Most were short, and power was back on within a few hours. A few lasted a day or two, but some lasted much longer.

The old FEMA program had been replaced by a much faster and more resilient one. Even then, being without power for that length of time got everyone's attention. Even with outside help, interruptions of that magnitude were causing communities to feel uneasy about their ability to handle such crises.

By the end of the first week of November, yet another crisis had arrived. There were multiple reports of a new strain of bird flu. This time, the flu was not affecting layer hens and increasing egg prices as it had done several years before. This time, the specific strain of the virus was hitting turkeys—the turkeys that were still too small to harvest for Thanksgiving. Once again, the carrier of the disease was determined to be migratory birds, but this time, they were flying south.

Sandhill cranes from Canada and the upper U.S. were in their annual migration south. Potentially ninety thousand birds were flying over the farm fields of the Midwest. Ninety thousand birds had a natural process to excrete their waste while in flight. Many of those birds dropped a virus, which did not harm them, but that was a death sentence to certain species below.

The *Turkey Flu*, determined to be an AI gain-of-function, lab-developed virus, had effectively wiped out thirty percent of the Midwest turkey population. The price of Thanksgiving turkeys had risen beyond what was affordable for many families.

People could generally be appeased when they could blame a natural disaster on Mother Nature herself—but not so much when they couldn't. The obvious question then, if not Mother Nature, who then, and why, and what could anyone do about it?

Biological warfare had been internationally outlawed after WWII. However, now with AI technology and gain-of-function labs, things were changing. Mankind was, unfortunately, not only finding ways to save lives but also developing very effective and seemingly natural ways to take lives.

****

By early December, the concern for America's ability to manage concurrent crises was starting to rumble to the surface. What if multiple crises, from different directions, all hit at once?

The official position from the federal government was that there was no credible proof that the power shortages were from anything other than ice storms. The *Turkey Flu* was still under investigation. Citizens were encouraged to avoid letting the fear-mongering by a few create unnecessary panic among the masses.

People needed a distraction from the negative. A positive message of self-help might just work to calm the winds of worry. Who better to provide that than a jolly old Santa and his media-savvy elves? In a very swift and positive, though not always so subtle, approach, Christmas advertising took on a new focus.

Commercials often featured Santa and Mrs. Claus using products necessary for some phase of becoming prudently prepared. The elves were often seen wrapping gifts of specific supplies or equipment to facilitate an aspect of food security. People of all walks of life were encouraged to view or re-view the complete summer series that the crew had posted during the past summer. Veterans' groups were posting clips from the old WWII victory garden campaigns as public service announcements in an effort to encourage self-reliance as one's patriotic duty.

****

It was early morning on December twenty-fourth. A fresh inch of snow had fallen the night before. A smooth blanket of white crystals covered the landscape outside the old brick farmhouse. Inside, Caleb had stoked up the fire in the fireplace. Lucy had fed Pup and joined Caleb in the living room. Uncle Joe was helping Aunt Millie with breakfast.

A moment later, they were all sitting at the table. Some time back, Aunt Millie had insisted that they exchange the old rectangular table for the new round one. She had said their old table kept them divided on sides instead of united in a circle. Uncle Joe extended both hands, one to Caleb and one to Millie. Lucy did the same, with one hand to Caleb and the other to Millie. The four of them were now united as one.

Aunt Millie had just started, with only one word out, when she was interrupted, as Caleb cleared his throat and began, "Dear Lord, we thank You for another peaceful night of rest. We thank You so much for those at this table who are not only united by our hands but also by our hearts. May our hearts always be united with Your love and care. Thank You this day for our food and all the blessings of this life. In Your Son's name, Amen."

When heads lifted, everyone wiped their eyes. It had been many years since Caleb had led a prayer in the Burns' house.

They soon finished breakfast, the table was cleared, and everyone went into the living room, finding seats facing the fireplace. Moments later, Millie glanced over to Lucy, who seemed to be deep in thought. "Everything okay, Lucy?" she asked.

Lucy turned to face her. "Aunt Millie, eight months ago on this day, I was in Chicago—alone. I had no one to pray with, no one to eat breakfast with, no one to sit by the fire with, and no one to look forward to spending the day with. Oh, yes, Aunt Millie. I am very, very okay."

About that time, Caleb's cellphone chirped. It was Janice Higgins. Caleb mouthed her name to everyone sitting in the room. "Good morning, Janice. What brings you to Welcome on unsecured phones?"

She responded, "Oh, just an old-fashioned unsecured Christmas greeting. Is everyone nearby?"

"We're all sitting here in front of the fireplace: Joe, Millie, Lucy, and me."

"Put me on speaker, Caleb."

"Good morning, everyone. Janice Higgins here. I just wanted to call and wish all of you my very best Christmas greeting, and I hope you have a wonderful, special holiday together. I've watched you all from a distance the past few months, but I want you to know I've followed you as a friend of the family. I couldn't let the day go by without telling you that."

She continued, "There are no updates today. I'll connect in a few days. Just wanted to say Merry Christmas." They all said their goodbyes, and Caleb clicked off.

He smiled and said, "Well, that was mighty nice of the boss to drop in like that." Then Caleb looked to Lucy and said, "Hey, you want to put a few more puzzle pieces together?"

"Mighty nice of you to ask."

Joe and Millie watched them go up the stairs, down the hall, and into the puzzle room. Joe and Millie turned to face each other.

"Merry Christmas, Joe."

"Merry Christmas, Millie."

Chapter 35

The Clock Still Ticks

The Welcome crew had been very successful in getting the conversation started. The commercial side of society could now exploit the concepts and keep the interest and activity alive. The Welcome team and the summer crew could now focus on phase two—once Washington decided what phase two would look like.

Caleb continued to meet regularly with his counterparts within Mother Hubbard's board of directors. The concern for a real SEMP hitting Earth had not diminished but only slowed slightly. Earth had finished its wintertime tilt to the north and was returning to its summertime position. Once again, the solar flares would likely have a greater impact in the northern hemisphere. The clock was still ticking.

It was the last Thursday in March when Caleb called a meeting of the project's inner circle. Joe, Millie, Lucy, Angela, Alison, and the five of the Welcome team met at The Nest. He wanted to share the latest from Janice on the SEMP and to talk about plans regarding phase two of the Welcome project. Phase two would now need to include a more flexible agenda based on those updates.

Caleb began, "As dictated by international agreements, there are no military bases on Antarctica. The U.S. does, however, maintain three year-round research stations on the continent and two research vessels that occasionally anchor off the coast. Those five research units supply us with very meaningful data on solar activity. The Southern Lights have been just as active as the Northern Lights in our hemisphere. Most recently, that activity had been intensifying. If it should continue to increase at its present rate, we may well need to change the SEMP status from *likely* to *very likely*."

"Our immediate assignment is twofold. First, redirect our attention to find a new purpose for the camp, as though it will be a long-term, significant part of the project. Second is the ever-vigilant preparation for a probable atmospheric hit by a SEMP. With that in mind, I want us to also consider how we can best take care of our extended, unofficial assets of the Hubbard team."

"Do you mean the crew and their families and Hannah?" asked Lucy.

"Yes, exactly. We owe them that. Without their efforts, there would be no hope for perhaps millions of people."

Marcus considered telling them he had already prepared an apartment for Hannah in his big house, but decided to wait. The consensus of the group was that at the proper time, they would reveal the plan for the families to use the camp as their safe place. If and when the SEMP hit, it would be theirs.

****

By early April, the plans were coming together. It had been like playing two different card games at the same time, but using only one deck of cards. Task one was to find a new, ongoing use for the campsite without exposing its location. Task two was the completion of all things necessary to be able to leave at a moment's notice. Once again, the synergy of combined thoughts had found positive solutions.

The second week of April was spring break for students at Welcome High School. The crew was encouraged to spend that time in leisure activities with their families. As the SEMP threat increased, Caleb wanted two things for the crew and their families: good food to feed their bodies and great memories to feed their souls.

On the farm, Lucy made time to help Millie prep her flowerbeds. It was a lot of physical work, and Millie needed and appreciated the extra help. The time of physical work was also a great time for more of that girl talk that Lucy enjoyed so much. In all the drama and potential danger of the day, Lucy had never felt so safe and secure. Much of that peace came from the older woman beside her, bent over, pulling weeds, and sharing her wisdom with the girl from Chicago.

Lucy's mornings were the best. Sunshine through her bedroom window brought a gallery of masterful art. Outside, she saw framed images of long shadows from wooden fence posts instead of shadows from tall buildings. There were scenes of green grass and flower beds instead of paved streets and concrete sidewalks. On two easels, side by side, she could see on the first easel the image of a funeral when a man's dog was laid to rest. Next to it was a painting of a young woman holding the man's hand for the first time.

There was a rooster on the fencepost crowing to wake the world. Gone were the pigeons tapping on her window. Looking over the pasture fence and toward the house stood two burrows with three little goats at their feet. The gallery would change from time to time, but it was full every morning. What a different kind of wake-up service than what she left behind in Chicago!

Chapter 36

THE FULL PICTURE

With the status of the SEMP going from *likely* to *very likely*, Caleb asked Hannah to call a meeting of her parents. This time, the meeting would be at The Nest and would be only for the parents. Hannah explained to them that it would be a very important meeting. True to form, the parents had done whatever was necessary to make it there.

Hannah began by thanking everyone for coming and said she would get to the point, as there was a lot of information that needed to be shared. She made sure to reintroduce Caleb, Lucy, and the Welcome team. If they had not already met them, she was sure their names were part of their children's conversations at home, and she wanted to put faces to those names.

"Let me first thank all of you for coming on such short notice. It was just a year ago that you took a leap of faith and allowed your sons and daughters to be a part of what we call The Welcome Project. I also want you to know that what your sons and daughters have done thus far has had immeasurable benefits for literally tens, if not hundreds, of thousands of people across America. As of this week, there are thousands of youth groups who have accepted the Welcome challenge. They are duplicating what your sons and daughters have been sharing."

"The reason for this meeting tonight is to share with you the yet untold, larger motives behind both the project and the ongoing social media presence. Two weeks before school concluded last spring, I was approached by Lucy Moore. She had been recruited by our federal government to connect with some local neighbors right here in Welcome. Their mission was a simple one: Train a million or so people as soon as possible to acquire as many skills as possible to grow their own food. If time allowed, they were also to train them to harvest, preserve, store, and prepare that food. This was to be done not as individuals, but in clusters of individuals, like the cluster your children have been modeling at the camp, and as they have shared on their websites. The reason for all of this was to help prepare local communities for what appears to be a very likely, clear and present danger to the American food supply."

At that point, parents started murmuring among themselves. They began asking a lot of questions, talking over each other, noticeably irritated that they had not been informed of everything at the beginning. The noise continued. Hannah calmly held up her hand high in the air, but said nothing. A couple of the parents noticed what she had done, and as before, they, likewise, held up their hands. Soon, the room was completely silent.

"Thank you," she said. "If everyone will give us a minute to explain, we can answer all your questions and assure you why things had to be done the way they were."

We need to share with you tonight why it is now so important that all of you become active partners with your children's efforts as well. At this time, I want to reintroduce Caleb Burns, who is the lead on the project. He and the others will answer your questions and explain the opportunities that you have to be engaged in during this ongoing national security project.

Caleb stood to address the group. "Before we begin the question and answer session, I suggest that everyone grab a drink and some of Ms. Robins' delicious snacks from over on the table."

They all got something to eat and then returned to their chairs. Caleb began. "I, like many, or maybe all of you, have always claimed Welcome as my home. I grew up in Welcome with my mother. We lived with relatives on a farm just a few minutes from where we now sit. I graduated from the old Welcome High School, went to college, and while there, enrolled in the ROTC program. When I graduated, I received my military commission in the army, which took me immediately to the wars in Africa. When I left the military, I returned to Welcome."

"Today I serve our country by invitation of the President's Cabinet, Department of Resources, and specifically, Secretary Janice Higgins. Most of you had the opportunity to meet and talk with her during Welcome's Independence Week celebration. In addition to myself, the entire team here in Welcome serves on behalf of Secretary Higgins. The project that your children have been participating in for a year now is much more than a competitive FFA challenge. It is a project of great national security."

"I will give you the quick version of the events that have brought us to this meeting tonight. On April twenty-first of last year, I was summoned to Washington, D.C. for a top-level security meeting to address a probable event that could have far-reaching consequences for our national food supply. This probable event would not come from one of our foreign adversaries, not from within our own country, but from ninety-three million miles away."

One of the parents put her hand to her lips and said softly, "Ninety-three million miles away … that would be the sun."

"Yes, Ma'am, the sun," Caleb acknowledged. He then continued, "The very likely event we are talking about is called a SEMP, a Solar Electromagnetic Pulse. Perhaps you are familiar with current news commentary regarding EMPs being used by our global adversaries. The latest concern has been the increased use of EMPs to deactivate some of our critical satellites."

"You may recall the phone service blackouts of last November and early in February of this year. Almost every phase of modern civilization is now dependent on hundreds of the most critical satellites. Not only would a SEMP take out all the satellites, it could potentially destroy all electronically driven devices if it should penetrate our atmosphere."

A parent spoke out. "And when exactly is this supposed to happen?"

Caleb said, "We have credible data that suggests it could be very soon. We may become lucky, and it could miss Earth completely. Another possibility is that it would hit only in certain areas on the Earth's surface. The worst-case scenario is that a very large one hits us in the western hemisphere over a great portion of heavily populated space and stops everything cold. Life as we know it would quickly return to the Stone Age. Looting and rioting would no doubt follow as everyone would attempt to store up as many essentials as they can. Some predictions have suggested that if a large SEMP were to hit, as much as thirty to forty percent of the population would be dead within twelve weeks."

The parents gasped audibly and began to whisper among themselves as they listened in disbelief to what they were hearing.

"Hopefully, the activity on the sun's surface will start to settle down soon. If that should happen, then the alert level will drop back down from *very likely*, to *likely* to *probable,* and finally all the way back down to *possible*. Even with all the latest and greatest AI-infused solar satellites that provide the data, the pulse will move at a pace too fast to give us any significant advanced warning. There will be no time for further preparation. At that point, if we are within the impacted area, life as we know it will quite abruptly come to a halt."

"Tonight, we have called you here to offer a proposal that should help you and your families survive the initial devastating blow, if one should occur. Over the past year, your children have given literally thousands of households a very precious commodity. They have given many in this country a newfound hope—the hope of having wholesome, fresh food regardless of interruptions that could prevent people from having any sustenance. In return, we offer to all of you and your families the campsite where they have been doing all their work."

"We have, for each of you tonight, an inventory of resources—both obvious and some not so obvious. As a group, you will need to make many decisions within a very short time. These are decisions such as first, determining how collective decisions are made for the group going forward. Second, decide the division of property. Even though you will all be working together, you will still need your own private family space. There are ten cabins, one machine shed, and one sizable dining hall.

"Third, establish at least a rough plan for division of labor. Who is going to be responsible for what in the immediate future? Finally, begin to answer the hard questions, such as, can you bring extended family members with you? More questions should at least be talked about before the event, and there are a lot of things that will come up totally unexpected."

"We propose that you approach tonight's topic with your children as a mock bug-out exercise. Suggest that with their help, you spend the next couple of days bringing some of your personal home essentials to the campground. We encourage you to listen to the voices of your children. They have proven themselves both as workers and leaders far beyond their ages. They know the site well and are familiar with many of its resources. They will be your guides when you get to camp."

"At this time, we want to turn the meeting completely back over to all of you. We ask that you start on some of those essential priority decisions. The team is passing out to you a list of physical resources you can count on in your initial planning. All of us are going back into the kitchen while you get started with your meeting. If you have a specific question essential to your decision making, feel free to step in and ask. Before you leave here tonight, you should at least get a consensus on how you plan to proceed from this point forward. For those of you who can start tomorrow morning, the team of mentors and Ms. Spargo will all be there early, but our role tomorrow will be primarily as observers only."

A heavy silence filled the room as the parents began looking through the notes they had just received and looked around the room at each other. They were clearly caught off guard by the significance of the decisions they were being asked to make.

The team stepped into the kitchen and began some of their own planning. They discussed whether any of the team members would be moving any of their own personal components of the project onto the campgrounds. Zack said he would bring six of his pedal-powered bikes to the campsite. Maria would wait before moving Bonita and Angelina to the little goat barn at the camp. They each went through their own inventories and discussed how best to proceed.

The meeting of the parents went late into the evening, but finally they emerged from the garage. After they had folded up the tables and chairs and put them against the wall, they approached the team in the kitchen, and one delegated parent spoke for all.

"We just want to thank all of you, and especially Ms. Spargo, for allowing our children and our families to be part of the project this past year. Regardless of how things turn out, we just want to say thanks." With that, they all shook hands as they walked past the team and left through the front door.

Chapter 37

The Race Is On

Early Wednesday morning Caleb got a call from Secretary Higgins. "Good morning, Caleb. We have new intel that may put a wrinkle in our time frames."

"Actually, there are two updates. First, we are watching closely some bad actors whose new pastime is micro-hacking. They start the game by shutting down all the cell towers within a small regional area. On average, the downtime is less than a minute, and then everything is back online again. So far, all the attacks have taken place in the southern hemisphere in countries where affected regions are still not totally digitally dependent. Since the blackouts are so short and the residual damage is so small, the problem has not caught the attention of global news services. Our growing concern is that they are successfully increasing the length of time that the systems are down before they bring them back online."

"If they keep perfecting their trial hits, it is only a matter of time before they take down a populated area within a developed nation. It would take only ten minutes of blackout to get everyone's attention. Even if they brought everything back online, such an attack would create immediate chaos. There would be a run on the banks and savings institutions. The hoarding of food and necessities would begin. Life would soon turn very ugly."

"Part two of today's update comes to us from Starbright. She says that within the next few nights, we are likely to see the most amazing light shows in the northern skies. We both know that such shows could well be a precursor of bad things to come."

"I hate to share all this by phone, Caleb, but I wanted you to know as soon as possible. The clock is still ticking, but I am afraid it might not tick for all that much longer. I am moving the SEMP status from *very likely* to *imminent*."

Caleb knew that there was nothing he or his team could do to affect a change in either of the events that Janice Higgins had just shared. They would stay focused on the important mission at Welcome.

He would have Angela and Alison increase their packing and shipping efforts of the items to be archived in the valley. Hard copies of journals and notes, physical photos and manuscripts, and newspaper clippings related to the project would all need to be sent as soon as possible. He would have Angela gather print material from the library—anything and everything about the times and people of Welcome, Indiana.

There was a new sense of urgency in all his thoughts. The old farm machinery would need to come to the campground for its new forever home. The Hubbard Command Center would need to be ready to evacuate and close at a moment's notice.

He had a midmorning meeting scheduled with the filming crew. From there, he would go to see Alison at K's before the lunch rush. She would be helping Angela with much of the gathering and packing of those things to be archived. He and Lucy were planning on meeting at K's for lunch at eleven-fifteen.

Everything went as scheduled. Caleb and Lucy enjoyed the early lunch and had finished just in time to avoid the noon crowd. When they stepped outside, the warm air felt good with its light breeze. "Hey," said Lucy, "Why don't we just walk over to The Nest. I need the steps, and with that lunch we just had, the walk will do me good." They both maneuvered through the people coming in and started walking down the sidewalk toward The Nest. A few steps later, the air was filled with the squall of civil defense emergency sirens. Both of their hearts skipped a beat before realizing it was noon on the first Monday of the month. In Welcome, that meant it was test time for the tornado-warning sirens to be activated.

One of the big orange megaphone-shaped sirens right above them wailed with its cyclical scream. They turned and faced each other, both holding their hands over their ears. There was no place to run. The sound was everywhere. There was no escaping the unrelenting decibels. So they stood there on the sidewalk, partway between K's Diner and The Nest. Hands over their ears, they waited until the screaming siren finally stopped.

She looked at him. He squeezed her hand and said, "Let's go." They walked on toward The Nest without saying a word. Caleb was too busy wrestling with the thoughts inside his head to find the energy to talk. He knew that when *IT* did happen, there would be no loud sirens of warning. There would be no loudspeakers heard from cruising police cars, because neither the sirens, nor the speakers, nor the cars would be working. There would be no sounds of planes overhead or the noise of machinery and equipment working. The only sound that would be heard would be the sound of people screaming—because they would not be able to accept the overpowering silence.

****

Meanwhile, out at the Burns' farm, Aunt Millie had also turned her attention to the inevitable exodus of Welcome. Unknown to Caleb, she had been boxing a few tangible mementos of his days on the farm—including pictures from the time he and his mother first moved there after the crash.

Millie had included memories of his school days: grade cards, certificates, and awards, clippings from college, ROTC awards, and copies of his enlistment papers. Her emotions flooded her soul as all those moments and all those years flashed before her.

She was also including pictures of Lucy from the short time they had known her—Lucy Moore from Chicago, the girl who had come to Welcome to find a secret government project. While she was looking, she had found her way into the hearts and lives of everyone on the Welcome team. She had become Aunt Millie's Lucy as well. She was the one and only person she would entrust her precious Caleb to for the rest of his life.

She and Joe had talked it over. When the time came for everyone to go, they would be staying in Welcome. They were resigned to accept whatever would happen. They had lived a long and wonderful life together.

The thought of starting over was an exhausting one for folks their age. Why would they even want to start over? They had also agreed to tell no one until it would be too late for anyone to try and convince them differently.

Chapter 38

DRESS REHEARSAL

Early the next morning, the campsite was swarming with activity. The parents had told their children that the project had been going so well that Ms. Spargo suggested a break for two or three days. She was suggesting that the individual families engage in a little competition game of their own. They were to assume that a civil emergency was about to happen. The work that the kids had been doing all summer had prepared them very well for the food component of the survival game. Now, each family would put together a trial run for the other components of the game.

Each family would have an individual shelter. Beyond that, they would have to prepare for family hygiene, non-motorized transportation, clothing, and a whole variety of other needs that would be required to survive this disaster. Each family was to work together as a family team to achieve as many of the essential activities as shown on the contest sheet. The family with the most tasks checked off would be the winning team and earn an unknown but very essential prize.

Ms. Spargo thanked them all for joining in the competition and gave a little pep talk to start the day. She suggested the students serve first as tour guides and show their parents around the camp, then reconvene in forty-five minutes back at the dining hall. The Welcome team all stayed on the dining hall porch and observed.

Everyone was quickly spreading out in all directions. The kids were leading their parents around the camp and spending extra time at the areas for which each had been most responsible. The crew was all so proud of what they had accomplished, and the parents were truly amazed at what their children had achieved in such a short time. The rest of the first day was spent with families trying to accomplish as many of the survival tasks as possible.

The second day began with families unloading some of the essentials brought from home and neatly stockpiling them in the back of the dining hall. It was there that the day before, everyone had agreed on where their designated spaces would be. After that, it was back out into the campground with parents overly eager to accomplish some meaningful tasks.

Before long, the student crew withdrew from the activity and started talking among themselves. Rachel, leading the group of nine, approached Ms. Spargo. With her familiar, assertive position of crossed arms, Rachel said to her teacher, "We need to talk."

"Of course, what seems to be the problem?"

One of them said, "It's our parents."

"Yes," said another. "They are acting way too seriously for all this just to be a game. Really, Ms. Spargo, what is actually going on here?"

Ms. Spargo thought a minute and then said, "Follow me." She led them over to a rock at the base of the dinner bell, just a few yards from the dining hall porch. "You see this rock?" Ms. Spargo asked, "Can any one of you pick it up and carry it by themselves?"

"No," they all answered.

"Could all of you together pick it up and carry it?"

"Probably not," they all answered.

"Why not?" She asked.

"The rock is too heavy, and we aren't strong enough yet to carry it. Maybe in a few years, when we are bigger and stronger, we will be able to."

"You are absolutely right, and I believe you will surely be able." Ms. Spargo continued, "This morning, your parents are all carrying a big, heavy rock."

Rachel interjected, "So, just tell us what it is."

"I can't, Rachel. The answer to your question is too heavy for you to carry right now."

"So what can we do?" They all wanted to know. Ms. Spargo considered the situation and then said, "I've got an idea."

Their teacher shared what she had in mind. This time, they picked Robby, or Robert, as his parents called him, to be their spokesman. Even though he was only a year older than some of them, he was the oldest and just as tall as most of the parents.

A few minutes later, all the parents were back in the dining hall, and it was time for lunch. Before anyone had a chance to start eating, Robby went to the front of the room and turned on the hand-held mic. "Can I have everyone's attention for just a minute, please?" His voice had changed so much over the last couple of years; he sounded as adult as anyone in the room. He cleared his throat and began.

"We think you parents are carrying a very heavy load this morning—a secret of some kind that you think is too heavy for us to carry. Maybe you are right, but we would like to help all of you carry that heavy load so it can be lighter for you. We have grown a lot this summer. We are a lot stronger than we were just a few months ago. So... think about it, and give us a chance to help you carry whatever this heavy secret is that you are pretending is just a game."

The parents went into a huddle. A moment later, their decision was made. Robert's father walked over to him and, pointing to the hand-held mic and said, "May I?" Robert handed him the mic. Looking at the crew all sitting together, he began to speak. "Of course you're right. You have all grown so much this summer. You are changing so quickly in front of our eyes, from children to young men and women. We are so proud of each one of you. The truth of the matter is this: It is you, all of you, who have been carrying the heavy load this summer. It is you who have grown so strong that you haven't even realized the weight of your load and the size of your mission."

The crew all looked at each other as if to say, "What is he talking about?"

Robert's father continued, "Apparently, there is a great likelihood that what you have been sharing throughout the summer may be the saving hope for the lives of millions of people very soon." He went on to explain the SEMP and the potential crisis if it were to hit North America.

When he finished, Hannah stood and stepped in front of the crew. "I must take this time as well to tell you how blessed I feel that your parents entrusted me with all of you. We have no assurance of what all the tomorrows have in store for us, but one thing I do know for sure is this: Your work here in this old 4-H camp has given hope to millions across this great land of ours. You all have truly put an unquestionable heartbeat into the words 'Learning to Do, Doing to Earn, Earning to Live, and Living to Serve.' Congratulations on a job well done."

From that point on, everyone shared and carried the load together. For the next three days, they all worked as one cohesive team, preparing for the unknown. One thing they were all quite sure of—whenever it happened, however it happened, they would all face the unknown together.

It was lunchtime on the third day of the bug-out blitz. They had been working exceptionally hard, and everyone felt satisfied with what they had accomplished. It was then that Caleb suggested they take the remainder of the day off and get some rest. He knew the day would never come when he would say, "We are finished. We have done all we can do." He also had overheard some of the crew and their parents talking about a special light show that was to take place in the city park after dark."

It was to be a light show under the stars. This time, it was not a creation of laser light technology but rather Mother Nature herself. The Northern Lights had been increasing all week, and tonight was predicted to be the best show yet.

It would be a tailgate party of sorts. The crew had been planning on going as well. Everyone in the park would be enjoying the light show tonight, while a few in the park would be viewing it as a precursor of a crisis to come that would change Welcome, Indiana, forever.

Parents and their children soon left the camp and headed home. Lucy said she would ride back to the farm with Uncle Joe and help Aunt Millie with some of her chores. After Joe's old truck rumbled through the gate opening, the team began to leave as well.

Caleb turned and walked a few yards out toward the cabins and stopped at an old light pole. He leaned up against it and began looking out over the campsite at all that had been done in such a short time. His mind had started racing and wrestling with a thousand thoughts when he heard a familiar voice. "Mind if I lean on this side and share the view with you?" It was Jenny.

Without changing his gaze and still looking straight ahead, Caleb said, "I thought you left with the rest of the team."

"Nope," she said. "I saw my big brother mosey out this direction and decided I'd better go look after him. I hope he doesn't mind."

"He doesn't," Caleb said.

Caleb pushed off from the light pole and said, "Why don't we walk back up to the dining hall. We've been standing all day. My legs are tired." She took his hand and they walked up and sat down together in a cushioned double glider on the porch. Caleb reached around her shoulders and pulled her in close. Jenny lay her head against him and neither said a word.

A moment later, Jenny said, "She loves you, you know?" No response. "She loves you, and it's about time you let her know that you love her just as much. It's okay, Caleb. You both have to stop fighting it. So, get out of here, and don't stop till you tell her. Promise me?"

A very long exhale made its way out of Caleb. "I promise," he said. "I love you, Sis."

"And I love you, Big Brother. Now get out of here. I've got a couple of things to do before I go home." Caleb left the porch, got in his truck, and headed out toward East Harvey Road.

When Jenny saw his truck turn left off Bickett and onto Mulberry, she went inside the dining hall. Walking over to an old comfy couch, she dropped herself down and began crying as she had never cried before. Was it possible she had lied to herself about her true feelings for Caleb? No. It had never been about romance. It was only just a sister's love. The sad truth was that Caleb had been such a big part of her life, she would now need to find a way to make herself whole again. A few minutes later, she got up from the couch and started sweeping the dining hall floor. She had so much adrenaline that she needed to use up. Two hours later, she walked over to her truck and said, "Rufus, let's go home."

Chapter 39

It's All About Hope

Jenny left the camp—exhausted. That had been her plan. Get physically exhausted, mentally exhausted, and emotionally empty. Usually, when she arrived home, she parked Rufus on the street, but tonight she drove on up the driveway and into the patients' parking area. She got out of the truck and closed the door. Her hand lingered a moment too long on the door handle, and she started to talk to Rufus. "Rufus, old boy, you look extra tired and dirty tonight. Maybe tomorrow we get a couple of the kids to give you a good wash, okay?" As her hand left the door handle, she got a glimpse of her own reflection in the door mirror. She paused and stared.

It was then she thought she heard Rufus say, *'Jenny, old girl, you look a might tired and dirty yourself. Sure, the kids can give me a washin' tomorrow, but you can't wait till tomorrow. If you want to crawl in and set yourself on my seats in the mornin', you better get your own washin' done ASAP.'* She was hallucinating now, talking with a pickup truck.

As she walked through the backyard to enter the house from the back porch door, her mind was flooded with a rollercoaster of emotions about the idea that very soon they would all become time travelers. They would leave this place they had come to call home and never come back. Over the last few years, they had become one hundred percent invested in making their homes the perfect place to survive a potentially unknown crisis. Now the potential had a name. It was getting close to having its own estimated time of arrival. Now, here they were, getting ready to leave at a moment's notice.

She stopped and scanned the yard, imagining all the animals that had spent time in the carriage house infirmary. She saw Pete and Marcus tapping the big maple trees near the front yard fence. They loved collecting the sap and transforming it into their delicious syrup. She looked over to the table under the big tree, and there they all were. They were meeting with a stranger named Lucy. The innocent, ambitious young writer from Chicago was meeting all of them for the first time. She had no idea what she had just gotten herself into.

It had barely been a year, but Lucy had changed all their lives in ways they never dreamed possible. Lucy had changed Jenny's life perhaps more than any. Until two hours ago, she hadn't realized just how much. Her thoughts were jolted awake when her wristband began vibrating. She looked at the screen. It was Caleb.

"Caleb, what's up?"

"I just talked with Janice. Time of departure—tomorrow morning. Call the whole team—everybody. Meet at the dining hall at camp at 0600. Try to get some sleep."

With that, the screen went blank. Immediately, the auto-drive inside her head kicked in. She called the other four and simply said, "Emergency meeting at my place tonight, ASAP!"

Once everyone arrived, she would delegate a lot of what Caleb knew would need to be done.

Within fifteen minutes, they were all sitting at the outside office table under the big tree. Tonight, there was plenty of light from a nearby streetlight and the full moon peering over the treetops. "Maria, you call Alison. She is to go to K's before opening time. Get a dozen or more breakfasts-to-go and bring them to camp. Pete, call Preacher Bob. Marcus, call Hannah. Zack, call Angela. Have her tell the media crew to head out for home ASAP. Everyone is to be at the dining hall at 0600. Let's get these calls done, and then we have some of our own plans to talk about."

Soon, all the calls were completed. Jenny was not at all surprised when Pete reached under the conference table and retrieved two brown paper sacks. He knew that even the healthiest of eaters would occasionally need some comfort food if under stress. Anticipating just that, he pulled from his sack three dozen cookies and a few other treats to nibble on. From the other sack, he pulled out several bottles of water.

Jenny began the conversation. "So here we are at the moment of truth. It's hard to believe that only eleven months ago, we sat at this very table meeting Lucy for the first time. We knew exactly why she had been directed here—even though she had no clue. As of tonight, that reason is emerging into reality. I think what I would like us to do is to take turns going around the table. We need to talk about what to anticipate and what our mindset should be when we get to camp in the morning."

Pete began, "I think maybe I should say something first because it may seem like a compromise to our original mission statement of deploy, prepare, and withdraw. Yes, I know our whole existence here, and especially these last few months, has been about creating a way to give people hope. I think the first two parts of the mission have been achieved. Actually, after the success of the social media campaign this past summer, I would say it was achieved very well. But I've been thinking a lot lately about all the people here in Welcome after the SEMP happens. True, we have given them hope for their bellies, but they are going to need so much more than that. Every day they are also going to need a different kind of food—a hope within their hearts and souls."

"There is going to be so much upheaval in everything. Panic, fear, defeat, and all the other negative emotions can tear our wonderful town of Welcome apart. They will need hope beyond the moment— beyond the day. I want to be here with them to help them find hope when it appears there is no hope. Besides, my namesake, another Peter, of the first century, and a terrific seed sower by the way, said it like this: *'But in your hearts revere Christ as Lord. Always be prepared to answer everyone who asks you to give the reason for the hope that you have. But do this with gentleness and respect.'* Welcome may run out of bread someday, but it should never run out of the Bread of Life that can sustain their hope. Besides, I hear that as of tomorrow, that little storefront church downtown is losing its preacher. I'm thinking about applying for the job." And with that, Pete sat down and said no more.

Maria was the next to speak. "You all know that my family gave up everything they had to come to this country when the border was open. They made many sacrifices to give me and our family a hope of a better life than was ever possible before. They fought so hard to give me a home where I could make choices about what I wanted to do. So I chose to join the U.S. Army and fight so others around the world could also have such hope. I learned many ways to fight to win. Now I think it is time for Maria to stay and fight for the people she knows and loves, and also maybe for Angelina and Bonita and their kids. Welcome is their home too, you know. So, yes, I was planning on staying as well."

Jenny turned and looked at Zack. "So, Zack? What are you thinking?"

He held up a *one moment please* finger in the air, swallowed hard, and finished the cookie in his mouth. "I was thinking," again, he paused. "I was thinking, Pete, those are the best cookies you have made in over six months." Everyone had a little chuckle and was thankful for the break from the tension that was creeping into the conversation.

Zack took a drink of water, set the bottle down, and began again. "For the last two months, I have been working very closely with a bunch of young people who actually like working. I don't mean just with their hands, but with their hands and their minds—designing, creating, and making things work. Give these kids a problem to solve or a project to build, and watch out. I am so proud of them, but they are not done yet. We still have supplies and materials to work with, and we can do so much more.

He continued. "If the SEMP hits and shuts things down, these young, healthy kids can be a big part of fixing things. They are eager learners, but they still need direction. Their parents will have their hands full just dealing with all the chaos. The SEMP will make most cars and trucks useless, so I am thinking the bike rental business could really take off like never before. It would be fantastic if there were a kid who had someone to help him learn how to manage it. Truth is, I have been thinking about hanging back and maybe, you know, helping them finish what they have already started. We all came here with a mission about food. Now it seems like it has become more about people, purpose, and relationships. I was thinking about signing up for another tour of duty."

Heads nodded in agreement. Jenny was still nodding hers when she noticed that all eyes were now on her. Maria spoke up, "Jenny, I guess it is your turn."

From left to right, her eyes scanned them all. Visual memories dashed by at digital speed—the times of laughter and tears, of celebrations and mourning, of work and play. There was no denial; they had become a united body of souls and minds and hands and hearts. Jenny cleared her throat and said. "Well, was there ever any question? I mean, somebody has to look out for this bunch of misfits."

With that, they all knew the meeting was over. They were all united in their resolution to stay. They would all go to the camp tomorrow morning as one.

Chapter 40

Time to Go

Joe, Millie, and Lucy were already in the kitchen when Caleb came in. "Did anyone get any sleep last night?" "I did," said Lucy, "Pup came into my room, jumped up on my bed, and snuggled in right beside me. I think he maybe knew something was up." Millie handed everyone a hot biscuit, egg, and sausage sandwich. "You have to eat something before we go down to camp." No one argued the point and began eating as Millie started pouring their coffee.

Caleb started, "Joe, you and Millie take the old truck when you head down to camp. There are no electronics in it that are affected by an EMP. That way, those who stay behind will still have transportation as long as they have fuel. The good news is we have a lot of fuel stored at camp. Swing by K's and see if Alison needs help with the food she's bringing to camp. Everyone, put your personal bug-out bags in the half-cab of our pickup. Lucy and I will join you at camp as soon as we finish up here."

Moments later, Caleb and Lucy were headed down Harvey Hill Road toward Welcome. "So, Lucy Moore from Chicago, does this now give you an answer to Pete's question?"

With a puzzled look, Lucy said, "What question was that?"

"The one when he asked you, 'Is it possible that you ended up in Welcome because God had a reason to have you here—a reason that would save the lives of so many of His children? You said you wanted to write a story that could make a difference in the lives of many average and ordinary people. Well, you just have, and you did it in record time. Because of your ideas of how to deliver that message through the kids' website and social media, you have impacted the lives of tens of thousands of homes. That's more than any book you would have ever written, and you have given them a chance for survival. You have given

213

them a gift that no amount of money could ever buy. You have given them *hope.*

He reached over and took her hand. He held it firm, but lovingly, and said, "I am so proud of you."

Still looking straight ahead, Lucy said, "Careful there, Major, two hands on the wheel. Keep your eyes on the road."

"Yes, Ma'am," he said as his thoughts returned to the meeting only minutes away.

They continued down the winding road in silence. Moments later, they arrived at the campground and noticed that almost everyone was already there. They walked over to the dining hall and stepped up onto the porch. Hearing a familiar sound, they all turned to see Joe's old truck pulling into camp and stopping just behind Caleb's pickup. The truck doors opened up, and everyone's serious faces took on a smile as they saw Pup jump down out of the truck and start wagging his tail in anticipation of being a part of whatever was going on. Then another car pulled in, and to Lucy's surprise, it was Preacher Bob. Even the preacher was part of this secret government project.

Alison pulled in last. Pete and Jenny helped her bring in a few boxes and bags of food for later. There were also breakfast rolls and coffee to help calm them in an anticipated stressful meeting. Lucy surveyed the group and noticed Hannah sitting with Marcus. The two were holding hands. She smiled at seeing how the puzzle pieces were starting to fit together.

Caleb stood in front of the dining hall tables and looked out over the group assembled before him. His mind momentarily flashed back to the war—a platoon of soldiers sitting in front of him, waiting for their orders. That group of people would die for each other because they knew each would die for them. He cleared his throat and began.

"This is it, folks—the moment of truth. You have prepared all that you could. You have helped all those in your charge as much as possible. I am so proud of all of you. The way you have carried out the mission is amazing. Now it's time for all of us to go."

The path will be too crowded if we all go at once. Angela, you, Preacher Bob, and Alison head on out. Truman is waiting for you. He'll open the door and get you on your way." They all quietly got up and made their way out of the dining hall. The rest of the team was standing closer together now, waiting to hear their orders.

Caleb turned toward Hannah and began, "Hannah Spargo". As he said her name, Marcus reached in behind her at the waist and pulled her closer. "Hannah Spargo, this great country of ours owes you so very, very much. You and your young army of students have given your all. Without your efforts and dedication, there would be little, if any, hope for many thousands of people. On behalf of Secretary Higgins and the President of the United States, we thank you. Secretary Higgins also extends her personal invitation for you to join us in a new location of safety and security. It is your choice to stay here or come with us."

Hannah replied, "Believe it or not, that is an easy choice. I am staying here in Welcome. Welcome is my home, and the students are my kids. I could never abandon them—not now, not after all they have done these past eleven months."

Marcus moved behind her and wrapped her in his arms. He smiled and added to her response. "I guess you all know by now, I won't be going either. I'm staying behind with this wonderfully complex and unpredictable woman. She has already furnished one of the rooms in my house as her private apartment space. It was all about a lesson I learned from Aunt Millie: 'If you have extra rooms in your big house, you should take in boarders.'" He grinned at Lucy.

It was now Jenny's turn to speak. She stepped closer and took Caleb's hands into hers. Her eyes were wet, and she struggled to keep her composure. "My dear brother and friend forever, I speak on behalf of all the team. We are all staying here, together, to see this thing through. We have to see how well the theory works in times of a real crisis. That was the mission all along. For all of us, this is simply the second phase of the mission. We will be okay, I promise."

She then turned to Lucy and they embraced. Between the sniffles and tears, Jenny whispered in her ear, "Take good care of him. Love him with all your heart, not for me, but for the two of you." She smiled and added, "If you do want to thank me, your old sister Jennifer never had any nieces or nephews. A few of those would be nice." They both laughed and then separated.

Caleb then turned to Joe and Millie. "Well, I guess it is just the four of us. We had better get going."

Uncle Joe looked at Aunt Millie and then said to her, "Why don't I tell him? I still outrank him."

She smiled, "So you do." Gesturing toward Caleb, she said, "Go ahead, Joe." He cleared his throat and began.

"Son, if there's one thing I've learned from Millie, it is this: If you both agree on the same thing that needs to be done, then it's probably the right time to be doing it. We've both known for some time that this day would probably come. Millie and I decided back when the campground took on a life of its own that it was time for us to downsize. Welcome is our home, and we want to stay here with our children, all five, or, I mean, all six of them. Marcus has already converted a couple of the rooms on the ground floor of his house into an apartment for me and Millie. Don't you worry. We will be just fine."

Caleb knew there would be no changing their minds. He should hug them goodbye. He let out a long, slow breath and, turning to Lucy, said, "Time to go".

They stepped down off the dining hall porch and were halfway to the truck when they heard a rustling sound behind them getting closer. They turned to see Pup in full charge, dragging his leash and heading straight for them. When he got to their feet, Caleb went down on one knee and started ruffling Pup's head as they had often done in their play. Caleb looked up to Lucy to sense her thoughts.

Tears were now flowing down her cheek. Looking to Caleb, she simply said, "Your call."

For a moment longer, Caleb rubbed his face with Pup and scratched his ears. Then he held Pup by each side of his face and spoke directly to him as though he would understand every word. "A few months ago, I met this amazing person who has filled all the space in my heart—even the one from losing Sadie. Remember me telling you about Sadie? Well, now Lucy and I have to leave, and that is going to leave a space in the hearts of Uncle Joe and Aunt Millie. Because you are such a wonderful Pup, and because they love you so much, you are the only one who can make their hearts whole again. It's a big job, but I know you can do it, okay?" And with that, Caleb turned Pup around, pointed him to everyone on the porch, and said, "GO!"

As they turned the truck around and headed out of camp, they looked toward the dining hall. Everyone was waving goodbye, with Pup sitting at ease between the feet of Uncle Joe and Aunt Millie. Leaving camp, they turned out of Bickett and onto Mulberry Street. Minutes later, they were passing K's diner and heading out of town.

Caleb fought hard to keep his mind from imagining the chaos and fear that would be in the streets and in the homes they were passing. It would all happen so fast and without warning. The shock of the unknown would first paralyze the people. The fear would quickly change to panic, and then, sadly, the panic would turn to rioting. He looked over at Lucy, staring out the truck door window. "Hey," he said. She turned to face him.

"Did I forget to tell you I have dinner reservations for us this evening?"

"Sure you do," Lucy said back, thinking he was just trying to distract her from the obvious.

"No, I really do—at a nice quiet place with candles on the table and music from live musicians."

"I don't think so, Mr. Burns. Those are my lines for your imaginary dinner at the Red Rope Inn. Remember?"

"Oh, so they are. Sorry ." Then Lucy said, "I'm okay, Caleb, I really am. I have been okay all morning, ever since we started to leave the farm and go to town."

"Why then?" he asked.

"It was when you told Joe and Millie to put their bags in *our* truck.'

Looking a little confused, Caleb said, "Alright, but what does that have to do with being okay or not?"

Lucy gave out a big sigh. "Caleb, when you say *our* pick-up truck, are you saying the truck is yours and Pup's?"

"No, of course not. I meant mine and yours—mine and yours, Lucy. That is what I meant. I guess I have felt it was *our* truck for some time now."

"Well, Caleb, now you know why I felt okay all morning." Lucy took a deep breath and smiled as she quietly thought to herself, *Men are so difficult to communicate with.*

They continued up the hill road and passed the old, rusty mailbox with the red letters BURNS. Caleb drove past it without hesitation. Lucy turned in her seat and looked back. Caleb said, "Don't look back. We're not going that way." Moments later, they arrived at the entrance to the old Red Rope Inn. As he had done before, he pulled the truck over to the side of the road near the big tree where Truman was still on duty. Caleb and Lucy got out of the truck.

Truman approached and said, "Good morning, Major. Morning, Miss Lucy." They took their packs from the truck and set them on the ground. Truman continued, "Angela, Bob, and Alison left about forty-five minutes ago, so they should be there before long."

Caleb said, "Truman, take our bags and put them on Jasper, and head on out. Leave Marigold tied up outside the tack room. Lucy and I will bring her along with us when we come. When you get to the end, set the closure charge for two hours. Also, be sure to hang Jasper's collar in the breezeway above the door.

"Affirmative," Truman replied in a tone that assured Caleb that Truman had also gotten an unspoken direction."

"Lucy, you go with Truman to the stable. I'll be there shortly."

"Where are you going?" Lucy asked.

"To hide the truck. It'll only take a minute."

Lucy followed Truman to the back of the inn. She saw two smaller structures—both made of stone. The first was the spring-house, and the other was a long, open stable. It was once used to board the horses of those who traveled to the inn. At the nearest end of the stable was an enclosed area used as the tack room. Its purpose was to store the harnesses, saddles, and grain to feed the horses.

Marigold and Jasper were both tied up in the stable area next to the tack room. Truman told Lucy to stand over by the spring-house while he took Jasper inside the tack room. As he started to open the door, he turned to Lucy. "Just stand right over there by the spring-house and watch for Caleb. He should be here any minute."

Lucy stood and waited—and waited—and waited. Finally, she had had enough of waiting and stepped over and opened the door to the tack room. But where was Truman? Where was Jasper? They were nowhere in sight. She knew they had both gone in and neither had come out through the door.

Just then, Caleb emerged through some brush at the edge of the woods and walked toward Lucy. She was alone and looking scared. "Truman went into that room and didn't come out. He and Jasper are gone." She was pointing to the door of the tack room. "He and Jasper just disappeared, Caleb. Gone, vanished!"

Caleb took her by the hand and said, "Follow me. It's okay. I know where they went." Lucy and Caleb stepped into the empty tack room.

Lucy, still seeing no Truman, said, "Now what?"

The back wall of the tack room was constructed of vertical wooden planks. A few scraps of old harness still hung on nails at the far left side of the wall. There was one lone horseshoe hanging on the far right side of the wall. Caleb reached up and turned the horseshoe to one side, and several boards started to move as one. The wall boards were actually a sliding doorway that moved to one side, revealing yet another door. This one was steel-plated and looked a lot like the one in Uncle Joe's barn.

Lucy stiffened and said, "Oh no, not again. The last time I went through a door that looked like that, I promised myself never, ever again." Sensing her anxiety increasing, Caleb thought it best to bring the stress level down before opening the door.

He thought for a second and then said, "Forget the door, Lucy. There's something else I have to know before we go any farther."

Chapter 41

The Ballroom Dance

"The first time I brought you here and we picnicked in front of the Inn, you shared your imaginary vision of us eating in the great dining hall. You talked about the musicians coming to our table just as I had asked for a dance. Do you remember that?"

"Of course I do, Caleb, but what does that have anything to do with all of this?"

"I never heard your answer."

"What are you talking about, Caleb?"

He again insisted, "I need to know what your answer was going to be."

Confused, Lucy said. "I was going to say 'I would love to dance with you, Mr. Burns', but what does that—"

Caleb interrupted her, took her by the hand, and said, "Follow me."

A few steps later they were at the back porch of the old inn. He led her up the porch steps, through a back door, and into the old, primitive kitchen. Through that room's door, they entered the room where meals were prepared just before being served. Caleb faced her, held both of her hands, and said, "On the other side of this door is the grand dining hall and dance floor. Before we go in there, I have to know: Do you trust me enough to take you dancing?" He repeated himself. "Do you trust me enough to take you dancing on the other, unseen, side of the door?"

Still quite confused as to what had gotten into Caleb, she said, "Of course I do. You know I do. Of course, I trust you to take me dancing."

He smiled and said, "Then, shall we dance?"

He opened the door into the grand hall and dance floor. It was a huge room with two floors to the ceiling. The room was but a ghost of its former opulence of nearly two hundred years ago. Cobwebs hung from the fragments of old chandeliers. The room was void of any furniture, tables, or chairs. A few doors were hanging tall and built-in wall cabinets with doors hung crookedly by a single hinge looked as though at any moment the doors would crash to the floor—creating a loud noise for an earless room.

Caleb smiled and said, "Lady's choice. You pick the dance, and you pick the music." He held her close and waited. Seconds later, the music must have started. She lay her head against his shoulder and began. From the cadence of her steps, he thought it must be a waltz, and he joined in.

They danced without saying a word—each in their own thoughts. They moved about in the room with their eyes closed. There was no worry of stumbling over the unknown and unseen. It was a floor void of doubt and fear. After a few moments, the music must have stopped, as Lucy lifted her head from his shoulder and simply said, "Thank you."

They left the dance floor and returned to the stable. He untied Marigold and led her into the tack room. The metal door still stood exposed, waiting for a code to be punched into its keypad. Caleb turned to Lucy and once again asked, "Do you trust me to take you dancing on the other side of this door?"

She looked at him, swallowed hard, and said, "Yes, I do."

He punched in the code. The door slid to one side revealing a long, mostly dark tunnel. The floor was smooth and the walls had small dim lights about every hundred feet. Lucy clinched Caleb's arm and cautioned, "I can't do this."

"Sure you can. It's just over an hour's walk. Besides, we have Marigold here to lead the way. We will be there in plenty of time for supper."

"And where is *there*?" she asked, with a short breath of apprehension.

"Do you remember a few weeks ago? We were sitting on the couch, and you described to me an imaginary place you would like to have someday as your home?"

"You mean my Fair Haven paradise?"

"Yes, that's the place. That is where we are going. We won't be eating at Harry's, but I do have reservations."

Lucy looked at Caleb and said, "I still don't know if I can do this."

Caleb took her hand again and said, "Remind me what it was that our little friend Rachel said about being brave?"

"She said it was okay to be scared. Brave people are scared, too. They just go ahead and do what has to be done anyway. I get it, Caleb. I have to try. So long as the lights stay on, I should be okay. But, if the lights go out, I am terrified of total darkness."

"Not to worry. Like I said, we have Marigold. Marigold here is one of the bravest burros that ever lived. She is so special in many ways, almost magical in some. I'm convinced that she can see every bit as good in the dark as she can on the sunniest of days."

"She's a very, very special burro. You hold onto her reins on the right side and I will do the same on her left. We can leave the navigation to Marigold. Everything will be fine, Lucy, I promise." With no further reason for delay, Caleb said, "Let's get going. We are on the clock." He gave a pat on the rump of the burro, and Marigold started leading the way.

A few yards later, Lucy asked, "What do you think gives Marigold her special abilities?"

"One story goes that the burros were used to carry the slaves' belongings through the cave, and so they no doubt made many, many trips back and forth. Was it possible the burros developed some kind of memory that would allow them to navigate in the dark, just as Marigold can do now? If she is a descendant of one of those burros, then maybe."

Lucy interrupted, "Do you really believe that?"

So far, so good, Caleb thought silently to himself. *Keep her talking. Keep her mind engaged in conversation and not about how dark the cave is.* That is exactly what he did for the next half mile through the cave. At that point, everything changed.

Without warning, the little lights on the wall went out. It was total, complete, and suffocating darkness. Lucy screamed, "CALEB!" She continued screaming his name as she began an immediate and total meltdown.

In that split second, he moved around behind Marigold and reached for Lucy. In the dark, he turned her body to face his own and pulled her close. He put both arms around her and held her tight.

"It's okay. I've got you. It's okay. I've got you. We are almost there, but right now I need your help. I am going to tell you a story of how we are going to get out of here, so listen closely. Close your eyes, so you can watch and see everything I'm going to tell you."

He began, "There once was a little boy named Johnny, who lived in a big red brick farmhouse right here." He placed the end of his forefinger in the center of her back and gently pressed to mark the spot. One day, Johnny walked up the hillside road and found an old abandoned guest house called the Red Rope Inn. Right here."

As Caleb told the story of the boy walking, he slowly moved his finger on Lucy's back to trace the boy's movement. He continued the story. "One day, Johnny discovered a cave behind the Inn. The cave was right here." His finger moved to the cave.

Lucy was starting to cry less and listen more.

"The opening to the cave was small but big enough for Johnny to squeeze through. The cave was dark. Johnny reached into his backpack and pulled out his flashlight, a pencil, and a small pad of paper. As he explored the cave, he made notes." Time for the finger to move again.

"Not knowing how long the cave was, Johnny counted his steps. At three hundred steps through the cave, the hard stone floor became rough with gravel, right here". The finger moved. "Then the floor was smooth again, so he walked on for another six hundred steps to right here." The finger continued to move. "What do you suppose he found here?" Caleb asked to get her mind engaged in the story and not frozen in her terror of the darkness.

As he told the story, his finger continued to move. The more it moved, the bigger the circle was drawn on her back. From time to time, Caleb would make a statement that obviously could not have happened. Lucy would correct his blunder. The blunders were working too.

In the darkness of the cave, where no one could see, the tears rolled down the cheeks of Major Caleb Burns. His mother had taught him well. It was she who told him stories on his back. It was her stories that had quieted the nightmares of the broken little boy after the crash that killed his father.

Lucy was starting to relax now, and her breathing was almost normal. Soon, Caleb had taken little Johnny all the way through the cave, from one end to the other and back again. As he told the story, he mentioned five points along the way, all recognizable in the dark. They were points of sound, smell, or temperature change, which were all able to be sensed without the need for sight.

The boy had documented the number of steps between each of his reference points. Over that summer, little Johnny had learned to travel the length of the cave in total darkness and still know exactly where he was and what to expect next.

Relaxed now, and with eyes still closed, Lucy asked, "Did all of that really happen?"

Caleb assured her it had. "Was his name really Johnny?"

Caleb replied, "Yes, named after his father. His name was and still is John Caleb Burns."

She hugged him tighter than ever before and asked, "Can Marigold really see in the dark?"

"Like I said, she can see every bit as good in here as she can outside on a bright, sunny day."

They continued on with Marigold leading the way. Now Lucy too, was engaged in the challenge to use her senses and count steps in anticipation of the next expected mile marker.

Forty minutes later Lucy said, "Do you hear that?"

"What?" said Caleb.

"It sounds like the tinkling of small bells." Marigold picked up the pace.

"Easy girl," Caleb tried to restrain the burro's obvious excitement.

"What is it, Caleb? What's wrong?"

"Good news, Lucy. We are going to make a right turn just ahead, and you are going to see a ray of daylight." Lucy's heart began racing. It was almost over. "Just hold on to Marigold. She knows where she is going." A few yards ahead, Marigold turned to the right and delivered her two companions into the last section of the cave.

Several yards ahead was daylight streaming through an open

window within the cave's end wall. Lucy looked up to the open window. She had sensed that was where the sound was coming from. Her eyes were slowly adjusting to the light, and then she saw it. Hanging in the open window was Jasper's collar. Attached to his collar were three bells. The breeze through the window was ringing the bells for Marigold to hear.

With eyes now adjusting to the faint, soft light, they were both able to see the large wood door before them. As they stood facing the door, Caleb put his arm around Lucy's waist and said, "Are you ready?"

"Not quite yet, said Lucy, "Just a couple of things I need settled first."

Totally surprised at such a response, Caleb said "Okay, what is it?"

"You promised me that day at the Inn that you would always tell me the truth, right? My first question is this: Can Marigold see in the dark?"

Caleb smiled. "As I have said, she can see just as well in the dark as she can on a bright, sunny day. The truth is, she is blind as a bat and can see nothing in either case. So my comment about her sight has always been truthful. However, like the bat, she has some other senses that make up for her inability to see. Those big ears of hers can hear the sound of Jasper's bells a very long distance away. She is quite happy to blindly follow Jasper wherever he goes."

"Anything else?"

"Yes," she said. "In the old inn, you ask if I would trust you to follow you through a door and onto an unknown, haunted dance floor, and I said yes. In the stable behind the inn, you asked if I trusted you to follow you through a door into a dark scary cave, and I said yes. And now once again you are asking if I am ready to go through one more of your terrifying doors, into a place where I have no idea what to expect. Well, Johnny Caleb Jasper Burns, the answer is *yes*. Wherever you go, I will go, and in whatever valley you lodge, I will lodge. Your people will be my people, and we will love and share the same Lord God forever."

Caleb took her in his arms and held her as he had never held her before. Their eyes met. Just as he started to ask her a question, there was a loud obnoxious bray from an increasingly impatient burro. Caleb said,

"I hate to say it, but maybe we should continue this conversation tonight at dinner."

"Promise?" Asked Lucy,

"I promise."

Caleb reached for a rope dangling through a hole in the wall near the door. He pulled it. The sound of a ringing dinner bell could be heard through the door. He then retrieved two pairs of sunglasses from a rack mounted on the cave wall. "Here, put these on. We have been in the dark so long that your eyes will thank you. It will only take a few minutes for everything to readjust."

There was a creaking sound as the door very slowly began to open.

Chapter 42

The Promised Land

The door opened only slightly. A voice on the other side said, "Just checking to make sure you have your shades on."

"Thanks for the caution," Caleb said back to the young voice on the other side of the door.

"Truman arrived an hour ago and said he thought you two would be the last to come."

"Affirmative," said Caleb, with a sound of sadness in his voice. Sensing the momentary loneliness, Lucy squeezed his hand. The door continued to open, little by little, as they made small talk to pass the time. Marigold came closer and pushed her muzzle through the widening crack of the door. A pair of hands on the other side took hold of her reins and pulled her on through. Now the two burros began an opera of braying as Jasper's collar was put back on his neck and the two long-eared friends were reunited.

Finally, the door opened completely, and they stepped out of the cave and onto a terraced area. Spread out before them was the most breathtaking view of the valley below. The girl who had opened the door said, "Welcome to Fair Haven."

Lucy said "Fair Haven? I can't believe it."

"Well," the girl said, "We actually call this little place Pleasant Valley, but when Caleb told us you liked the thought of Fair Haven, I thought I should let you down slowly."

Lucy looked to Caleb, punched him in the arm, and said smiling, "You are something else Caleb Burns."

They stepped to the edge of the terraced landing and together viewed the valley that lay before them. "Lucy, tell me what you see," said Caleb.

She started to describe her view. "I see rolling green hills just like the ones we left in Welcome. I see a little town down there in the valley. There is a road going in, but I don't see any—" She abruptly stopped. "I saw this place the other night, didn't I, when you asked me to close my eyes and describe my own port in the storm?"

"Well, I must say your vision in the dark seems to have been remarkably accurate."

The young woman at the cave door spoke up, "Caleb, Molly is over behind that patch of trees. She has been waiting for you all morning. Somehow she knew, and, well, she insisted on taking you down to check in."

Lucy felt like she had just been punched in the gut. A few minutes ago she embraced the man she wanted to spend the rest of her life with, only to hear now that someone named Molly had been waiting for him all morning.

"Are you okay, Lucy?" Caleb said as he saw the color drain from her face.

"Sure, why wouldn't I be," Lucy responded with a little edge in her voice.

"We can take our glasses off now," he said as he took her by the hand and headed toward the trees.

When they reached the other side of the cluster of trees, Lucy saw no one there—only a small horse hitched to a carriage. Caleb brought Lucy up to the front of the horse and said, "Lucy, I want you to meet Molly. Molly, this is Lucy."

Lucy blushed, threw her arm over the horse's neck, and said, "Molly, you are one beautiful horse." Not sure what had just happened, Caleb helped Lucy up into the carriage seat. He untied Molly, stepped up into the carriage, and the three started down the hill toward the small community below.

As they descended the hillside, the carriage bounced over the rough terrain. Lucy's mind flashed back to the night Caleb had taken her to Harry's for supper in the *Batmobile* luxury car, and now she was on a bumpy carriage ride. She just smiled and reached over with one hand and held onto his arm.

They soon came to a group of small buildings at the beginning of what appeared to be the main street. Caleb stopped Molly and got out of the carriage. He went around and helped Lucy out and safely to the ground. A young man came and took the reins of Molly and said to Caleb, "If you like, I'll take Molly and stable her for you, Mr. Caleb."

"Thanks Roger, I appreciate that." Caleb turned to Lucy, "I need to go in here, check us in, and get any updates. Rest here on the bench. It shouldn't take long." Lucy sat down on a slatted park bench beneath a big shade tree to wait. It felt good to get off her feet after all the walking they had done. As soon as she sat down, she noticed a wire enclosure attached to the building Caleb had just gone into. The enclosure looked like the flight cage back at Marcus' place. She got up and walked over.

As soon as she got there, she saw him. It was Avogadro. "Well, well, well. Look who's here! So this is where you've been going every day." He scooted sideways on his perch and came over to her. He cooed a few coos as though he was telling her something. "I know what you mean," she said to the pigeon, "I miss them already. I just want to always know that they're okay. So I am going to depend on you to keep us informed. Marcus said that, for an animal, you are very dependable."

Her conversation with Avogadro was interrupted by a voice behind her. "Young lady, I am glad to see you finally made it." She turned quickly to see who was talking. He tipped his hat as a courteous greeting and continued. "Do you also know how to speak pigeon? Not too many folks can do that, you know." Standing there was an old man in bib overalls holding on to the bridle of a donkey. He looked familiar, but she was having a hard time placing where or when she might have seen him. "Me and Hosannah here have been waiting to catch up with you. I just wanted to thank you for helping all of us find the boss's boy. It is so good to have him back and hear him talking with his Father again. I hope finding him didn't create too much excitement for you. Be sure to take good care of him, for all of us, okay?"

Lucy's forehead wrinkled with confusion. "What does he mean, me taking care of the boss's boy?"

The old man turned the donkey, and the two started walking away. As he did, Lucy spotted something in the luggage bags slung over the back of the donkey. Something orange sticking out from under one of the canvas bags caught her eye. *Cheetos!* It was in a similar luggage bag to that of the old man she met at K's—the old man that was looking for his Boss's son. Was this old man just now one of his contacts that he spoke of having?

As she was trying to figure out what had just happened, she heard Caleb's voice. "Okay Lucy, we are all checked in, and now we're ready to move on to temporary quarters."

She grabbed Caleb by the arm and asked, "Do you know who that old man is? She turned to point, but then saw no one.

"Lucy, there are no old people in Pleasant Valley. The oldest one here now is Angela, but she is in her early sixties. Is everything okay?"

She hesitated, "Sure...everything is fine." They continued to walk along on the wide sidewalk. They walked past a clinic, a hardware store, a fabric store, and a consignment gift shop.

Caleb stopped. "Well, here we are, our temporary quarters for a few days. It's Pleasant Valley's one and only guest house— locally referred to as *The Hilton.*

They walked in to a spacious and beautifully decorated lobby area. Through open doors on the left, the lobby connected to the gift shop. Through similar open doorways on the right, the lobby connected to a dining area. Caleb and Lucy stepped to the registration counter. "Good afternoon, Major," said a young lady behind the counter. "We have been expecting you. Here is your key. And this must be Ms. Moore. Welcome to Pleasant Valley, Ms. Moore," the young lady said as she handed Lucy her key. As they turned and began to leave the service counter, they heard voices.

"Hey, Caleb, Lucy, you made it." It was Angela and Alison coming into the lobby from their rooms. "Hey, girl," Alison said, "Come with me, and I'll show you around this place. Those two probably have to talk business anyway."

As they started to leave, Caleb spoke out. "Lucy, I'll meet you right here at six-thirty, casual dress, okay?" She gave him a big thumbs-up. The two hurried on up the stairs and along the second floor landing.

Angela turned to face Caleb. He was watching Lucy's every move.

"So, it's a real date tonight?" said Angela, "It's not another one of those pretend business meetings like before, is it?"

"It's a real date," said Caleb.

"Well, it is about time," she said.

"Yes, Angela, you are absolutely right. It's about time."

****

Promptly at six-thirty, they met in the lobby. Caleb offered his arm to Lucy and then escorted her into the dining room. "There's no surprise guest for me to meet tonight, right?" Lucy asked.

"No," he replied. "I am at a loss for a surprise such as the last time. However, I can assure you that the food here is surprisingly the best in town. Will that suffice?"

"Only if you take me dancing afterwards". The waiter came and took their order. The meal was everything that Caleb had promised. As they ate, they spoke only of what lay ahead—nothing of what or who had been left behind.

In honor of the new arrivals, the dining hall had live music for the evening.

It was good, slow music for two tired people to dance by, and so they did.

When the dancing was over, Caleb said, "Would you like to go for a walk?"

Lucy feigned a frown, "What, you didn't get enough walking through the cave today?" He started to say something when she put her finger to his lips and said, "Shhhh. I would love to go for a walk."

They held hands, and Caleb led the way down the sidewalk of Main Street. Actually, it was the only street, but Only Street lacked the same appeal as Main Street. Besides, everyone knew that the sun came up at one end of the street and went down at the other, so there was no need to even mark it as West Main or East Main. If that were not enough for giving directions, at the west end of Main Street was a large gazebo situated in the middle of the wide street. There was still plenty of room on either side of it for any foot or horse traffic to easily pass by.

Caleb led Lucy up the steps of the gazebo and, pointed to the curved benches lining the perimeter, and said, "Let's sit a spell." They sat close together on the bench, and soon Lucy snuggled in a little closer. Caleb put his arm around her. They sat there watching the sun go down. It was a beautiful sunset.

"It's so quiet and peaceful here," said Lucy.

"So, have you found it?" Caleb asked.

"Found what?"

"Your port in the storm, your Fair Haven?"

"Caleb, Fair Haven is not just a place to be found. It's so much more than a place. It is a feeling of calm and peace and hope. More than all of that, it's a presence of love. Yes, Caleb. I have found my Fair Haven. What about you?"

"That depends," he said.

A little surprised by his answer, Lucy asked, "Depends on what, may I ask?"

"It depends on whether you say *yes.*"

"Yes to what?"

"To becoming my wife. It depends on whether you will share your peace and your hope and your love with me—the two of us together for the rest of our lives. Will you marry me, Lucy?"

She threw her arms around him, and they kissed for a very long time. When they finally separated, Lucy said. "Caleb, three times in the past twelve hours you've asked me if I would follow you through doors into places of uncertainty on the other side. First, it was through a door in an old, haunted inn. Then it was through a door into a cave of near total darkness, and finally it was through a big wooden door into a world lost in time. So, if there is any doubt, I promise, I promise to walk beside you. No need for a collar with bells. Together we will start a new life— not in Fair Haven, but in our new home called Pleasant Valley."

****

The high hills surrounding the valley gave the sun a bad reputation. It was as though the sun got up late every morning. In reality it took the sun forty minutes longer to rise above the hills and show its shining face. For the new arrivals from Welcome, that was just fine. The journey there had filled a long, hard day. The extra sleep was a good thing.

After breakfast, Caleb offered to show Lucy around the valley. They would take the carriage, and Molly could do the driving. It was midmorning, and the road they had taken brought them to an open meadow filled with wildflowers, a few young trees, and an apiary of bee hives. Caleb gently tugged on the reins, and Molly stopped. He got out of the carriage, went around Molly, and helped Lucy to the ground.

They walked side by side, holding hands, walking toward the patch of wildflowers. "Shouldn't we tie Molly to that little tree?"

"No need to," said Caleb, "I put her in *park* when I got out."

Lucy shook her head. "I have so much to learn."

A minute later they stood waist-high in the middle of the most beautiful spring wildflowers. Lucy said, "I feel like we are characters painted into the middle of some master's famous artwork." Then immediately she said, "No, I take it back. We *are* in the middle of *The Master's* artwork. He takes care of the flowers of the field and the birds of the air. If He takes care of them, He promises to take care of us as well."

Caleb held her in his arms and said, "Lucy Moore, I love you so very, very much."

At that exact moment, as they were holding each other, *IT* happened. Everything changed in a split second. Thousands of birds took flight from the surrounding woods, meadows, and pastures. The sky darkened as their deafening wings shadowed the ground below. Molly reared up with her front hoofs pawing the air. There had been no boom or blast or violent shaking of the earth. But they both still knew *IT* had happened. They continued to stand in the middle of the wildflowers— silently holding each other for a long, long time.

Epilogue

The music stopped, and the bride turned to face the groom. They came together then turned and faced the preacher. She was wearing the same dress she wore the night Caleb had taken her to Harry's Place. It was the perfect wedding dress, thanks to Angela, who had done a little forward thinking and made sure it got shipped to the valley. Theirs would be the first wedding in Pleasant Valley, but now that *The Event* had happened, there would be more weddings to celebrate in the months and years to follow.

The summer would fly by in a blink, then the cold months would soon follow.

There was no time to dwell on what was happening outside the valley, as there would be crops to harvest and store. There would be food to preserve and set aside for winter use. Firewood needed to be cut, split, and stacked for winter heat and fuel for the kitchen stoves.

When the snow began to fall in southern Indiana, Lucy found time to, once again, get back to writing . This time it would be a novel—a story about the adventures of a young woman who headed out of the big city one day to find a little excitement. It would be a story about the *hope* that was found among people who came together and learned to worked together so that someday they could survive together.

One winter evening, Lucy was writing at the kitchen table while Caleb was working on the floor. He was sanding a cradle that would need to be finished by late spring. He stopped his sanding and watched Lucy write. He enjoyed so much watching her write. The words in her mind were first filtered through her heart, then on through to her pencil, and finally onto paper.

After a little while, he broke the silence and asked her, "How's your manuscript coming?"

"Pretty good, so far," she said. "I have most of the chapters in some form of an outline."

"Do you have a title for it yet?" he asked.

"Maybe," she said. "I think I might call it—*Before It Happens.*"